Burning for You

Rylee Adams

Contents

Chapter 1

Three Years Ago

My arms pumped beside me and my legs were kicking wildly, surging me forward. I propelled through the water to the extent my sides were burning.

Water was burning my nose. My limbs felt like lead, resulting in my body wanting to sink faster than the Titanic. I urged myself through it, needing to beat my opponent.

Shouldn't have had that second piece of chocolate cake...

I could see his figure in my peripheral vision and it fuelled me into focus. I let the world around me fade. All I could see, was me and the bank. All I could think about was winning. Finally, after what felt like an eon, I reached the part of the bank where I could touch. I sprang to my feet and began to bound over the waves, literally neck and neck with Carter, fighting my way through them viciously.

I had to win.

He is an athlete and in comparison to me, is pretty fit. I speed walk most afternoons or jog, but I wasn't exactly bulk like him. Okay, so he kind of had puny arms and a six pack due to his skinniness, but still. He was a lot more toned than most of the guys his age and trust me, he wore the look well. I had to prove that I could beat him. At least once. It was always so close, but he always got me in the end.

This time, it was going to be different. My breathing was shallow and heavy, my heart was galloping wildly, threatening to leap out of my chest any moment.

"You can't beat me, Lace," his voice taunted as we both furiously leapt over the waves. All I could see was the white foam left over from the crashing waves and a tangle of our legs. The sun was beating down on my skin and although I was still drenched with water from the swim, I could tell sweat was beginning to form on my forehead. My long, blonde hair was trailing down my back, sticking unattractively to my skin. "I can't help it, I'm a professional."

"You - wish!" I panted heavily, my lungs swelling with the air I was consuming. He made this kind of activity look easy. Me on the other hand...

Only a little further, I told myself encouragingly.

My feet pummelled on the hard sand as we both drew closer to our destination. I dived forward like superman and dove head first into the sand, sliding across my belly. The sand felt raw and rough against my skin, but at the moment, it hardly even registered in my mind.

Gradually, I came to a halt, my head hitting the trunk of a tree. I gasped out, flinging my hands up in some sort of attempt to protect myself. It wasn't a bad hit, but it still hurt. I blinked a couple of times, trying to get my vision to clear, before I coughed, slapping my chest. I rolled onto my back, completely winded. I closed my eyes, my body aching and throbbing from the exertion.

"What!" Carter gasped out dramatically, collapsing beside me. I peeped through my half open eye, to witness his own popping out of his head. His head was whipping back and forth, from the land to the water, as though he was watching a tennis match. "You never win!"

"It's just what I like to call," I said, my voice a little shaky. I slowly reeled into sitting position, ignoring the stab of pain in my abdomen. I pretended to brush a piece of dust off my shoulder and stuck my nose in the air. "Skill."

He scoffed, crawling over to me, rolling his eyes. "You think you're skilled?"

"I know I am."

He chuckled and I frowned at him, not appreciating his attitude. He smirked devilishly and tantilisingly slow, crept toward me. I gulped, my face become blank and my eyes widening to the size of saucepans.

Before I had a chance to respond to his hands coming up, like two serpents launching for attack, he had me flat on my back, with my hands pinned above my head. This was a move Carter had perfected over the years and used on me frequently. His face was mere inches from mine. Our breaths mingled together and I blinked in surprise.

"Skilled, huh?" he asked me, his voice coming out husky. His hot breath fanned my face and I couldn't help let my eyes wander to his lips.

"Yep..." I trailed off, losing track of my thoughts.

This tended to happen when I was in close proximity with Carter. My thoughts melted into a puddle and my heart felt swollen. I battered my eyelashes up to him, drinking in all his features. His perfection always seemed to dazzle me and I became entranced. I could stare at him all day.

"What's this then?" he murmured, all joking sliding from his face, being replaced with seriousness, which I must say, was rare for him.

He edged his face closer and brushed his lips against mine fleetingly. Although it was only a peck, it felt amazing to me. His kisses always did. A swoop of tingles rolled down my body, through my stomach and down to the tips of my toes. My heart stuttered in my chest and my breath became hitched in my throat. He pulled back, smirking at my reaction and I stared up at him breathlessly, my eyes dilated.

Our friendship was hard to describe. Carter and I have been inseparable since we were both born. Okay, truthfully that's not quite accurate, as he is three months older then I am, but close enough.

We've known each other our entire lives. Our parents are best friends and we even live next door to each other. Having your best friend, live so close, is amazing. His house was practically mine and vice versa. Family dinners and get togethers were very common between us all.

Sometimes though, our friendship evolves into something a little more... intimate. We change our status to friends, to being in a relationship, quite regularly. Whenever we choose not to be together, it was completely fine with the both of us. Whatever the circumstance, there was never any awkwardness between us.

We're never really labelled 'boyfriend' or 'girlfriend'. We're those friends that nothing can get in between. I know a lot of our friends envied what we had.

I, myself, have never had another boyfriend, bar Carter. I was still innocent in more ways than one. I can't really say the same for Carter though. Even at the age of fourteen, he is a lady killer. His golden locks and smoldering eyes, left many girls weak at the knees and me feeling very smug about the attention he gives me. He hasn't gotten with many girls yet, but he has a long line after him already.

He had that golden, beach tan and blond, floppy hair that just had you begging to run your hands through. We both had gotten braces at the same time, (and had been nicknamed the 'Gruesome Twosome' for a year), which meant we both had matching, pearly white teeth. I had been absolutely devastated upon hearing the news of getting braces. Everything was very dramatic, tears were shed and I had been a distraught mess. Although when I did finally get braces, it wasn't bad at all. I had convinced myself I would look ugly and no one would like me or want to be my friend.

So, in order to stamp on my pity-party, Carter had the brilliant idea of also getting braces, although he hadn't overly needed them that much. The crooked tooth on the right side of his mouth was enough to convince his parents and wah-lah, we became braces buddies. Which had my feelings developing for him at a more increasing pace.

Now that, was a true best friend.

He rolled off of me and I clambered to my feet, wiping the excess water and dirt that clung to my skin. I tilted my head back and stared up at him, loving the height difference between us. He placed his hands on my hips and lent down, kissing the tip of my nose. He drew back and smiled at me. I wrapped my arm around his back and he did the same around my shoulders.

My father, Ben and his Dad, Matt, built a cubby house for us when we were about six. We still used it. Our cubby isn't a little hut up a tree, that only was big enough for two toddlers. We had expanded on it over the years and it was practically an apartment. Our town was pretty big and was sectioned off to 'north' and 'south' islands, which was divided by a great bridge. The bridge wasn't very long and the water to swim across it, as you've just heard about, isn't actually that long of a swim. This part of town had a bunch of houses along the beach. Our parents co-own a couple of holiday houses along here, so having the cubby sanctioned outside, was super convenient.

For years, we have always raced across the water, in battle. This 'hut' was our Haven, basically. We spent so many nights here, it wasn't funny. If we wanted to hang out, or were upset, or anything, we met up here.

It was our tradition.

I trailed behind him wordlessly as we climbed the ramp that led us to the entrance of our little home. He opened the door and like the gentleman he is, let me go through first. I smiled sweetly at him.

"Why thank you," I said in a British accent, sucking my face back and attempting to look posh. He laughed, but soon sobered up and did the same.

"You're welcome, My Lady." he responded back without a blink.

I let out a bark of laughter and entered, with him hot on my heels. It wasn't fancy place or anything, but it was cosy and completely ours. It had wooden floor boards, a T.V, coffee table, mini fridge, benches, and all the essentials we need. We had a key to the door and everything, so it was all legit.

(We left the keys in a secret area - wouldn't want to lose them on the swim over!)

We literally had spare clothes here, so we wouldn't have to drive over the bridge and get them. That's how often we come here. It was more than our second home.. We spent more time here together than with our own families.

Carter went and fetched the towels for us from out back, while I ringed my hair out through the window, letting the cool breeze wash over my body. He re-emerged and chucked it at me. I caught it easily and threw him a grateful smile. We both toweled off in silence, before I hung them out on the railings, which were located at the front of the hut. I re-entered and grabbed his hand, loving the jolt of electricity that ran up my arm at his touch. Our fingers were interlaced as we strolled over to the lounge. We decided on the movie Jaws, (very ironic) and switched it on. I snuggled up beside him and sighed in content, completely satisfied with my day.

Carter had this indescribable scent to him, that made my stomach do back flips. I loved it so much, that I even slept in one of his jerseys. I could live here, with Carter, for the rest of my life and be the happiest girl in the world. I know that's sloppy and cliché, but it's true.

I turned to him and pressed my lips, softly against his. I pulled back and erected my pinky finger. I hovered it near his and he grinned, following suit.

"I promise..." I began in a low, soft voice.

"That we..." he continued without hesitation, already had knowing what I was going to say.

"Will be..." I whispered.

"Best friends, forever." he finished, wrapping his arms securely around me. He tenderly, kissed my forehead and I closed my eyes, in pure bliss.

Being in his embrace, I just knew, no one could ever hurt me.

Now

I bit into my apple, as I one-handedly shoved my books into my bag. Attempting to zip it up, I continued to demolish the remains of my breakfast. I chucked the core into the bin and made my way back up my stairs, humming my new favourite song of the month. Quickly brushing my teeth, I double checked my reflection. I stared at myself for a few moments, allowing myself to actually take in my appearance.

My tan was golden and shined under the bathroom lights. My greens eyes stared unemotionally back at me. I had soft, red lips and a scatter of freckles underneath my eyes. I had long blonde hair, that tumbled down to the length of my elbows. My cheek bones were high and my collar bones stuck out so much, I could probably poke someone in the eyes. I have had numerous people confront me about being 'anorexic', but it was just my build. My whole family was thin, so I wasn't an exception.

I sighed, shrugging off my thoughts. After being somewhat satisfied with what reflected back to me, I skipped back down the stairs and swooped down, shrugging my bag onto my shoulders. I located my mother, who was ironing her work uniform and planted a quick kiss on her cheek. I had to stand on my tip-toes, due to her being ridiculously tall.

"See you, Mum." I sang.

"Bye, Lace." she smiled back, her bright blue eyes dancing.

Mum and I had look pretty alike. I had her golden hair, her tan and tall, thin build, although her legs ran longer than mine ever would.

I waved over my shoulder and walked briskly out to the front. I wrenched the front door open, a wave of the fresh, morning air washing over me. I took a big gulp, inflating my lungs. I smiled into the crisp, morning air and closed the door behind me. I took a couple of steps down onto my path and piled into my car, sliding across the cool leather seat, which feel smooth on my skin. I briefly checked over everything, before ramming my keys into the ignition. My beast rumbled to life underneath me and I adjusted my mirrors. I turned and rested my elbow on the seat, so I could see better. I began reversing, before slamming on my breaks. The car jerked to a halt and my body lurched forward. I growled in anger, ripping the hand break up and cutting the engine. I got out and slammed the door shut behind me with more force than necessary.

"I had a lovely evening," his familiar voice floated towards me again, making me clench my fists at the mere sound. "I'll call you."

I would bet you my car, he wouldn't.

"Thanks Carter," the blonde bimbo giggled, running her fingers down his toned arm. He gave her his player smirk, that seemingly nowadays was indented into his skin, making it his trademark. He seemed to never be able to smile genuinely anymore.

"Hey," I called out angrily, marching towards him, my lips spread into a thin line and my eyes narrowed dangerously. "Your one-night-stand is yet again, blocking my driveway!"

He shrugged nonchalantly, smirking down at me. I used to love the fact that he was about a head taller than me, it had made me feel small and cute.

Now, it just frustrated me. It made him have more power than me and I hated it.

"So?"

"So, this happens almost every week!" I screeched, anger pouring out of me. I shot my hands forward and shoved him in the chest. He staggered backwards slightly, but only took a couple of seconds to compose himself. He always had had good reflexes. Probably due to the gruelling years of football games he has endured. "I'm sick of it! They have the entire street to park, but coincidentally find themselves in my way."

He exchanged a look with the doe-eyed twit, before looking back at me in amusement. "Someone clearly has their panties in a twist..."

The girl giggled, the bubble of laughter filtered through the air, making me want to slap myself in the face. With my eyes burning, I dragged them from Carter and to her, shooting daggers. She gulped and took a step back, obviously receiving my 'back-off' signals.

"Me and my panties have nothing to do with you." I bit out, my voice low. My eyes found themselves glued back to his bright, blue ones. I used to fall into them, feeling as though they were as deep as an ocean, but now, I could hardly stand to look into them for more than a couple of seconds. "You made that perfectly clear."

His cocky expression wavered for a second and I thought I saw something flash across his eyes, but his mask was back on before I could study it too much. He was always good at covering his emotions. It was one of the things I hated about him.

"Are you done yet?" he asked, sounding bored.

"Just get your hook up out of my way," I said, swivelling my eyes to hers, looking at her distastefully. "Before I make her move."

She scrunched her face up and I took a warning step towards her. She sighed in defeat and turned away from us. She stormed over to her pink Bug and sidled in. Of course she owned a car like that. It contrasted with her barbie doll look perfectly. She waved at Carter, who waved back instantly and blew her a kiss.

I vomited a little in my mouth.

She drove off, thank the Lord. I sighed in relief at not having to rip my claws out completely this time, like I have had to previously. I spun on my heel and marched back towards my own 2008 Lancer, without another word to him.

"Oh, not sticking around for a chat?" he teased, following me like a bad smell. I gritted my teeth together to the extent it was actually painful.

"No. Thanks."

I didn't turn to look at him again and shut the door in his face. Without a backwards glance, reversed and took off, practically burning rubber. My nostrils were flared and my grip on the steering wheel was so tight, you could see the whites of my knuckles.

Okay, so you're probably wondering how I could go from being best friends for sixteen years with that boy, to not even being able to stand the sight of him.

Well, this is just the beginning of mine and Carter's very complicated relationship.

Chapter 2

S ince the beginning of my day was unfortunately ambushed by my ex-best friend and neighbour, Carter Williams, I found myself stomping into school with a look of death etched onto my face.

"Uh oh," my boyfriend Aiden said, the smile dropping from his face instantly, upon seeing me. That's comforting, my mere expression is enough to spread my negativity. "An incident with Carter?"

"How did you know?" I grumbled, letting out a puff of air, my cheeks feeling hot. I was flushed and riled up, not having even endured through my first class yet.

I let my eyes roam over the boy who stood in front of me. Aiden was tall, with broad shoulders. He had an olive complexion with dark, brown eyes. He was cute and the exact opposite of Carter's 'golden boy' look, which is probably what drew me to Aiden in the first place.

"Because you always have that look after being around him."

"Yeah well, he brings out my dark side." I hissed, angrily brushing my hair from my face. I sighed heavily, rolling my tongue across my teeth. "Let's talk about something else. How was your dinner last night?"

"Yeah surprisingly alright," he said lightly, wrapping an arm around my shoulder. Automatically, I leaned my head onto his shoulder, seeking his comfort. "His family isn't as bad as I made them out to be in my head."

I rolled my eyes. "I told you. You really should-"

"-Listen to you more, I know."

I laughed, coming to a stop and snaking my arms around his waist. I tilted my head back and he kissed me softly on the lips, before allowing me to snuggle my head into his chest. I sighed, closing my eyes.

I liked Aiden. A lot. We get along really well and he always makes me feel good about myself. Except... he never did make me feel as alive as Carter did. No matter how much I tried to convince myself I liked Aiden, it never compared to what I had felt for Carter. I think that boy has permanently printed on me, as disturbing and revolting as that sounds.

But I could push through it. Aiden, admittedly, had been my rebound at first, but I generally did like him. Just not... how I liked Carter.

"Holla, Lace." My best friend greeted, waving Aiden off. He chuckled and stepped back, releasing me from his capture. Mercedes replaced him instantly, wrapping her arms around my neck, strangling me, before letting me go. She beamed brightly at me. "How are you this morning?"

"Don't get me started," I sighed, shaking my head.

"Carter?" she deadpanned.

"His name is like Voldemort's. I shudder at the sound of it."

She snorted with laughter, rolling her eyes.

Speak of the Devil and thus he appears. Carter rounded the corner, his arm slung around an unfamiliar brunette's shoulders, laughing at something she said. His hair was extra floppy today, falling messily onto his forehead. His lips were tilted up into his usual smirk and he walked, confidence oozing from him. The too-bright sun shone down on him. He made it look like he was in a music video, whereas I felt flustered and gross. I let out a puff of air, as if that would somehow cool me down.

He nodded at me in greeting and I flipped him off in return. A couple of witness' around us chuckled and I turned, gritting my teeth. "Aiden, let's go."

"Okay," he said, catching onto my tone.

Mercedes had already taken an exit route to her class. Aiden slipped his hand into mine and my nails bit viciously into his hand. He winced, but I couldn't slack my hold. Not when he was in my vicinity. I tugged on his hand and dragged him after me.

Once away from him, I let out a breath, letting go of Aiden's hand. I felt his gaze on me as I began pacing, flexing my fingers back and forth.

"This thing you have with Carter... it's very unhealthy. Why don't you guys attempt to salvage your friendship? You hate to admit it, but I know he still means a lot to you. You were best friends for forever."

"Really? Were we?" I snapped rudely, my anger sizzling. "I hadn't realised that. And no, we cannot 'salvage' our friendship."

"Okay..." he trailed off, visibly biting his tongue. "Whatever you say."

I stopped, my breathing heavy. "Look, I'll see you later. I'm going to class early."

With that, I stalked off towards my locker to get the books I needed. I know Aiden was just trying to help, but I couldn't force myself to be polite when I was like this. I grabbed my books, yanking them out and slamming my door shut.

I turned and came face-to-chest, with the one and only, Carter Williams. I exhaled heavily, looking up at him. "What do you want?"

"Just wondering if you're okay," he said. Although his words were kind, his tone was implying that he didn't really care, he was just trying to stir me up more. He was successful. "You didn't seem the happiest when I saw you this morning."

"Carter, you and your fake sympathy can kiss my a-" I was interrupted when the bell buzzed loudly, cutting me off.

He smirked, obviously enjoying my response. I elbowed him out of the way and marched to my classroom, fuming.

I just needed to get through the day, without getting suspended for inflicting pain on other students, or myself.

The rest of my school day cruised by uneventfully. There weren't really any more Carter incidents, if you don't count me stomping on his foot when he put his arm around me at the canteen line. He, better than anyone, should know not get in between me and my food.

I was striding towards my car, before my hand was swallowed by someone else's. They tugged me back and with a gasp, I staggered. I clenched my fist, positioning myself to launch as I was spun around on my heel. Fortunately, to where Aiden was grinning at me, so my violence wasn't needed.

"In a rush?" he joked, his eyes roaming my face, drinking in my features.

I jerked my shoulder up in response to his question. "I could really use a long run to calm myself down."

"What about this?" he asked me, his voice dropping so that it was low and husky.

He took a step forward and gently, brushed his lips against mine. They began to move together in synchronisation, and before it could start to get good, I pulled back from him and smiled, tilting my head back to see him better.

"That was pretty soothing, yes."

"Good." he grinned, leaning down and kissing me once more, before giving me my own space again. "Did you want to go to the movies or something tonight?"

"Yeah, that sounds good. Text me the details."

"Okay, cool." he said, smiling.

I turned from him and resumed the short trek to my car, eager to just get home and sweat my anger out with an intense run. One that will make my legs wobble in pain. Running, was my distraction from the world. It made me numb, which was perfect. It was easier to hide your thoughts when you couldn't tell what you were feeling. It probably wasn't healthy, but it works well for me so I am going to stick with it.

I collapsed into the driver's seat and plunged my key into the ignition. Upon getting home, I discovered that I was alone, which meant mum was staying back a bit later to finish up with some of her work. She worked at a primary school across town. I did work experience there with her when I was in year ten last year and could see why she loved it. The school was beautiful. It was small and the kids were all lovely.

My father, Ben, worked as a real estate agent. He was good at his job and sold a lot of houses and properties. He worked out of town a fair bit as well, because in this town, there weren't a heap of opportunities. Therefore, he wasn't home as much as I would have liked. I still got to see him though, which was good enough for me.

Shredding my school uniform off, which was just a white polo shirt and black bottoms of your choice, and slipped my tights on. I grabbed my exercise singlet and arm band, which suctioned onto my skin. I rammed my iPod into the little pocket and jammed the earphones into my ears, cranking up the volume. I threw my long, blonde hair into a high pony tail, that trailed down my back and past my shoulder blades. I began to do some lunges and stretches, warming up my muscles, before putting them through my run.

Grabbing my joggers, I sped walked out the door, loving the feel of the cool air washing over my body. As soon as I was down the porch steps, I was off and running. My eyes glanced towards Carter's house, which only fuelled me more. I picked up my pace a notch, loving the numbing feel that began spreading through my veins and muscles. I kept going, doing twenty minutes longer than I usually did, which really pushed me to my limits. My sides were aching and my legs burning. I jogged all the way back home, up the steps and didn't stop until I was literally inside and couldn't run any more.

I could hear mum in the kitchen, but I was too sticky and sweaty to go there yet. I peeled my sweat-drenched clothes from my skin and deposited them into the laundry basket, I turned the water on freezing cold, before stepping in. Gasping at the icy water running over my skin, I leapt back. I didn't heat it up anymore, however. This was what I needed. Numbing cold, that would make me forget everything. I sighed, the water running through my hair felt amazing.

After spending longer than necessary bathing myself, I stepped out and toweled off. I slipped into a loose singlet and my comfy pants, before emerging out. I stepped into the kitchen, the smell of chocolate biscuits filling my nostrils and making my stomach growl with hunger. My mouth watered and I licked my lips, already able to taste them. My mother, Elizabeth, could cook amazing wonders.

Okay, going for an intense run like that and then wanting to eat chocolate probably sounded funny, but running for me was more like a release of emotions, rather than for exercise purposes. Her back was to me. Her hands were spread out and she was leaning heavily, onto the kitchen counter, her shoulders shaking. I paused, confused. I then could hear it. Faint crying and sniffling, making it evident something was wrong.

"Mum?" I asked softly.

She stiffened upon hearing my voice. She took a moment to hastily wipe at her eyes, before turning to me. If she was crying, it was something bad. Us Adams girls never cried. If something sad was happening, we didn't cry or get upset, like most others.

We get angry and fought back.

Therefore, her crying, was not a good thing. At all. Her cheeks were tear-stained, whilst her eyes were tinged red and were puffy. I swallowed nervously, edging cautiously towards her, as if she was a time bomb, ticking until destruction.

That's how serious her crying was.

"What's happened?"

"Your grandmother..." she whispered shakily, wiping at her eyes again. "She's had a stroke. They don't think she's going to make it. I have to go and... try and look after her. She's really not well, Lace."

My mouth dried out, as though all the saliva I had, suddenly was retracted. I stared at her for a few moments, not knowing what to say.

So, she continued.

"Your father and I are going to go and look after her-"

"Um, what?" I interrupted, confusion lacing my words. "You and Dad? Am I going?"

"You're a senior now," she said, shrugging. "I couldn't ask you to miss days off school like that. They're too vital."

"I don't care, I'm going."

"No, Lacey." she said sternly. "You're staying here and going to school. That's final."

I gritted my teeth together, biting back a retort. It probably wouldn't be the wisest decision to pick a fight with her when she was so vulnerable. I sighed, running my fingers roughly over my face, suddenly feeling tired.

"So, I'll live here by myself. That's not going to get boring or lonely." I bit out sarcastically, folding my arms across my chest. I couldn't break down about Grandma right now. I need to be strong in front of mum. So, I did what I did best. Became selfish.

"You're not staying here by yourself," she rolled her eyes, smiling even. Maybe I was being a good distraction. She wiped at the corner of her eye. "You're only seventeen. I don't want you living here alone for that long."

"Where am I going then? Mercedes never said anything at school..." I trailed off, furrowing my eyebrows together.

"You're staying with the Williams'." she said in an obvious tone. "Didn't Carter tell you?"

Time slowed down. All I could hear, was the continuous thudding of my heart beat in my ears. Her lips were moving, but no sound was coming out. I was stumped on that mere sentence. She couldn't do this to me...

"What?" I asked, my voice cold and low.

She stopped, mid-sentence, raising her eyebrows. "You're staying with the Williams'."

"No. I'm not."

"I thought you would have been delighted?" she asked me, confusion lacing her voice. "You and Carter are so close."

"Used to be close. Past tense, Mum."

"What?" she asked distractedly, turning and getting her biscuits out of the oven. I glared lasers into her back as she did so. Was she that blind?

"Have you not noticed the silence between us when they come over? How I'm never home when we go there? I hate him, mum. I have for the last year."

"What are you talking about?" she asked me. I don't think she was even processing my words. "They're practically your family. Staying anywhere else would be ridiculous."

"Staying there, would be ridiculous!" I cried out, throwing my hands up in exasperation. "You're not making me live there!"

She opened her mouth to reply back, when the front door swung open and heavy footsteps could be heard ascending toward the kitchen. I turned just as dad entered, dressed in his suit. He placed his briefcase down and went straight up to mum.

He gave her a quick kiss, before sweeping her up in his embrace. They stayed like that for several moments, before I couldn't take it any longer.

"I am not staying there!" I shrieked, my voice coming out panicked and high-pitched. I don't care if I sounded like a whiny brat. I think I deserved it after this double bomb shell.

"Honey," dad started. "Please don't cause a scene. This is hard enough for your mother already. You better get packing, our plane leaves in a couple of hours."

"Are you even listening to me!?" I cried, angry tears flooding my eyes. My breathing was heavy and my chest was heaving. I could murder someone right now. "I am not living there."

Dad turned and looked at me fiercely. "Lacey, you will not speak like that in this house. Stop being so selfish."

"ME!?" I screamed in outrage. "Have you not noticed-"

"LACEY." he barked out, effectively silencing me. "Go upstairs and pack your bags. Now."

We had a heated stare down, for several moments, before I snapped my head away. I rolled my tongue across my teeth, agitated.

"How long will I be gone for?" I murmured quietly.

"What?"

"How long?" I said, pronouncing the words tantalisingly slow, my voice dripping venom.

My arms were shaking in rage. My hand was twitching with the impulse to hit something. Someone. His eyes flared with warning and I bit my lip, to stop myself screaming out in anger and actually going on a rampage.

"A couple weeks."

"A couple weeks?" I echoed incredulously, my body about to explode in anger. "No fu-"

"Lacey." It was my mother who spoke this time. Her voice was timid and soft. She pulled back from dad's touch, looking pale and fragile. When mum looked pale, you knew something was wrong. Her bronzed skin looked off-colour and her eyes weary. "Please. For me."

Clamping my mouth shut, I swallowed a lump that had seemingly lodged itself in my throat. Tears of frustration burned my eyes. My hands clenched in fists, I turned, striding from the room. I marched stubbornly up to my room and slammed the door shut.

My vision began to turn red at the sides I was so mad. I opened the door and slammed it shut again. This continued a couple more times, before my knees gave out, causing my body to sink to the ground in despair. Pummelling my fists into the floor, I grabbing my pillow. I threw it forcefully to the ground and smooshed my face against it, before screaming as loud as I could. My throat burned and my hands were aching in pain.

My father's words whirled around my mind, like a cyclone.

I was going to be staying, with my enemy, for a couple of weeks, possibly more. I drew my thighs up to my chest and buried my face into them.

If I was insane before, I don't know what I am now.

Chapter 3

Carter's P.O.V:

"Can't I just stay..." The girl trailed off in a whisper, biting her lip seductively, twirling her long hair around her finger. "A little longer? Even if it's just ten minutes?"

I rolled my eyes at her forwardness, knowing exactly the double meaning she was implying. We both knew if she did, it would sure as hell be longer than ten minutes. I am Carter Williams, after all. I have a reputation for a reason.

"Sorry babe. I have things to do, people to see."

She pouted childishly at me. She ran her fingers up my arm, trying to convince me otherwise, as though her mere touch was enough to persuade me. Yeah, she was no Lacey Adams. No girl could do that to me, other than her. I quickly pushed all thoughts of Lacey into a file in the back of my mind, which wouldn't be opened any time soon.

I snapped back to the present, as the girl's eyes roamed over my chest, her fingers walking all down my torso and sighed. This one was going to make it difficult to ditch. This is why, one should never do a booty call before it's ten p.m. It was an amateur move on my part.

"Look, seriously, you need to go." I said, my voice dropping from the charming tone it usually was, becoming blunt. I grabbed her hand, stopping it from sinking any lower and gave her a warning look. "I'll see you out."

I wrenched myself out of her touch, ignoring the flare of hurt that flashed in her eyes. Rolling from my bed, I chucked on a shirt, the closest one I found and peeped out the door, making sure mum wasn't around. After the coast was evidently clear, I stepped out and ushered her along with me, trying to be as silent as possible.

She paused, causing me to run into the back of her. I grunted slightly in surprise, before staggering backwards. She turned and stared up at me, between her long lashes, chewing at her lip. I resisted the urge to slap myself in the face repeatedly.

Did she not understand the word 'no'? Actually, probably not. I don't think it would exactly be in her vocabulary.

"This way." I barked, ignoring the way she flinched slightly.

Her face fell at my obvious rejection. Well, it wasn't exactly rejection, we both already got what she came here for, but seemingly, she wanted to go again. Usually, hell yeah. But God, her clinginess was enough to turn me off.

Brushing around her, I took off towards the window door at the end of the hall. I quietly slid it open. After successfully doing so, I turned and swept my arm through, implying that she goes first. She just stood there rigidly, blinking in confusion. I closed my eyes, feeling a head ache begin to accumulate behind my eyes.

Got yourself a keeper here, Carter.

"Can't I just use the front door?" she asked, her eyes wide.

"No?" I said like she was stupid, my impatience bubbling to the surface and beginning to trickle into my veins. "Look, climb over the railings, there is a vine thing on the side of the house, pretty much a ladder. It will hold you, I go down it all the time."

She laughed humourlessly, shaking her head. "You're not actually asking me, Rebecca, Queen of the school, to climb down a vine? You've got to be joking."

"Do I look like I am?" I remarked challengingly, quirking an eyebrow at her.

She stared at me in shock for a couple of moments, processing what I had just said. Her face twisted into a scowl and her eyes narrowed at me. Oh, I'm trembling.

"You're such a jerk Carter Williams!"

"But you already knew that."

"But-I-You-" she began spluttering incoherent words, clenching her fists. "Y-you pig!"

I snorted despite myself. I couldn't help it, she was entertaining, to say the least. "That's the best you got?"

With that, I turned and slid the door shut behind me, satisfied upon hearing the click, informing me it was locked. I glanced over my shoulder, staring at her furious expression. I gave her a smirk before I waved enthusiastically. I began padding down the hall, chuckling to myself. No doubt, she will be mad, but if I called her to 'hang' again, she'd come running.

They always do.

I took a second to observe my surroundings. I lent back on the wall as I surveyed the place. I loved my house. It was unnecessarily massive for only three people, with two stories splitting it through the middle. The bottom half consisted of the kitchen, lounge and master bedroom, where my parents live. I have the whole top floor to myself, so that's how I have so many girls come through, without them knowing.

Well, most of the time. My parents were hardly ever home, so I only had to hide them sometimes. My father was a Doctor, which forced him to endure long hours at the hospital. Sometimes, he wouldn't be home until two in the morning and would be up and off to work again, before I was awake for school. So, it was pretty obvious that I didn't see him that much.

I spent more time with mum, but yet again, she was hardly home much either. She was a flight attendant at the nearest Airport, which was a twenty minute drive from here. She travelled all over the countryside, staying at places for days or weeks, whichever suited.

So, I lived by myself a lot, in this massive place. Luckily, we have a cleaner, Kim. I would be in a lot of trouble if I didn't have her. It was pretty sweet actually. I even had my own lounge, bathroom and gym room up here. It was the perfect place to bring the boys over and just smash the X Box and watch footy on a Friday night. They seemed to love coming here as well. I had a hard time sending them home.

It used to be great when Lacey came over...

I mentally slapped myself upon even thinking her name. I didn't want to be regretting what happened between us. She was the one who was holding the grudge, not me. Yeah, what happened shouldn't have, but what's in the past is in the past. I can't change it. She doesn't see that though. She seems to think I can just invent a bloody time machine and go back, to before everything was screwed up and fix everything.

Jogging down the stairs, the smell of bleach and disinfectant abused my nostrils. I gagged, scrunching up my face. I followed the source of the smell into the kitchen, where my mother was scrubbing excessively. She had long gloves on, that reached her elbows and the daggiest clothes I've ever seen her wear. My mother always dressed as classy and nice as she could, so seeing her in this was quite shocking.

Cocking my head to the side for a moment, I only now noticed the house was immaculate. Spotlessly clean. I couldn't see hardly one spot of dirt anywhere. Since when did my mother do the cleaning, when we had our own personal cleaner?

I furrowed my eyebrows questioningly. "Er- mum?"

"Hmm?" she responded, keeping her back to me.

Mum and I were pretty alike in the looks department. She was tanned, blonde and had bright, blue eyes, which I luckily inherited. I had her same golden tan, hair and eyes, that could 'light up a city', as Lacey used to say. There I was again, thinking about her. It was like my mind automatically switched to her, even after all this time.

I ran my hand through my hair, annoyed at myself. I wish I could just get over all the emotions I felt, whenever I saw her, but it was like she had permanently printed on me. Like she was embedded into my brain and no matter how much I pretend I don't care, it will always be there, nagging at me, reminding me of what I had. Before I screwed it all up.

"Why are you cleaning the house like the Prime Minister is coming over?" I asked her, snapping myself out of my emotional turmoil and back to the present. I found it easy to lose track of time and get side tracked easily, whenever my thoughts wandered to the beautiful blonde who lived next door.

"Well, she isn't a Prime Minister, but she will be staying here for quite some time. I wanted the house to be at least nice."

She? My ears instantly perked up.

"Who?" I instantly asked, intrigued, attempting to suppress the smile that was fighting its way onto my face. "And where is Kim?"

"Lacey." she said in an obvious tone, turning around and planting her hands on her hip. "Didn't she tell you at school? And Kim's on holiday leave."

"No..." I trailed off, my eyes wide and my heart jerking in my chest. Lacey... Lacey Adams, my ex girlfriend/best friend of sixteen years, who I was now practically enemies with, was going to come and stay with us?

What?

"Lacey?" I echoed, shock coursing through my veins.

"Yeah. She'll be here in an hour or two. You can help if you like. I could use an extra pair of hands here. I'm not used to cleaning like this." she laughed as if this was just a normal day and my life wasn't just about to flip upside down. "Almost sad isn't it? How much we rely on Kim to prepare the house for us."

"That's what she's hired to do." I said distractedly, picking at my nails, which was a nervous habit I'd unfortunately picked up. And rubbing my neck. Both signs that I was nervous and I hated it. Lacy used to think it was 'cute'.

I swallowed, leaning back into the wall for support. Was that why Lacey was so angry at me today? Well, she was angry at me every day, but seemed almost more so today. But she would have said something, right?

"How long will she be here for?" I asked through gritted teeth, trying remain calm and act as casual as possible. Yeah I loved stirring up the girl for laughs, but having her live with me... could I pretend to not care with her here all the time? It was going to be a slap in the face of what happened, every single day.

"I'm not sure," she sighed, wiping the back of her hand across her head. "A couple of weeks. Liz's mother isn't well."

"Oh." I said slowly, feeling something stab at my stomach. "Is she okay?"

Mum just shook her head sadly at me, giving me a tight-lipped, grim smile. "They wouldn't travel all that way if she was."

I clenched my jaw, determinedly looking away from her intense, blue eyes. Lacey's family was like my own. Hearing the news of Liz's mother's illness was unsettling. I sighed, rubbing my hands roughly across my face.

"I thought you'd be excited having Lacey here?" she asked me.

"I am." I forced out with a smile, lying through my teeth. "I'm just surprised. You know, I didn't get to talk to her much today to hear about it."

She smiled at my response. "Lacey is such a lovely girl. It's so nice you guys have remained friends for so long. You guys were always perfect together."

Perfect. That single word, swirled around inside my head and I felt like I couldn't breathe. Yeah, we were once, before I blew it. My parents were oblivious to my life at all costs, apparently. They had no idea of the falling out we had. I must be one hell of an actor at those dinners. Do they not realise she doesn't come over at all anymore?

Well, I guess they're never here to realise...

Begrudgingly, I picked up some gloves and soap, making a face as I began to clean. I wouldn't do this for just anyone, but mum asked me and I always had this undying feeling to impress the girl I love.

Loved.

Past tense, remember Carter? A voice in the back of my mind whispered, slapping me with remembrance of that day, over a year ago, that still haunted my sleep and gnawed viciously at my brain.

Lacey and I, together, under one roof.

Well, this should be interesting...

Lacey's P.O.V:

Kill. Me. Now.

I stood outside his house, one foot on the porch step, the other firmly on the path. It was like my own body was refusing to enter the house of death. Okay, frankly the house is actually really nice and I loved it. His family were beautiful and like my own. Despite this, nervousness spread through my veins and pumped in my blood stream. I swallowed a lump that had seemingly lodged itself into my throat. I closed my eyes and counted to ten. That, was an Anger Management exercise I had learnt, when mum had sent me to get help, to get over my 'issues'. (Little did she know, the boy she was sending me to live with was mostly the cause of these 'issues').

My parents were just about to leave. I could still see them bustling around in the house. If only I hid until they left, then I could crawl back into my house and just live there. I can just pretend to have lived with the Williams' the whole time and they wouldn't know a thing!

I grinned at myself. I do consider myself a genius at times. I heaved my bag back onto my shoulder and walked down his drive way. I kept going until I found the small pocket of shadows, that their dividing fence held.

Planting my bag down, I sat down roughly beside it. I drew my thighs up to my chest and just began humming to myself quietly. I had just closed my eyes and rested my head down, when I heard a rumble of a car. Snapping my head up, I peered out behind the fence. My mother was sliding into the Taxi. Huh, it must have entered the other side of the street, I hadn't heard it approach. I watched my parents buckle up, before the Taxi sped off.

Smirking devilishly to myself, I sprang back to my feet. Suddenly, all the nerves and the feelings of trepidation that had been accumulating inside me, vanished. It was replaced with cheerfulness and a rush of elation. I didn't have to go and live with him! Oh, the freedom.

Okay, that was dramatic, but oh well.

Unable to wipe the smile from my face, I found myself walking the familiar path back to my house. I walked up to the porch and tried to open the door. As I figured, it was locked. I shrugged my bag off and went to locate the key.

I dug around in the dirt of the pot, digging my fingers around it. A frown formed on my face when I couldn't find it. I felt my heart pang. No... they couldn't have taken it. Breathlessly, I began clambering everywhere, lifting the mat in front of the door, moving all the furniture around. I ignored the aching in my hands and the loud noise I was making.

Alas, I found nothing. I sank to the ground, my hope being crushed. I felt my face crumple as my previous feelings began rushing back into me, making me feel like I had been hit by a truck. My eyes began stinging and I gritted my teeth.

So much for that plan.

I rose to my feet and grabbed my stuff again, trying to keep my cool. With my knees high and my face twisted into a scowl, I marched back across to his house, determined to make the best of a crappy situation.

I would be okay. I would be fine. I would get through this. I had hardly opened the door, before he met me. A grin instantly lit up his face and I sighed deeply through my nose.

"Lacey!" he burst out. He swept me up in his embrace, smooshing my face into his hard chest. "I'm so glad you're here! Sleeeeep over!"

I ignored the flare of heat in my abdomen and pushed him roughly away. I frowned up at him and his over-the-top display of affection. He looked at me warningly and I gave him a baffled expression. Why was he looking at me like that? It's hardly like he thinks we're friends again, because I'm forced to live with him, right?

"What are you doing-" I began, when his mother, Miranda, bustled around him.

I couldn't help let the genuine smile cross my face, upon seeing her. She wrapped her arms tightly around me.

"I am so happy to have you here Lacey! You and Carter, together, this is going to be a blast!"

"Yeah," I said, forcing a laugh, beaming to the extent my cheeks hurt. "We sure will!"

She patted my cheek, before hugging me again. "It feels like I haven't seen you in forever! That must mean I'm not home enough!"

Again, I forced out a chuckle. "Pfft, feels like only yesterday."

She laughed, smiling from ear to ear. "Well come on in! Make yourself at home - although I needn't have to tell you, it practically is!"

Well, that may have been true in the past, but it wasn't now. I didn't say anything though. She quickly went off, doing something else. Carter opened his mouth to say something, but I turned my back to him and began mounting the stairs. I didn't look back and continued to walk, until I reached the spare bedroom. I shut the door, so he wouldn't follow me and dumped my stuff on the ground.

I sank to the ground, my hands shaking. I rolled my lips into my mouth, forcing myself to breathe. This would be fine. I would just avoid Carter, go to school, spend heaps and heaps of time out with friends.

I'd be fine.

I unzipped my bag and began unpacking, when the door was rudely barged open. He entered, smirking at me.

"Heya' roommate."

Producing a sweet smile, I turned and face him. "Carter."

"This is going to be so exciting!"

"Yeah. Highlight of my life." I deadpanned.

He grinned at my reply. "You'll see. You'll learn to love me again."

I froze and his face twitched. I don't think he was meant to let that one slip. We both stared at each other in silence for a moment, before his smirk was back on his face, as though nothing had happened.

"Be right back," he said, waving at me girlishly. "I'm just going to go downstairs and get some snacks, so we can do each other's nails and braid our hair!"

I stared at him blankly, as he clapped his hands with enthusiasm. He turned and swiftly left my room. I face-palmed myself, falling backwards onto my bed.

These were going to be the longest days of my life.

Thankfully, I had thought ahead and eaten dinner before I came, so I avoided that awkwardness. I stayed in my room, 'settling in', as I had called it. I was pretty much all unpacked, but was doing it at a painfully slow rate, as if waiting for my parents to come home and say they've just played a practical joke on me.

After saying in the room, longer than I should have, I thought I should go out and try to be at least civil. With a heavy sigh, I ripped the door open and wandered down the stairs and out to the lounge room, where I could see the T.V light flickering.

I entered and Miranda beamed at me in greeting. "Hi honey. We're just watching some Underbelly. Do you still like that?"

I felt a smile tug onto my lips. "Yeah, it's great. What season are we watching?"

"Razor." Carter answered.

I absolutely loved Underbelly - especially Razor. It was one of my favourite T.V shows. I collapsed down onto the lounge. Carter was on the left, so I made sure I was very far to the right, in non-touching distance. Because unfortunately for me, my body still reacted lustfully to him, as if we were still in a relationship. But, my mind was sharp and knew I couldn't let myself be close to him. I may be strong, but I'm still a girl with hormones. I need to be careful.

I felt his eyes rest on me and blatantly ignored the fact. I let myself get absorbed in the show. At some stage during it, Carter announced it was his bed time and retired up to his room, but it hardly even registered in my mind. I was too consumed.

Using the extra space to stretch out, I extended out my body, leaning my head on the arm rest. I let my eyes close for a few moments. Well, that's what I had intended. About an hour passed, before Miranda was shaking my arm gently.

"Honey, I think you should go to bed." she murmured.

"Hum," I replied, yawning. "Good idea."

Dragging myself into standing position, I shuffled up the stairs. Tiredly, I entered my room, needing to change into my pajamas. I sat roughly on my bed and felt my body hit something. Jerking up, I spun and my eyes widened.

A jar of Nutella was perched on my bed, adjacent to it was my absolute favourite T.V series, Prison Break. A note was placed beside.

' I know you always eat Nutella and watch Prison Break when you're upset or angry. I thought you might have been both.' -Carter.

I felt my heart swell inside my chest. I nibbled at my lip, trailing my fingers over the note. That was surprisingly sweet. I let my eyelids flutter closed. Maybe this wasn't going to be as bad as I thought. Maybe we could try and sort things out...

Oh God. Carter just won me over with buying me food and a present. I was so weak. I lent down, scrunched up the note angrily and threw it across the room, pegging it roughly against the wall. It ricocheted off the wall, to the desk, before landing its final destination on the floor.

If he thinks he can 'seduce' me with sweet talk and gifts, he has another thing coming. I scrunched up my face, my skin heating up.

It was so on.

Chapter 4

Light flooded into my room, piercing through my closed eyelids. I groaned, rubbing at my face, scrunching up my nose.

"What the hell?" I grumbled groggily, still unable to comprehend what was happening. "Where am I?"

"Rise and shine!" an overly cheerful voice boomed, causing me to wince. It was way too early for this. My body jerked, my eyes snapping open. Carter? It took my still-asleep-mind a couple of moments to process what was happening.

I rolled onto my side and snatched at my phone. I squinted at the screen. It became evident it was six thirty am, which is an hour earlier than I usually wake up. I blinked at it for a few moments, trying to understand what this meant.

"You've got to be kidding me..." I trailed off moodily.

"Nope." he replied, popping the 'p', positively glowing at me. "Up we get."

"No."

"Yes!"

"No." I snapped, smothering myself with my blanket.

Maybe, if I play dead, he will leave me alone...

Before I could even blink, the blanket was ripped away from me, instantly being replaced with the harsh, morning air. I gasped in shock, my mouth popping open. I curled myself up in a ball, embarrassed to only be wearing a shirt. I know he has seen me many times like this before, but things were different now.

"Why are you doing this to me?" I ground out in annoyance.

"Um, since your car has no petrol and I'm your ride?"

"Since when do you go to school early?"

"Since I have to work out now for football." he chirped, clapping his hands enthusiastically and rocking back and forth on the balls of his heels.

"I'll walk."

"Not an option. Get up!"

"No!"

He sighed, planting his hands on his hips and pursing his lips at me. "This could have gone a lot easier."

"What do you-" I began, but my words died off when I let out a cry of surprise. Carter swooped down and wrapped his arms around me, hauling me over his shoulder. My stomach swooped and I squeezed my eyes shut. "CARTER! Put. Me. Down!"

"Not yet."

"Urgh!"

He began casually walking down the hall. My face was directly in line with his bottom, which was disturbing. I began pummelling on his back with my fists, shouting angrily at him to put me down. Apparently, he didn't get the hint.

"What's going on?" Miranda asked, emerging up the stairs.

I peeked at her through his legs. She had a nightie on, securely wrapped in a golden robe. Her platinum blonde hair was mounted in a bundle of ringlets, piled on top of her head. Her face was flawless perfection. Obviously, she had to work today.

"Oh, you know, just making sure someone's hygiene is up to scratch. Can't arrive to school with someone stinky- ouch!"

Miranda chuckled as I pinched him hard on his back. His grip around me tightened and I squeaked in surprise, feeling my ribs almost crack under the impact. I sometimes forget how strong he really is.

"Well, I'll leave you guys to it..." she trailed off, amusement clear in her voice.

"Oh, thanks a lot!" I yelled out sarcastically, yet again, earning another laugh.

Carter resumed walking and I found myself staring at the bathroom floor. I had my lips pressed into a thin line, a crinkle on my forehead. Gently, he lowered me down to my feet. He took a step back and dusted his hands, as if to say 'job well done'. We stood there, silently, before I slapped him in the chest.

"Ouch!" he laughed, shying from me. "What's that for?"

"For dragging me out of my warm and toasty bed!" I huffed, folding my arms. "I was having a good dream about Michael Scofield you know!"

Upon saying the main star of Prison Breaks name, last nights events came rushing back to me. The chocolate, the T.V series, the note. How sweet it had been...

"Aw, you're so cute when you're grumpy." he teased, reaching out and ruffling my hair.

My breath hitched in my throat. Firstly, due to the compliment and secondly, because he always used to do that to me. I used to pretend I hated the gesture, but I secretly loved it. It was kind of our... thing, as lame as that sounded.

We both paused for a moment and I cleared my breath uneasily. It was weird how easily we just fell back into that. "Hum. Well. This has been... Um, I'm going to shower now."

"Er- right." he said, rubbing the back of his neck, a flush creeping up his skin. "Just don't take too long, okay?"

"Mmhmm." I said, pointing at the door.

This time, he received my signals and trailed out, without another word. I lent heavily on the door, biting my lip softly. Sometimes, staying angry with him was hard. I mentally shook myself and pushed away from the door.

No it wasn't. I hated him. Anger comes with hate, right?

Shedding my clothes, I stepped inside the shower cubicle. The warm water ran over my muscles, deknotting all the muscles that had bundled up during my almost-like-coma. I inhaled a large, lungful of the steamy water.

I avoided getting my hair wet, since that would slow my getting ready process down. Carter was annoying, yeah, but if our roles were reversed and he made me late for school, I would get pretty annoyed. I rushed through my morning routine and was making myself some toast, when Carter appeared in the kitchen. He smirked at me cheekily.

"Nice shower?"

"Yeah. Thanks." I grunted.

He rolled his eyes, not dropping the smirk for a second. I edged around him, placing all the items away, when he pressed his hands onto my hips. I froze, the vegemite jar almost slipping from my hands in surprise.

His hands sunk lower and onto my bare legs, his fingers walking across my skin. Instantly, causing it to heat up at his mere touch, making me lick my lips in anticipation. I tilted my head back, pressing myself further into him.

I then snapped back to reality.

I jolted backwards, colliding with him. He jerked in surprise and I slammed the fridge door shut, spinning on my heel. I narrowed my eyes at him warningly.

"What are you doing?"

He opened his mouth, but no words came out. Huh, that's a shock. Cater Williams always has something to say.

"I was just-" he began, but Miranda entered at that moment, interrupting him.

"You better get going soon Carter." she said, her eyes glued to her watch. "Don't you have to be there by seven thirty?"

Frowning, I brushed past him and began nibbling at my toast. I was ready, I just needed to demolish these bad boys, before I could go. After doing so, I trailed wordlessly after him and out to the car. Awkwardness hung heavily between us, as I sidled into the passenger seat, fiddling with the hem of my skirt. Oh and also, I was going to be at school, ridiculously early this morning. Yay for Lacey! I was going to beat about ninety nine percent of the teacher population there.

"Sorry about this morning." he murmured quietly.

If I hadn't been so wired, I probably would have missed him saying anything completely. I turned in surprise, my eyebrows raised.

"It's okay. You had to get here early." I shrugged dismissively. "I would have done the same."

"You mean pick me up over your shoulder and throw me into the bathroom?" he smirked.

"Yeah, what else would I mean?" I asked with an eye roll. "Because you don't weigh a tonne or anything."

"Hey!" he cried out, faking hurt. "This is pure muscle baby!"

"Sure it is."

His mouth fell open and I laughed, shifting back from him again. My laughter died off when I realised how easy things were falling back with him. How easily I could forget everything over the past two years.

That night when everything changed...

I pushed my thoughts roughly into a file at the back of my mind, which wasn't going to be opened anytime soon. I would not forgive him. That easily, anyway. Wait, what was I thinking? Urgh, get me away from Carter before I turn weak again! I thought urgently, my fingers twitching at the handle. But, no, I wasn't quite suicidal yet, so I would have to wait it out.

"I actually meant sorry about the thing in the kitchen." he muttered.

"What?" I asked, trying to recall what happened. When I did, my mouth fell into an 'O'. "Oh yeah. Right. Um... it's okay."

"Really?"

"Really."

"Good." he said, a genuine smile taking place on his face. "We're going to be living with each other for a while. I don't want us hating each other every minute, or it's going to be a living nightmare."

His words hardly registered through my mind, because I was just too absorbed up in his beautiful smile. I hadn't seen him actually smile, without his trademark smirk, probably since the day of my sixteenth birthday... before everything went wrong.

"What?" he asked, quirking an eyebrow. "Is there something on my face?"

Yes, something beautiful.

"I-er-what?" I stammered like an idiot. "Oh. Nothing. What were you saying?"

He stared at me in amusement. "Am I dazzling you with my good looks again?"

My cheeks turned hot. Was I that obvious? A grin lit up his face at my lack of control on my emotions. He looked pretty smug about it.

"Always had that affect on you..." he trailed off.

"Do not!" I protested, although I was lying through my teeth. "You're so narcissistic!"

He burst out laughing, slapping the steering wheel. I frowned at him, blowing out some air and turning the opposite direction of him.

"You're too funny Lacey."

"Yeah. Should be a comedian."

He grinned again and silence lapsed again. I felt my heart throb and I tightened my grip on the seat, rolling my tongue across my teeth. I hate how nice this felt. Not yelling or fighting with each other. How good it was to just spend time with him.

How much I really had missed it...

Thank God, school loomed ahead of us. Well, not exactly, I didn't want to be here, but anything to get out of this car and away from Carter would be a blessing. He was having strange affects on me and if I stayed any longer, this hate act was going to become tough...

The car hadn't even hardly stopped, before I fell out of the car, almost face planting. I reefed my bag out behind me and swung it onto my shoulder.

"Slow down hot stuff," he laughed. "What's up with you?"

"Nothing!"

He frowned at me and I mentally slapped myself.

"Okay..." he trailed off. "Well, I have to go. Meet you here after school?"

"Sure. Yeah." I said, turning from him.

"See ya."

"Never wanna' be ya," I muttered, striding from him.

The further I walked from him, the clearer my mind got. I breathed a sigh of relief. I was getting a bit ahead of myself there. I shook my head, hardly realising my hands were shaking. Why did my body go so strange, being with him?

"Hello beautiful," a voice whispered in my ear, causing me to jump about a metre in the air. I slapped my hand to my chest, whirling around. Aiden, stood there, grinning from ear to ear. "Got your text, so I thought I'd come early too. I don't need to go to practise this time, it's only for the first line."

I smiled, grateful for this thoughtfulness. "You didn't have to do that."

"I wanted to." he smiled.

He stepped forward and brushed his lips to mine. His fingers trailed down my cheek as our lips moved together. He pressed his hands on my hips and images of Carter bombarded my brain. I stiffened, stepping back as if he had poisoned me.

A look of hurt flashed behind his eyes, before he quickly masked it. "Sorry... I didn't mean to... go too far or anything."

"You didn't. It's okay." I said.

You're just not Carter...

"You okay?" he asked gently, swallowing my hand up in his.

I nodded in attempt to shake away my thoughts. "Fine."

"Well, since you ditched me the other night about the movies, we should go see one tonight?"

Ditched him? When did I... Realisation soon dawned on me. That was the night I had to move into Carter's. That then blatantly reminded me, that I still haven't told Aiden about my new sleeping arrangements. He knew Carter gave me a lift this morning, but didn't know it was due to us having recently become roommates. I gulped slightly, averting my eyes, feeling guilt accumulate in the pit of my stomach, making my skin itch.

I was a horrible girlfriend.

"Yeah, that sounds good." I said, forcing a smile.

"Okay, I'll pick you up at seven?"

"No!" I blurted, my voice rushed. "I mean... I'll meet you there."

"Okay?" he asked, confused.

To distract him from asking further questions, I stood on my tip toes and pecked his lips. Before I could move away, his hand wrapped around the back of my head holding there. I let him kiss me for a few moments, before I successfully pulled away.

He grinned at me. "What was that for?"

"I don't know." I lied, shrugging. "Want to go get some food?"

"You know me, I always want food." he laughed, slinging an arm over my shoulder. I lent my head onto him, sighing.

I wish I could just get over Carter.

Why, I didn't take the opportunity to fess up and just tell Aiden about me living with Carter this morning, was beyond me. I was regretting it already. I had to walk to the movies, while the cool night air slapped me in the face, reminding me of my lies. Well, my non-truth-telling, I suppose.

My body began shivering in the cold. I wrapped my arms around myself in attempt to keep in some of my body heat. My teeth chattered as the icy wind made my hair swirl restlessly around my face. I gritted my teeth together, trudging on. The cinemas were only a couple of minutes walk from my place, but it felt like forever when it was this cold. The weather of our town was nice but annoying at the same time. The sunny days were really hot and humid, forcing you to go swimming majority of the day to cool off, whereas the nights were harsh and cold if you weren't indoors.

I was glad I brought my coat, as I was enveloped in it, it's warmth slowly seeping into my skin. I cupped my hands around my face, trying to protect it from the harsh winds. Eventually, the cinema came into sight and I let out a breath of relief, increasing my pace. I stepped inside, the warm air washing over my body. Aiden's eyes widened and he rushed towards me, a frown evident on his face.

"You walked here?" he cried out angrily, causing curious bystanders to glance over at us. I hushed him, inclining my head, so we could get out of the entrance area. When the doors opened, a swoop of the night's air filtered in.

"Yes."

"Why? I offered to pick you up!"

I didn't want you to see me in Carter's house.

"I felt like I needed the exercise." I blurted.

He just gave me 'the look'. "Lacey, you exercise like an athlete and are skinnier than a twig. Why are you lying to me?"

"I'm not!"

"Lacey-" he began angrily, but the guy behind the counter cleared his throat, effectively gaining my attention.

"Lacey? Is that you?"

Upon hearing my name, I pivoted around. A small smile broke out on my face when I noticed Jim, a former peer of mine. I went up to him, leaning on the counter, glad he gave me an excuse to walk away from Aiden.

"Hey! I didn't know you worked here?"

"Started last week," he laughed, beaming at me. His eyes slowly rested on Aiden and he quirked his eyebrow. "Is Carter with you?"

I felt Aiden bristle beside me. "No, this is my boyfriend, Aiden. Aiden, do you remember Jim? He went to our school a couple of years back."

"Vaguely." he said, smiling politely. "Nice to meet you, man."

"Yeah same. What movie are we seeing tonight?"

We paid and he printed our tickets off. We split off and I found myself seeking out some popcorn and chocolate. Like, come on, you can't watch a movie without popcorn. After stocking up on my supplies, we headed inside. I collapsed heavily down onto one of the seats, leaning back. After a few moments, I felt Aiden's hand slip onto my thigh. He began gently caressing it. I shifted slightly, moving as far away from him as I could. I felt his gaze on me, but promptly ignored it.

I don't know why I was so touchy today, but I couldn't stop myself.

My body was tense as we sat there. I was dreading every moment, as the movie slithered by, slower than a snail. My foot was tapping restlessly and I was looking anywhere but at the screen, just wanting to leave. I continuously played with my sleeves, my skin still feeling like ice from my walk. I don't know what is is, but everything with Aiden felt so forced and unnatural.

Everything was already getting so complicated.

I slid my shirt up and ran my fingertips over the jagged scars that would permanently damage my skin. Swallowing uneasily, I tugged it down so my scars were firmly covered once more.

Finally, the credits began rolling across the screen and I was out of my seat, as if it was on fire. I rushed out of the room and out into the cold air, waving over my shoulder at Jim. I kept going until Aiden grabbed my hand, hauling me back.

"What is wrong with you lately?" he snapped at me, clearly annoyed.

I wrenched my hand from his, shaking my head. "Nothing. I'm just tired. I'll just walk home. See you tomorrow."

"Are you crazy?" he hissed, reaching out for me again. "You will freeze!"

I side passed him, but halted. He narrowed his eyes at me. We had a heated stare for a couple of moments.

"You're being dramatic."

"Come on, I'll drive you home." he sighed, pinching the skin in between his eyes, obviously frustrated with me.

Exhaling through my nose, I slowly nodded. "Okay. Thanks."

I followed him to his car and climbed in, facing away from him. He kept attempting to start a conversation with me, but gave up after my short, blunt replies. I don't know what was wrong with me, but there just was something not right. For some reason I was feeling guilty, as if I was cheating on Carter, despite us not having been together for almost a year. I felt like Aiden is just an excuse to distract me from my true feelings. It was wrong and I was only beginning to realise this.

The car came to a stop and I didn't move. I felt uncomfortable and out of place. He sighed, running a hand through his hair, agitated.

"Is it me?"

"No."

"So it's you?"

"I guess so?"

He groaned, face-palming himself. "You're confusing me."

"Like I said, I'm just tired." I looked nervously at my house, where it was pitch black and looked almost neglected. I hoped he didn't notice. "See you tomorrow."

"Wait!" he said, as I flung the door open and struck my leg out. I paused, looking back. "Goodbye kiss?"

I lent forward and pressed mine to his briefly, before scrambling out of the car. I made sure I walked to the porch and waved. He did a U-Turn and exited my street. I roughly ran my hands over my face, as I walked with dread towards Carter's house.

My body slipped inside the door and crept up the stairs as quiet as I could. I tip-toed through the hall, hardly breathing. I silently went to the bathroom, brushed my teeth and emerged into my room, eager to get out of these close and into my nice, toasty pajamas.

My heart leaped inside my chest as I jumped about two feet in the air. My T.V playing. I registered that it was, in fact, Prison Break. My eyebrows shot up and my eyes swivelled towards my bed, where Carter was sprawled out, dead asleep.

I just watched him for a moment, shaking my head. Quietly, I walked over and switched the T.V off, the room instantly returning to its dark state.

I stripped down and changed my clothes, before doing the worst possible thing.

I crawled into bed beside him.

Chapter 5

Being in his embrace felt amazing. His arm was securely draped around my waist, his face nuzzled into the crook of my neck. I could feel his warm breath, fanning across my skin, making my stomach flip flop every time he exhaled.

I really had missed this. Just being with him. I know how stupid it was of me to have done this. I know it went by everything I stood for about our friendship, but I had had a lapse. He has always been and would always be my weakness. I moved slightly, trying to slither out from his capture, although my whole body screamed at me to stay where I was.

I already knew that when I get out of his vicinity, my brain will defog, causing my hatred and anger to come flooding back and I will be normal, once again.

Or, so I hoped.

"Morning gorgeous." he mumbled into my skin, his thumb rubbing circular patterns into my arm, making me tilt my head back and close my eyes, loving the rippling sensation my body was experiencing.

My breath hitched in my throat. All I wanted to do was wrap myself further around him and grab him, not letting go again. The desperation to be with him again was gnawing under my skin to the extent I was almost cringing.

Why was I so stubborn? Why couldn't I just let myself be happy with him? Even at the best times of my life, I am never quite as happy as I was, when Carter had been my best friend. He was the missing part of me and without him, I would never be right.

Before I had time to realise what he was doing, he moved his head, his lips pressing against the corner of my mouth. Every single muscle in my body protested at me to lean forward. Kiss him back with all I had, but no. I couldn't.

Thoughts of Aiden bombarded my mind and it was like a trigger inside me. I gasped, shoving him roughly from me. He let out a cry of surprise and I toppled backwards. My head slamming against my bedside cupboard, the side of my face piercing with pain. A scream escaped my lips at the sudden impact. I laid there, sprawled painfully on the hard, wooden floorboards, winded. I felt hot blood trickle down the side of my face. I closed my eyes, my entire face stinging.

"What the hell Lacey?" he demanded, maneuvering over the side of the bed so that he could see me. "You're bleeding!"

I clambered to my feet and staggered backwards, the world spinning slightly. I blinked, trying to steady my vision, but my body kept swaying. He leapt to his feet and steadied me, wrapping an arm around my shoulders. I blinked, my eyes rolling back slightly.

There was so much blood. I didn't think a cut would be able to have this much blood flow.

"Jesus," he muttered, swooping me up bridal style into his arms. He used to always do this to me. My stomach swooped at the gesture. I let my fingers run over his bare chest for a moment, loving the feel of his defined muscles underneath them.

"Usually go by the name Lacey." I muttered.

"Okay, I think you need to go to the hospital. Looks like you're going to need stitches." he informed me as we made our way down the hall. "Hold on, stay here for a moment. Hold on to the rails, I'm just going to get mum."

He gently lowered me down and made sure I was holding the rails, before he rushed off, in search of Miranda. My head throbbed painfully. I raised my head, and gingerly touched where it was aching. Upon removing my hand, a fresh coat of blood stained my skin.

My stomach clenched and my mouth watered. I was going to be sick. I needed to sit down immediately, before I puke everywhere. Slowly, I moved towards the stairs. Somehow, my feet got tangled and everything else after that was a blur.

One minute, I was just walking, the next, I was rolling down the stairs, bouncing down them painfully. I gritted my teeth as my head copped another blow, before I fell into a heap at the bottom, gasping for breath. Black dots danced across my vision and my entire body ached.

Well, this was one way to start the morning.

We had been in the waiting room for over two hours and I was getting pretty over it. I sat there rigidly, arms folded across my chest, determinedly looking the other way. Carter was positioned beside me, texting someone on his phone. He hadn't spoken another word to me since my falling down the stairs, due to me blatantly ignoring him.

Since Carter's father was a doctor here at the hospital, he had made regular checks on me, to make sure I hadn't bled to death. Okay, that was a bit dramatic, but you should see the blood. My head was like a broken tap. I hadn't had my stitches put in yet, but he made sure they saw me and that I was okay. I was light headed and my vision was fuzzy, but I was alright.

My phone buzzed yet again and I didn't bother trying to fish it out of my pocket. I felt Carter's gaze flicker towards me. "Are you going to check your phone? This is like the seventh time it has gone off."

"I don't want to talk to anyone."

"Suit yourself." he sighed, resuming back to his phone.

"You don't have to stay and baby sit me." I snapped, closing my eyes tiredly. The urge to just curl up in fetal position and cry myself to sleep, was growing stronger with every minute. "You don't have to miss out on school because I fell over."

"Like I'm just going to leave you here." he scoffed, making me re-open my eyes. He was looking at me incredulously. "We may have our differences now Lacey, but despite everything that has happened between us, I obviously still care for you. I'm not going anywhere, whether you like it or not."

My mouth fell open at his little speech. He turned away from me again and continued playing his new app that he was obsessed with.

Silence lapsed between us again and it was another half an hour, before the doors pushed open and Carter's father came rushing towards us. He looked very professional, dressed in his white, pristine uniform. He was tall and tan, just like his son. He had bright, piercing blue eyes and dirty blond hair.

"Lacey, did you want to come on through?"

I nodded and stood up. Automatically, Carter rested his hand on the small of my back and guided me through one of the numerous corridors through the hospital, as if I were made of glass. I ignored the flare of heat underneath my skin. We made our way to a small room. I sighed, not wanting to deal with this right now.

Stitches on my face. How attractive.

"This might sting..." he muttered as I collapsed down on a seat.

'Sting' was an understatement.

"What the hell happened to you!?" Mercedes burst the second I walked in the hallway of school. I had been ignoring the rude stares of people all morning. She rushed up to me, waving her arms frantically, examining my swollen and bruised face.

My head looked like a balloon. I had a wicked set of bruises, scattering across the left side of my face. The ugliest stitches I've ever seen was plastered across my skin, the colour too disgusting to describe.

To say I looked nice today, would be erroneous.

"Fell over, hit my head on my bedside table and then fell down the stairs." I explained simply, not pausing my stride.

"What!?"

Luckily, the setting in my house was quite similar to Carter's, so she didn't question my story, because it could have easily happened in my own house. That then reminded me I still hadn't told her about my recent 'moving'.

"Why have you been ignoring mine and Aiden's texts?"

I shrugged. "Didn't want to talk to anyone."

"You're so lame." she said in annoyance. "Did you know Carter missed school too? Aiden was suspicious."

And Mercedes would have absolutely loved that.

"I'm sure he was. And yeah, because he was with me at the hospital."

"WHAT?" her voice echoed down the corridor and a couple people glanced over at us. I frowned at her and she quieted down. Just because I needed more attention today. "You were with Carter yesterday?"

"Well, it did happen at his house..." I trailed off, wanting nothing more then to just turn around and leave.

She planted her feet and ripped my elbow back painfully. I stopped and scowled at her. Her eyes were bulging out of her head. Okay, I could understand her lack of understanding right now, but I was not in the mood to explain it.

"Since when have you been going to Carter's house again?"

"Since I'm living there for a few weeks."

It actually felt good to talk to someone about it, although it was more like an investigation rather than casual chit chat. I know I should have told them both as soon as it happened, but it was as though if I didn't talk about it, it wasn't real. But, unfortunately for me, it was and I just need to deal with it.

"You have got to be joking."

"Does it look like I am?" I questioned, my voice bland.

"Why have you waited to tell me? You're a pretty slack friend."

"Yeah, well, you get that." I said, walking forward again.

"What is wrong with you lately?" she snapped at me, irritation lining her voice. "This isn't the usual Lacey..."

"Thank my recent life style changes for that."

"Okay. Whatever." she said, stepping back from me. "Call me when you're normal again."

"Sure."

Aiden then materialised by my side, grinning from ear to ear upon seeing me. His face soon fell once his eyes landed on my face. Oh, that's comforting. You could probably put me in comparison with Shrek right now.

"Hey babe, why have you been dodging my texts... what did you do to your face?"

"Oh, she is PMSing right now. Don't bother speaking to her." Mercedes said, her voice blunt. I swivelled my eyes to her.

I winced at her voice. I was on pain killers, my head was throbbing painfully, a head ache was accumulating behind my eyes and I had had the worst sleep in history last night. Yes, I was in a bad mood. Yes, I was taking it out on my best friends, but I couldn't stop. I was too riled up and angry to filter my thoughts.

"Umm...?" he trailed off, his eyes switching back and forth between us as though he was watching a tennis match. "What's going on?"

"Lacey, care to explain?"

Mercedes always had a thing for Aiden, so when he asked me out, we had a major falling out. We were normal again, obviously, but I know if I ever broke up with him, it wouldn't be long before she would try and hit on him. Whenever Aiden and I had a fight, I couldn't help notice she'd play on whatever I did, to make me look like the bad guy. I was getting so damn sick of it.

"You and Aiden are so close, why don't you?" I said emotionlessly, shouldering around her. "Adios."

"Lacey, wait!" Aiden called behind me, but I did what I was best at. I ignored him and marched down the hall. I noticed Carter flanking me, in my peripheral vision, and turned to him. He stared at me with concern.

"You okay?" he asked, just as the bell buzzed loudly, signalling the start of school. I turned and kept going, walking straight out the exit.

I needed a cleansing day. I kept going until I was back at Carter's place. I shredded my clothes and slipped into my tights and singlet. I jammed my headphones in my ears and flew down the stairs, just itching to get out of the house again.

Running would be my distraction.

My feet pummelled against the ground as I pushed myself to go harder and faster. My breath was coming out in short, fast pants, my sides burning to the extent I thought I was going to pass out. My head complained the whole way and blackness began edging my vision.

Pushing myself like this wasn't healthy, but I was going to do it anyway. I felt the numbness slither into my veins and through my muscles.

This was my therapy and I sure as hell needed a lot of it.

Chapter 6

One Year Ago

I was so excited, I could scream. I had been waiting for this day my entire life. I was finally sixteen. With my grin spread from ear to ear, I let out a big whoosh of breath, effectively blowing all of my candles out.

Cheers erupted from my friends and family that gathered around me. My cheeks were aching as I had been smiling nonstop ever since I woke up. Which had been Carter belly flopping on me and screaming that the house was on fire.

A knife was shoved into my hand and before I knew it, I was slicing the cake up. After removing the knife, it became evident that it was dirty, making me smirk. I knew what came next and the prospect was exciting.

"Oooh, Lacey has to kiss the nearest boy!" one of my friends laughed childishly.

I grinned even wider, if possible and turned to Carter. I think it was pretty obvious why I demanded that my boyfriend be next to me while I cut the cake. I smashed my lips to his, ignoring the fact that both our parents were present. They've all seen it before. More cheers broke out around us. Our lips moved together, before I breathlessly stepped back, the taste of him still tingling against my lips.

I felt so exhilarated. The whole night had been a rush. The whole day had been. I didn't want it to end! He gave me a heart-stopping smile and I found myself gazing into him, my mouth agape. He rolled his eyes, smirking broadly.

"We all know I'm attractive Lacey, no need to stare."

Shaking my head, I snapped out of my trance. He always had that effect on me. He was ridiculously attractive. There were a couple of sniggers from my friend at his smart remark and my cheeks grew warm.

So far, my birthday had consisted of waking up and spending time with my family, unwrapping presents and such. I had gone down to the river with the extended family, (Carter's fam bam) and had lunch by the water. The smell of the salty sea and the feel of the freshly mowed grass brushing against my bare skin was still fresh in my mind, causing a sigh of content to escape my lips. I could close my eyes and still envision the whole scene in my head.

It had been perfect.

Afterwards, there was a party at mine. We had been playing childish games such a 'pass-the-parcel' and 'pin-the-tail-on-the-donkey' for laughs. Okay, when I say childish, I mean kids play it, but I still do as well, okay? Don't judge.

I let my eyes wander towards the clock, where it showed me it was a little passed six. A grin broke out on my face. Anything after this point, my parents were turning a blind eye too.

In other words, the real party gets started.

We were having a bonfire out the back, and all my friends were here already, milling around it. We were going to be drinking, yeah, but no way was I getting drunk. I wanted to remember every single bit of this night, because it would be the first time I would give something to Carter, that I would never get back.

We had been waiting for this moment, for so long now. The fact that it was now here, was still dazzling. Every time I thought about it, nerves bubbled in the pit of my stomach and my hands trembled with excitement.

The cool air was crisp, as per usual on my birthday. We always lit a bonfire for my celebration of birth due to it being the middle of Winter. I rubbed my hands together and watched the flames dance carelessly. I breathed into my hands, my hot breath fanning my face.

"Having fun?" Carter asked me, shrugging his arm around my shoulders. I turned to him, pecking him on the cheek in greeting.

"Yes, it's been amazing."

"Well, it will only get better." he smirked, winking at me confidently.

I gulped, my knees going weak. Oh God, oh God, oh God. I was so nervous that it was making me sick! It was actually hard to explain my emotions right now. I was nervous, hell yeah, but at the same time, I was so comfortable with Carter, I knew everything was going to be fine. He took off from me, to go socialise further and I stumbled towards the esky, withdrawing another premixed vodka.

Slowly, I made myself walk around the bonfire, in attempt to find a suitable stick, to cook my marshmallows on. After a few moments, I snatched one up and gathered around with the others, who were asking each other a series of questions. Carter sat behind me, his legs straddling me, chin resting in the crook of my neck. Every time he laughed, his hot breath would fan across my skin, causing tingles to erupt down my spine, making me shiver involuntarily.

"What are you doing later tonight Lace?" my friend Mary asked, taking a swig from her cruiser and tucking a strand hair behind her ear.

I felt Carter's fingers walk across my thigh and hoped my face didn't mirror my thoughts. My cheeks began to turn hot as I tried my best to act normal.

"Just hanging with Carter."

She began wiggling her eyebrows suggestively at me and I rolled my eyes in response. I think everyone knew what would be happening later, as disturbing as that was. My best friend couldn't keep secrets apparently.

Not long after, the fire dimmed down and the drunken teenagers began slowly, one by one, departing from my party. It was highly entertaining watch everyone, how stupid they get when they're intoxicated.

It was about eleven-thirty when everyone had gone. I sighed, pulling Carter behind me and up the stairs, biting my lip. I thought I would be tired by the end of the night but the elation coursing through my veins drowned out any weariness that had begun to seep in.

I went to enter my room, but he grabbed my hips, snagging me back. I gasped as he spun me and roughly smashed his lips to mine. I widened my eyes in surprise at his abruptness. Before I knew what was happening, he had me swooped up, so that my long legs were tangled around his waist, his hands supporting me so that I didn't fall.

He carried me into my room, gently shutting the door behind him. He laid me down on the bed, collapsing on top of me, his lips never leaving mine. Spikes of electricity shot through my veins, making me feel more alive than I had ever felt before. I was beginning to feel light-headed at the lack of oxygen I was enduring.

He made a trail of kisses from my jaw, to my neck, as I was gasping breathlessly, my fingers shakily running through his hair. Only seconds went by, before clothes were peeling off faster than the speed of light.

"Are you ready?" he murmured into my ear, his hands stroking me lovingly, sending waves of emotions through my body.

"I've never been more ready in my life." I whispered, my voice unable to go any louder.

My birthday ended in the most amazing way possible.

I awoke with a smile, plastered across my face. I inhaled deeply, stretching. When I didn't feel a body next to me, I stiffened, my eyes snapping open. I stared in surprise at the vacant space beside me.

"Carter?" I mumbled groggily, getting onto my knees, peering around.

No sign of him.

Huh, he might be in the kitchen. I hope he was cooking something delicious. I rolled out of bed and went to my bathroom, freshening myself up. I padded down the hall, surprised at the soreness I felt between my legs and into the kitchen, eagerly awaiting what I would find there.

No one.

Frowning, I maneuvered around the kitchen, my eyes roaming. I began restlessly searching the entire house. I was home alone. Obviously, my parents were at work, but where was Carter? With my hair, wrapped securely around my finger, I dragged my feet upstairs. The more I began to realise he wasn't here, the tighter the hair got around my finger. Twirling my hair was an annoying habit I'd somewhat adopted when I'm nervous.

I fell heavily onto my computer chair and logged myself onto Facebook. I went onto Carter's page, just to see if he had a status or something. My mouth fell open slightly at what I saw. He was tagged in a post, at two a.m this morning. I scrolled through it, my mouth agape.

He went to a party after we... after...

My lips spread into a thin line as I began to go through the photos. Numerous people had posted on his wall, saying how crazy last night was. Okay, I had fun at my party but it wasn't "crazy". Who even were these people? Surely I didn't have gatecrashers and not know about it. I sat there, a frown evident on my face. It only increased further when I began going through the pictures he was tagged in.

My heart skipped a beat in my chest. My eyes burned with tears. A photo, of him, with Mary... their lips locked together, bodies pressed. My stomach churned uncomfortably and I placed a hand to my mouth, wanting to be sick.

No... he wouldn't do that to me.

Carter has hooked up with other girls before. I was used to it. But if he had, we were never together at the time. And I was always okay with it. Carter and I were hard to keep up with. We were dating, back to friends, and then dating again within days. Our relationship was like the weather. But right now? We were together. Or, so I thought.

Slamming the lid of my laptop down, I clambered to my feet. I hastily wiped the tears away and let out a huff of air.

Don't make any assumptions, before you know the facts, I told myself firmly.

I began getting myself ready for school. Yeah, many of my friends were going to have some wicked hangovers for History today. I laughed at the thought, momentarily shoving the disturbing image from my brain, although it was almost an impossible task.

I did my make-up quick and left my hair, falling down my back in natural waves. I slid my uniform on and grabbed an apple for breakfast. If I didn't eat, I would be sick. My stomach was already feeling uneasy with what I saw this morning. I made my way out and stopped, realisation dawning on me.

Carter was supposed to be giving me a lift today.

I sighed and checked the time. School starts in five minutes. It was about a ten minute walk from my place, meaning I would be late. Grumbling under my breath, I began my trek to the school, dreading going there after seeing my own worst nightmare in photo-form just before. It was an overcast and dreary day, which made me further disgruntled. If it rained, I was going to be seething.

As if my thoughts triggered the large cumulonimbus cloud above me, patters of rain began to fall, seemingly landing directly in my eyes. Of course it would be raining today. Tucking my head in, I increased my pace, praying it didn't bucket down. Too soon, the rain got heavier and I was drenched. Was someone trying to make me lose my mind? My clothes stuck to my skin and my hair was glued attractively to my face. I scowled, wringing it out as much as I could.

Today, was obviously not my day.

Eventually, I arrived at school, later than I thought I was going to be. I scribbled my name in the late book and trudged down the hallway, towards class. I entered and eyes swivelled to me instantly. I must look like an absolute drowned rat. A few whispers broke out and I noticed a few people making kissing sounds, to see my reaction.

Of course, I remained as blank and indifferent as I could. I hoped I looked as stoic as I felt.

Setting my eyes determinedly forward, I handed my late note over to Mr Erikson and maneuvered my way down next to Mercedes. She was smiling down to her crotch, indicating that she was on her phone.

"Hey." I said quietly, sidling in beside her, ducking my head.

"Oh - morning! Bit late hey?" she laughed, quirking an eyebrow. "Busy morning with Carter?"

As soon as the words left her lips, she paused. Okay, so she obviously had saw the photos too. She gave me an awkward look, before glancing away.

"Who's party was on last night?" I demanded, avoiding her question.

"Someone in the year below us."

"Carter hooked up with Mary there?" I asked, fearing the answer, although I already knew it. Seen it, rather.

She refused to look at me and fiddled with her phone. "Umm..."

"Oh my God."

I was hoping it was a drunken mistake, a slight peck... but I knew I was just kidding myself. They were two, drunk, hormonal teenagers. Although that isn't an excuse, it's a definite factor.

Dread sunk into my veins as I flopped forward, my forehead hitting the table roughly. My good friend and my boyfriend. On the night of my birthday. The night I had slept with Carter for the first time.

How the hell could he do that to me?

Anger surged inside me, the more I thought about it. Okay, we were dating, so that extremely sucked, meaning he cheated on me. Secondly, on the night of my birthday. Thirdly, on the night that had meant so much to me.

It would have been different if it had been another night. Still horrible, but different.

I slammed my fist onto the table. I got up from my seat, rage flaring in my veins. People glanced over instantly. My 'I don't care' facade was slipping. Fast.

"Is there a problem Lacey?" Mr Erikson inquired, cocking his head to the side.

"Yes." I said through gritted teeth. "May I be excused?"

"What for?"

Without answering, I hauled my bag up and stomped out of the class, anger rolling off of me in waves. I was marching down the hall when I saw him. I skidded to a halt, my heart jerking inside my chest.

He was at his locker, leaning onto it heavily. His eyes were closed, his hair disheveled and his collar tucked in. Sucking in a breath, I rushed over to him, unable to stare at him without screaming any longer.

"Big night?" I snapped at him, slamming his door shut and jolting him awake. He stumbled backwards in shock, his eyes wide. He had dark circles under his eyes from his sleepless night. This only made me more furious.

"What?"

"Big. Night?" I said excruciatingly slow, trembling. My words were venomous and no doubt could cut glass.

"Umm..." he trailed off, looking around, rubbing his neck, looking nervous. Probably looking for ways to escape. Good. He should be.

"How could you?" I screamed, projecting my fist into the locker. Pain scattered across my knuckles in protest but I was so angry, I hardly felt a thing. "How could you do that to me? After sixteen years of friendship... after last night!"

"Lacey-" he started, looking pained.

He was so hung over I could still smell the stench of beer on his breath. This fact made me more angry, to the extent red was beginning to edge my vision.

"And with Mary. One of my closest friends." I spat, twitching. "You could have gotten with anyone, Carter. Anyone."

"Seriously, things got out of hand, okay? I was only going there for a little while, but I had a few drinks and one thing lead to another..."

"That is no excuse!" I screeched. "My God. I can't believe what you have become."

"Lacey-" he tried again.

"No seriously Carter. I will not... I cannot forgive you for this."

"Can I just explain-"

"Give me a reason, why you did it."

"Huh?"

"Give me a reason." I deadpanned, tears making me vision so blurry I could hardly see a thing. I blinked rapidly, my nose beginning to run.

"It just happened."

Oh wow. That's a good response.

"We're done."

"What?" he squeaked.

Yes, he actually squeaked.

"Done." I repeated firmly.

"Let's just talk about this-" he began.

"Not just done from our relationship. Done from our friendship."

His mouth fell open. "You can't be-"

"Serious?" I laughed humourlessly, physically feeling my bruised ego. "I am. I don't want this anymore."

With that, I jerked myself away from him and ran down the hall, tears gushing fluently down my face. I felt like I was five years old, running away from school crying. But I couldn't help it. It felt as though my heart had been ripped into two and ripped from my chest.

I hate Carter Williams.

Chapter 7

One Year Ago

Carter's P.O.V:

It was hardly a second over six a.m before I was sprinting down the hall and barging roughly through the door of Lacey's bedroom. I leapt on top of her and belly flopped. Our bodies colliding together with a painful smack, the pain hardly registering in my mind.

"THE HOUSE IS ON FIRE. GET UP LACEY!" I yelled at the top of my lungs, making my throat burn slightly.

She jolted awake, sitting up so abrupt our foreheads smashed together. I gasped and fell backwards, as I stared up into her wide eyes. Although pain skittered across my head, I couldn't help grin up at her.

"Ouch!" I laughed, as I shot up again and pinned her down roughly. "You're going to pay for that."

She frantically began trying to wriggle out from underneath me, as I began cackling with laughter. She stopped and let out a huff of air. Her 'grumpy' facade didn't work too well as a smile danced around the edge of her lips.

"I'd like to point out you're the one who jumped on top of me yelling the house was on fire!"

"I don't see your point."

"Thanks Carter." she stated sarcastically.

"You're welcome, beautiful birthday girl."

"Oh my God." she breathed, her eyes dilating in excitement. "It's my birthday!"

"It surely is." I beamed at her.

I edged closer to her and pressed my lips against hers, ignoring the fact that we both probably reeked of morning breath. This day... we have been waiting for sixteen years now. It was going to be the night we would finally be together, in more ways than one.

"Come on! I can't wait to see your face when I give you my present."

An excited grin stretched across her face as she clambered to her feet. Her golden hair was a tangle of curls that fell loosely around her face. She looked so hot. Her soft, tanned skin glistened underneath her bedroom lights and her lips were so red and inviting, that I almost wanted to lock her in her room and do it right here and now.

I smiled smugly as she was wearing one of my old football jerseys. She always had to sleep in a garment of mine, saying my scent was 'refreshing' to her. I always complained that she was creeping on me, but in all honesty, I was exactly the same. Okay, so I didn't go sleeping in her dresses or anything, that might be awkward, but I did have a bottle of her perfume that I occasionally sprayed around my room...

Entwining our fingers together, I pulled her after me. Our feet padded against the wooden floor as I tugged her along. We piled into the spare room, where I had her presents laying on the bed. A massive bouquet of roses was perched in the middle of the bed, with matching diamond earrings, necklace and a ring.

I had seriously spent about two years saving for those. I didn't work at the supermarket part time for nothing. Oh and saving for my car, but I may have blown half, or most of that budget on Lacey. Yeah, I won't be informing my parents of that one any time soon. Lacey's fingernails biting into my flesh effectively snapped me back to the present. I winced as she viciously tore up my skin. Guess she's preparing me for tonight? Just kidding...

"Oh. My. God." she gasped out breathlessly, sprinting towards the bed. "I love you. I love you. I love you."

"I know."

"No, seriously." she murmured, turning around to me, her face expressing all seriousness. She bit her lip softly. "I really do. Love you, I mean. More than I've ever loved someone in my life."

My mouth dried out slightly. I took two strides to her and cupped her face in the palm of my hands. Her skin felt soft underneath my fingertips. She was so fragile and little. I wanted to pick her up and hold her to my chest and just squeeze her. "I love you so much Lacey."

She smiled up at me as I gently pressed my lips to hers again. I pulled back and gave her a toothy grin.

"Okay, try them on!"

I didn't exactly need to tell her twice.

"No matter how long you stare at them, the diamonds aren't going to change..." I trailed off in amusement, as I watched her eyes. They had been glued to the diamond rock on her ring, for the past three hours during lunch. It was almost as though if she looked away, it would disappear or something.

"But every time I blink, it just gets even more beautiful." she breathed, in a complete daze, still not looking up.

"So, you like it?" I smirked, feeling pretty smug about myself.

Not many sixteen year old's were privileged in wearing a diamond ring on their finger. Nor many sixteen year old guys able to afford it. Well, in this town anyway. My parents could have just given me the money for it, it's not like it would damage the bank account, but it meant so much more to me that I worked for it. Lacey is the type of girl who deserved beautiful things in life. I vowed to myself I would try and achieve that whenever I can.

"Like is the understatement of the century!"

I rolled my eyes, but couldn't wipe the smile off my face. Whenever Lacey was happy, so was I and today, we were both ecstatic. I pulled her closer to me and hugged her, loving the feel of her being in my embrace. I kissed the side of her cheek and sighed.

"Tonight will be amazing."

"I'm so nervous." she whispered.

"Don't be. There is nothing to be nervous about."

"I know, but I can't help it."

"It will be the best night of your life." I teased, punching her lightly. "Well, any night with me would equal to the best."

"You wish."

I winked playfully at her and she rolled her eyes. The rest of lunch cruised by pretty uneventfully. The party was creeping closer and closer, with each second and I was getting seriously pumped. We'd already played some games, but the real party, was what I was keen for. Don't get me wrong, 'pass-the-parcel' can get pretty intense, but it wasn't exactly the highlight of the night.

Eventually, it rolled around the six o'clock and excited tingles were shooting through me. We'd had the cake and got a pretty cheesy photo kissing after the knife was dirty. It turned out pretty funny as it looked like she was about to stab me. Or well, everyone else thought it was funny. They weren't at the other end of the knife.

The parents began disappearing one by one as the rest of us teenagers were attracted to the huge bonfire set out the back, as though it was a magnet. The warmth of the fire radiated onto my skin as I inhaled a deep, smoky breath. I could hardly stand still, I was that excited. I just wanted the night to hurry up and end so I could be alone with her.

I really hope Lacey had a good day. She seemed to. Every time I saw her, her eyes were bright and her smile wider than I'd ever seen it. I saw her collapse down on the other side of the bonfire, so I leapt up and sidled in behind her, resting my chin on her shoulder. I inhaled her smell and sighed with content, snuggling closer to her.

Tonight...

I couldn't stop thinking about it. I couldn't wait for everyone to get out of here already. My phone had been going crazy all night, due to another party going on that I had been supposed to go to. Who in their right mind would hold a party on the night of Lacey's sixteenth? They must have been mad. Like I was going to ditch my girlfriend's party, just to go to a random one.

Before I knew it, as if the night was a blur, people were going home and soon, it was just us. As soon as I got the chance, I swiped her hand and dragged her up the stairs. Without any warning, I swept her off her feet and carried her into her room.

This was going to be a night we both definitely would remember.

My God, if my phone doesn't shut up, I'm going to throw it out the window.

I groaned as I removed my arm from around Lacey's waist and snatched my phone. It had been vibrating non-stop. I squinted down at the screen and saw that it was my best friend, Jacob. He knows how important this night is for me, so it must be pretty serious for him to keep calling me.

I pushed myself off the mattress and padded into the hall. I skipped down the stairs and out into the brisk, night air. The smell of the fire was still fresh and lingering in the air. I probably hadn't even been asleep long.

I dialled his number and impatiently waited for him to answer. "Hello?"

"Jacob, what's up?"

"Man, I've been trying to reach you all night!" I heard him yell.

It was a bit hard to hear what he was saying due to the noise in the background. In comparison to my silent surroundings, his sounded very static. I rolled my eyes. There wasn't much need to point out the obvious.

"I know, I've been a little busy..." I trailed off with a frown.

"I know. Andrew's here."

My mouth dried out. Surely, I hadn't heard him right. It was definitely the loud sounds affecting my hearing.

"What?"

"I know. He's been trying to find you, he has been causing heaps of trouble. I reckon he'll get the cops called on us soon. I think he's on something."

"On something?" I echoed.

"Drugs, man."

I began muttering profanities, rubbing my hand roughly across my face. Andrew had been one of my best friends for years. He had been the biggest player at the school. Us two were the footballers guys everyone wanted to be friends with. Our popularity status got to his head. He was obsessive, self-centered and ignorant.

Which girls adored.

We were really close, until the day Lacey became his new fixation. That was not on. Long story short, it ended with his nose broken, me with bruised knuckles, him expelled and me on a ridiculously long community service sentence.

As you can guess, we weren't exactly on the best terms. That was about a year ago. He liked to drop into town again, every few months and stir up trouble. I clenched my fists. The more I thought about him, the angrier I got.

"What is he doing?" I ground out.

"Throwing furniture around and yelling out for you."

I let out an exasperated sigh. "He just had to come tonight."

"Carter, you really need to be here man."

Agitatedly, I ran my hand through my hair. "Fine. I'll be there soon. Tell him to calm down."

"I've already tried."

I hung up and the grip on my phone tightened, to the extent my knuckles were white. I stormed back up the stairs and threw on a shirt. I contemplated leaving Lace a note, but thought better of it. I'll be back soon anyway.

Shrugging my jacket on while I bounded down the stairs, I made my way to the party.

It was about a ten minute walk, before the sounds of shouts and music alerted me. The cool night air was starting to make my skin feel clammy and dry. I sighed again as I maneuvered down the street and towards the party. Seeing Andrew again was not something I was looking forward to.

I entered and my eyes burned with the sudden light. Music thumped in my ears as the floor vibrated underneath me. It was such a stereotypical party it made me laugh. I so did not want to be here right now. I didn't want Lacey to wake up alone, especially after what just happened between us...

"WHERE IS HE?" a voice bellowed, which could be heard clearly over the loud bass. I flinched at his familiar voice and shuddered.

All I wanted to do right now was snuggle up with my girlfriend and spend the remaining hours of her birthday with her. But no, yet again, Andrew has bombarded his way into my life, trying to flip it upside down.

Shouldering through the crowd, I followed the source of his voice. I made it successfully into the living room, where he was tearing up the lounge. Literally. His eyes were stained red, his hands were trembling furiously. His back was tense and his Caucasian skin sweat-drenched. A slight shudder rolled down my spine.

More profanities left my mouth as I walked over to him, shaking my head incredulously. "Andrew, what are you doing?"

"Ohh, he's here. Guys, the man of the hour is here!"

"What are you talking about?" I frowned at him.

He stumbled towards me, his breath reeking so much of alcohol, it could knock over a horse. I grimaced as I automatically steadied him. He poked me roughly in the chest and pressed his face against mine. His eyes were glassy and his pupils scarily small. His face was flushed, his skin so red you could hardly see his light blond eyebrows.

"Oh you know. You're the famous one. You're the one who hit me, but no, I am the one who gets my whole life messed up!"

"Because you already had a record." I pointed out.

"Come on, golden boy. Let's show us how bad ass you can be. Oh wait..." he said, his words slurring together to the point I could hardly make out a word he was saying. "Your skank isn't here, is she?"

A growl tore from my throat as my hands projected out, pushing him. He toppled to the ground with a loud clash, causing everyone to stop. The music dramatically lowered so everyone could hear what was happening.

"Don't you talk about her like that." I ground out, my teeth clenched together painfully.

"Make me." His words were hardly audible but I still could understand him. His blond hair was greasy, due to the amount of sweat that was sleeked across his skin. Whatever he was on had him messed up. It physically pained me to see him go down this road. After having so much potential...

"I'm not looking for a fight, Andrew." I sighed, rubbing my hands over my face, feeling exhausted after today.

"Let's party hard!" he yelled out suddenly, hauling me to my feet. He began fist pumping fervently.

My eyebrows shot up with his abrupt mood swing. He reached for a vodka shot and sculled it. I frowned, due to him already being highly intoxicated. Before I knew it, a couple of vodkas were in my hand, my throat was burning and some had spilled down my chin. I blinked a few times as I chugged a few more back. Why, I was doing this, I wasn't sure. The more I drank, the more it dulled Andrew, as weird as that sounds. The fact that he was 'happy' again was pleasing.

I collapsed back onto the lounge, closing my eyes. Unfortunately I was still here. Every time I looked like I was heading out, Andrew threw some big tantrum, which turned violent and things began breaking. So, to keep the peace and for everyone's safety, I decided to stay.

I felt the lounge dip beside me and before I knew it, a pale hand was on my thigh. With my eyebrows raised, I swivelled my head to the side. "Mary?"

"It's a dare. No tongue."

"Huh?"

Before I could ask any more, she pressed her lips to me. I heard the click of a flash, before she pulled back. "Thanks Carter. I'm going to win for sure!"

I stared after her in shock as she sprang to her feet and ran after a giggling girl. I wiped my hand with the back my of hand, feeling dirty. Yuck. I rose to my feet and maneuvered to the bathroom. I splashed some cold water on my face, suddenly feeling weary. I cringed as I heard something break. I turned and emerged back down the stairs. Andrew visibly relaxed upon seeing me.

"Here man, take this off my hands." he said, shoving the drink into my palm. "Drink and stay here. I'll be back."

Without another word of complaint, in case it set him off, I sculled the drink. It burned my throat and stung my eyes. I gagged and the glass slipped from my hands. I leaned back on the wall. I didn't feel too good...

My skin was becoming clammy and sweaty. I could feel my hair was matted against my forehead. My mouth was hot and sticky, feeling dryer than sand paper. My eyes were so blurry I could hardly focus on anything.

That is when I blacked out into unconsciousness.

Chapter 8

Now Lacey's P.O.V:

My head hurt.

My face was still a blotchy and bruised mess from falling down the stairs. I winced as I gingerly prodded it with my fingers. I hadn't spoken to Mercedes since our argument at school and I was supposed to be meeting up with Aiden at the park about... five minutes ago.

Crap.

Sighing, I rose to my feet and slipped my iPhone into my back pocket. I already had a text from him asking where I was. I glanced in the mirror and sighed once more. My face was looking better, but it was still semi-revolting.

Fetching my red leather jacket, I slipped it over my shoulders and brushed a loose tendril of my hair behind my ear. Slipping into my shoes, I wandered through the door and past Carter without a word, our arms brushing due to our proximity.

His mouth opened as if he was about to say something, but I kept going. The cool air washed over my body the instant I stepped outside. I was thankful for it as my face had been flushed with heat. I stared at my Lancer and groaned, forgetting that I didn't have petrol. Grabbing my phone, I quickly texted Aiden that I was walking, so I may take a bit longer. The walk would probably do me good anyway. The silence of my surroundings and the cool air was pleasant.

Hastily brushing my hair back from my face, I turned and entered the park where we were supposed to be meeting. I could see him bent over, sitting on one of the swings, his elbows dug into his knees. I stood there for a moment, just watching him.

He was a good guy.

A nice guy.

He was popular, easy going and had a line of girls willing to do anything for him. Why, he stuck with me, I wasn't sure. I was moody, irritable and took my anger issues out on him. My baggage was heavier than luggage you'd take on an overseas holiday.

As if sensing my presence, he turned his head and smiled. I felt myself give him a small smile in return. He got to his feet and walked over to me. Without a word, he just wrapped his arms around me. I snaked my hands around his waist and just let my forehead press against his chest.

"I'm really sorry."

"No, I'm sorry. I shouldn't have got mad at you." he mumbled into my skin making me feel ten times worse than I already did.

"No, that's just it. You had every right. I was being rude and just... ugh. I'm sorry. Forgive me?"

He took a step back and rolled his eyes. "Like that is even a question. I love you, Lace. I would forgive you for anything."

I love you.

Three words.

Three, simple words that held so much meaning. Every time Carter and I had seen each other, we would always tell each other I love you. Saying it to anyone else felt weird and wrong in my mouth. My mind paused on the; "I would forgive you for anything," part.

Anything?

Like living with Carter, sleeping in bed with him and then practically kissing him?

To avoid saying anything in return, I grabbed his shirt and pulled him closer to me. I kissed him softly. He immediately responded, cupping my face with the palms of his hands. I let him kiss me for a few moments, before I did what I always did and pulled back.

"Have you spoken to Mercedes?" he asked me. "Since your little.. . episode the other day."

I shook my head. "Not yet. Have you?"

"Yeah, she messaged me the other night."

A frown instantly came across my face. Of course she did. I gritted my teeth together angrily as furious thoughts began whirling inside my head.

"What did she say?"

"Just wanted to talk about what was going on with you and I."

"Because she just loves getting in the middle of it, right?" I bit out, my voice venomous. I stepped back from him, my fists clenching at my sides.

"She isn't getting in the middle of anything."

"Oh, so you're on her side now, huh?"

"Lacey, can you stop jumping down my throat for two seconds?" he asked in exasperation, throwing his hands up. "I'm not taking any sides since there are none. I'm just trying to reason with you. Stop seeing everything as a threat."

I had nothing to say back. Because he was right. Like always.

I sighed, rubbing my temples with my fingers. "Sorry. Again."

He let out a soft laugh. "Are you okay? You seem really stressed."

"Yes. No. I don't know." I let out a breath, closing my eyes. "It's complicated."

Slowly, he reached out and pivoted me. He ran his hands across my back. "Jeeze, you're really tense."

He began moving his thumbs in circular motions across my back and I let out a soft sigh. I always told Aiden he could do this for a living. He ran his hands over my back, unknotting all my wound up muscles.

I felt my body relax as I leaned back into him. After a couple of minutes of silence, he stopped massaging me and wrapped his arms around me. His chin rested on my shoulder and he softly kissed the side of my neck.

"Feel better?"

"Much better." I confirmed, a genuine smile coming onto my face. "Thank you."

"Anything for you."

I turned and wrapped my arms around his neck. "You're great."

"I know." he laughed, a playful smirk on his mouth.

He leant forward and kissed me softly on the forehead. "I'm glad you came tonight. When you were late, I thought..."

"I wouldn't do that to you." I said immediately, frowning at him.

"I know, but I couldn't help think you were trying to... end it with me or something."

"No!" the word rushed out of my mouth before I could stop it. "No. Don't think that because it's not true. I don't want to break up with you."

He let out a visible breath of relief and grinned at me. "Thank God."

My arms wrapped around him tighter as I felt the need to hug his worry away. We stayed at the park for about another hour, just talking. It was good to just spend some time with him. We hadn't hung out and just spent time together for a while. We only ever really hung out at school, because I always blew him off any other time.

I really was a horrible girlfriend. I'd dump me if our roles were reversed.

"I have to get back."

"Okay."

"I'll drop you home."

"I'll walk-" I began, but he cut me off.

"Don't start."

Frowning, I followed him without further argument. We piled into his car and instantly, the warmth wrapped around me like a blanket. I snuggled back into his soft, leather seat and let me inhale his scent. The car rumbled to life and it wasn't until we were almost at my house, that I began to panic.

I really hope he doesn't question why the lights are off all the time. Maybe I could say we're saving power or something...

"Want me to wait, so you can see where you're going?" he asked me, peering out the window with a slight frown.

"No!" I said too quickly. I cleared my throat. "I mean, it's fine. Thank you. I'll see you tomorrow?"

"Yep." he smiled. The leather seats squeaked as he leaned forward, planting a kiss on my cheek. "Good night, Lacey."

"Night!"

I slid out of the car and made my way up my driveway. Despite my wishes, he waited. I began to turn the knob and waved, when he finally pulled away. I exhaled and let my head fall forward so that my forehead smacked against the wood of the door.

I hated lying. I don't know what it was, but I still didn't tell him the truth. I had the perfect opportunity to tell him tonight but for some reason, the words got choked up in my throat and refused to come out.

Turning, I dragged my feet with me towards Carter's house. I mounted the porch steps and entered. It was quiet and all that could be heard were the soft falls of my feet, as I mounted the stairs. I went to my room and was glad to see that Carter had found his own bed tonight and not mine.

I threw some comfortable clothes on before I emerged into the bathroom. I was rinsing my mouth out when hands found themselves on my waist. I choked on the water in my mouth in surprise. Carter chuckled as I hacked up a lung.

"Let me go Carter." I said in a quiet, firm voice when I regained my breath.

Anger surged inside me. I cannot believe I crawled into bed with him. He set up a trap and I fell for it, head first. The stupidity from me was enough to make me want to punch something. How could I do that to Aiden? It made me sick.

I finished brushing my teeth and turned. He stared arrogantly down at me, a smirk plastered across his face. I sneered up at him with distaste, wanting to wrap my fingers around his neck and strangle that smirk off of him. He brushed my golden hair from my face, his long, slender fingers sparking electricity in my skin, making my knees wobble together.

"Will you ever, forgive me?" he whispered huskily, his eyes intently staring into mine. His face was only mere inches from me. I just needed to reach out a little further to kiss him...

"Yeah. Over my dead body." I snapped, before throwing my arms out forcefully, shoving my hands into his chest, pushing him from me.

I need to go to bed and get myself away from him, before I go absolutely mental.

Mercedes' P.O.V:

I hated the fact that I was always the one who had to apologise to her. Although she was the one who jumped down my throat. But, it was Lacey. My best friend. I need to swallow my pride and just go and apologise.

It wasn't until I had pulled up to her house and was about to get out, that I realised she wasn't living there currently. I had completely forgotten she'd moved in with Carter. Did Aiden know? If so, why hadn't he said anything?

The temptation to blurt it out to him was increasing, the longer Lacey ignored me. But if I did that, I wouldn't have a best friend any more.

My phone vibrated against my leg and I eagerly grabbed it, hoping it was Aiden. When it wasn't, I felt my heart sink slightly. Ignoring the message from Mary, I went to my recent inboxes and began to read through my last conversation with Aiden. Seeing his name brought a small smile to my face, as it always did.

I hated, so much that it almost hurt, that he was with Lacey and not me. It sucked seeing them together everyday. Especially when she treats him like crap and he acts like she is the Queen.

Lacey is a good person and can be a great friend, but she can be snappy, rude and just plain mean sometimes. Her anger controls her. I'm probably not the best friend either, admittedly. We would be so much closer if Aiden hadn't come between us. And because of this, I know there would always be tension between us.

I loved him. She was the one in between us. In the back of my mind, I've always wanted to get back at her. Hurt her the way she hurt me. Exhaling loudly, I removed myself from the car and out into the crisp, morning air.

I wanted... needed to apologise to Lacey before school so it wasn't awkward. Dread filled my veins at the thought of facing her.

Slowly, I walked up Carter's driveway and climbed onto the porch. It took me a few moments to muster up the courage to knock. I waited for a couple of minutes, growing more nervous by the second. Maybe she saw me through one of those little eye things and refused to answer.

Raising my hand, I went to go knock again, but it swung open. My mouth fell open as I came face-to-chest with Carter. His torso was bare and slicked with water, from his shower I'm assuming. A towel was loosely slung around his hips, resting dangerously low.

I know I was gawking, but it was like my eyes had a mind of their own. How was it that Lacey got with the most attractive people ever? I gulped, my mouth suddenly going dry. I hadn't ever really spoken to Carter much before. He scared me with his coolness, as stupid as that sounds. He was like royalty in this town. After him and Lacey broke up, I lost all contact with Carter, not that we spoke all that much before it. He was either with his many guys friends or consumed with Lacey. He didn't have time for anyone else.

One look from him had girl's going weak at the knees, myself included.

"Take a picture. It will last longer."

"Huh?" I asked stupidly, snapping myself out of the trance I seemingly was in. My cheeks burned crimson when I realised what he had said. "Oh-I-err-umm..."

He sighed and glanced down at his watch. It was one of the nicest watches I'd ever seen. Of course.

"Look, school starts in thirty minutes and I need to make myself look even more fabulous than I do now. If we could speed this process up, that would be great."

"Um, r-right." I stammered like an idiot, my face getting hotter by the second. "Is Lacey home?"

"Nope." he said, popping the 'p'. "Her pet came and picked her up about ten minutes ago. Just missed them."

My lips spread in a thin line at his word choice. Describing Aiden as a 'pet' was not cool. Not when he was so, so much more than that.

"But, you're welcome to come in if you'd like." he offered, giving me a charming smile. His eyes swept over me not-so-subtly and I felt my heart rate quicken. Every girl wanted Carter Williams to notice her. I felt like I was beginning my five seconds of fame. "I could always use the company."

I stood there, blinking at him for several moments, his words slowly sinking into my brain. "You're asking me to come in?"

"Well, that's what it looks like." he pointed out with an amused smirk. "Unless you have something better to do, of course."

"Oh, no." I said with a nervous laugh, waving him off dismissively.

He stepped back and gestured for me to enter. With my heart thudding loudly in my chest, I stepped in. His hand touched the small of my back and I leapt a metre in the air. He chuckled softly in my ear, the sound making shivers run down my spine.

"What's your name?"

If I wasn't so nervous, I would have laughed. I had been to school with Carter for almost all my life and had been friends with Lacey for most of that time. The fact that he didn't know my name was incredulous.

"Mercedes."

I watched to see recognition or any sign that he knew me, but he remained blank. He nodded and smiled.

"Do you have to be at school early, Mercedes?" Goosebumps erupted across my skin as my name left his lips. I swallowed uneasily, feeling suddenly flustered.

"No, why's that?"

He smirked.

And with that, he dropped the towel.

Carter's P.O.V:

Again, I didn't think with my brain.

Lacey was going to slaughter me. Well, if she found out anyway. I don't know what got into me. The fact that she was out late last night with that twit, Adrian or whatever it is and he picked her up this morning.

I, was supposed to be taking her to school.

Not him.

The anger that fuelled me every time I saw them together was enough to make me think irrationally. Which is what excuse I'm using for if she finds out that I slept with her best friend. It was an impulsive move on my behalf, but hey, it's her choice to never forgive me. I wasn't going to stop living because of this.

I was surprised to see the girl when she arrived on my door step. I acted like I didn't know her, as usual, but I know she's been glued to Lacey's side for the past year. Which makes it ten times weirder that she gave in to me, after knowing everything between Lacey and I. Good friend, huh.

I dressed and finished getting ready, as Mercedes finished doing whatever she was doing. I packed my bags hastily and opened the front door, when she cleared her throat.

"Um..." she trailed off.

"What?" I asked, pausing and turning back to her.

"You're just leaving?"

"Yes?" I asked her, looking at her as if she was stupid. "School starts in four minutes."

"O-oh..." she trailed off, her face red with sweat glistening across her forehead. Her eyes darted around and I could tell she was freaking out after what just happened. I shrugged it off though, she's probably never done anything like this before school.

"Look." I said, running my hand through my hair. "It was fun, okay? Now go on and pretend this didn't happen. I'll do the same."

"Are you serious!?"

I just gave her a look, before I turned and walked out. "Oh and lock the door behind you. Thanks."

Striding out to my car, I slid in and pressed heavily on the accelerator. The car had hardly come to a stop as I heard the school bell buzz loudly. Hastily grabbing my bag, I rushed inside and made it into the hall.

I felt her presence before I saw her. I turned, seeing her mane of blonde hair cascading down her back. His arm was securely wrapped around her waist as she laughed at something he said. My teeth gritted together as I saw the picture perfect couple waltzing towards their first class.

Suddenly, I didn't regret this morning.

Not one little bit.

Chapter 9

Lacey's P.O.V:

The urge to punch Mercedes was increasing with every minute.

She wouldn't leave me alone, but every time I talked to her, guilt flooded her face and she would scuttle away. Every time I turned she was talking to Aiden and the sight of those two together made my skin itch. My hands trembled as I slammed the locker of my door closed.

"What's wrong diddums?" his annoying voice cooed from behind me.

Running my tongue across my teeth, I pivoted. His lips were stretched into his trademark smirk as he stood over me, arrogance rolling off him in waves. Just the sight of him made me want to strangle something.

Okay, so I was a little angry today, if that wasn't obvious.

I quirked an eyebrow at him as he stared intently into my eyes as if searching for answers within them. My face instantly became blank.

"You tell me?" I toyed, watching his reaction.

He swallowed, almost nervously. I tilted my head to the side curiously. There was something up. He let out a laugh which I immediately recognised was fake.

"Don't frown, Bub." he said, stroking the side of my face. "You'll get wrinkles."

I slapped his hand away. "I hope I do."

Relief flooded onto his face as if his question had been answered somehow. He smirked victoriously which made my frown deepen.

"Okay. See you this afternoon."

Frowning after him, I watched as he strolled from me casually. Well that was strange. Letting my body sag against the lockers, I sighed, running my fingers across my face. School was the last place I wanted to be right now. To feel my feet hitting the hard floor and my lungs burning is what I need.

The temptation to turn and walk out the door was so forceful it almost knocked me over. But, in reality, every time I got a little mad I couldn't just skip school. The bell signalled loudly overhead and a loud sigh left my lips.

Pushing past anyone who was in my way, I shouldered towards my history class. History and I were not a good combination. I was average at the class, yeah, but what made me hate it to the point of wagging most lessons, was an arrogant, smirking boy, who sat directly across from me.

It was infuriating that he was positioned in my peripheral vision. The swinging motion of his chair was enough to have me twitching. It was just the fact that it was him. All class he just sat there, distracting us fellow peers and making unnecessarily annoying noises.

And yet, he was still beating me, which made me want to punch myself. He didn't hand in any assessments or listen in class. The fact that he is unbeatable in the exams is so frustrating. I wish I had the ability to do absolutely nothing and succeed. He was one of the brightest people in our year. An absolute evil genius.

"Lacey?" Mr. Andrew's voice effectively snapped me out of my hating-on-Carter thoughts in which had consumed me. Which evidently is a regular occurrence for me.

"Er-what?" I asked, realising I had no idea what we were discussing.

He frowned at my lack of attention and leaned back in his swivel chair, maintaining eye contact with me.

"We're going through revision for your upcoming exam. Today, our focus is on Stalin. Tell me what year he died."

Lacey, you are in modern history, studying Russia in the early 19th century. Stalin died in... my thoughts urged.

"Erm-" I stumbled, trying to improvise. "1950..."

"1953." his smooth voice cut in and my fists automatically balled, my nails biting into my flesh.

My eyes snapped towards his. He smirked at me and winked, making my blood boil.

"Well done, Lacey." Mr. Andrews said sharply, emphasising my name as he stared at Carter.

"Welcome babe," his smug whisper came towards me.

Gritting my teeth, I refused to acknowledge him further. About ten minutes from then, he stood up. I watched his tall, lean body as he strolled to the front of the classroom, handing Mr. Andrew a piece of paper.

Mr. Andrews eyes widened and he let out an incredulous; "hmph."

Carter must have handed in his first piece of homework ever.

He stretched and threw a scrunched up ball into the bin, flexing so that every girl in the class had drool running down their chin. He made a show of taking a long, scenic walk back to his chair. Directly in front of me, of course.

Without my brain even processing it, my foot stuck out as he made some smart comment to a girl in front of me. His foot connected with mine and he stumbled. Not just tripped, but actually face planted into the carpet.

I snorted with laughter and covered my face. He groaned and rolled onto his back. His nose had a red mark where he hit the floor. Laughter erupted all around the classroom and must admit mine would have to have been the loudest.

Look, it was an immature year seven move, but it had to be done.

"My God you two!" Mr. Andrews sighed in exasperation. "I'm sick of it! Get out. The both of you."

"Me?" he asked in shock, making his way to his feet. He pointed at his chest incredulously, as though showing who he was would eliminate the threat of detention. "You're punishing me?"

"Just get out." he sighed, turning around and waving his hand to us as if we were merely flies in his way. Not finding this situation quite as funny anymore, I threw my chair back, grabbed my stuff, storming from the classroom.

"Did you have to?" he spat, slamming the door behind him.

"If you weren't such a jerk I wouldn't have."

"Oh so helping you in class is a crime now, is it?"

"It's not the act itself, Carter." I snapped, whirling around to him. "It's the way you do it. The way you do everything! God, you're so infuriating! The way you walk, the way you talk, even the way you smile is just so God damn arrogant that I want to get a baseball bat and hit you repeatedly over the head!"

His eyebrows shot up when I mentioned the baseball bat. We stared heatedly at each other for several moments. My chest was rising as I tried to gain control of my breathing again.

"You have issues." was all he said, before the bell rang and Mr. Andrews was summoning us inside, to most likely, make the situation ten times worse.

Definitely ten times worse.

"You have after school detention? What for?" Aiden asked me curiously, as he ran his fingers through my hair.

"I tripped Carter over in History."

His fingers paused on my scalp and I tilted my head back to see him better. I took a moment to observe his straight jawline and angular cheek bones. He really was an attractive boy. I was lucky to have him.

Was it bad that I had to keep reminding myself of that?

"Well..." he trailed off, biting his lip and giving me an amused smile.

"That was childish?" I finished for him.

"A little." he admitted.

I sighed, rolling my head forward again. I let out a puff of air as I watched the other students mill around, chatting in groups. Currently, Aiden and I were perched underneath the shade of one of the large, chestnut trees in the oval. It was perfect for the warmer days and was a popular destination at our school. The days were only getting hotter and hotter, while the nights remained frosty as ever. It was a dramatic change, to say the least.

"You're really worrying me." he murmured, much to my surprise.

"Me? Why?" I asked nervously, peering up at him under my lashes.

"You're just so wound up and not yourself at the moment. It's like every little thing makes you snap. I'm scared to even speak to you anymore. I feel like-"

I planted my finger onto his lips, effectively silencing him. I reeled into sitting position and wrapped my arms around his neck. I positioned my face so that we were eye level.

"I'm sorry. I'm struggling with my anger issues at the moment but I don't mean to take it out on you."

I love you. Just say it...

"I lo-" I tried to say. I cleared my throat. "I lo.. really like you Aiden. You're always there for me and I probably don't seem appreciative but I am. God, you're an amazing person and I am honestly so lucky to have you."

Oblivious to my tongue troubles, a grin broke out on his face. He lent forward and brushed his nose to mine, before gently kissing me.

"I love you."

I kissed him once more, before burying my face into his chest. We stayed in each other's embrace for another few minutes just enjoying being with each other.

"Oh. Isn't this cute."

My body stiffened as I heard his voice. I exhaled slowly and reclined back. Okay Lacey, turn over a new leaf. You're living with the boy for goodness sake. Just try being civil with him until it's over.

I don't want to lose Aiden and if I keep going, the possibility will only increase. So, I put on my nicest smile and looked up at Carter.

"Hello."

He raised his eyebrows and I felt Aiden's eyes on me. I tightened my grip on Aiden's hand, as if that would keep my anger in check. I just wanted to be normal Lacey again. I was sick of this hate-driven monster I had become.

"What's with the new attitude?" he questioned curiously.

"Just trying to turn over a new leaf. Anything you need?"

"I don't like it. Can you go back to hating me?"

A slight smirk twisted onto my face as I was putting him on edge.

I ignored him and rested back onto Aiden's chest. "Aiden offered to take me home so I don't need a lift from you."

"I was going to say we could go out for dinner or something?" he asked me, giving me a charismatic smirk.

"Why on earth would you suggest that?"

"It's a celebration. Duh."

I exchanged a confused glance with Aiden. I rested back into him further and sighed. "And what are we celebrating?"

"One week of us living together!" he exclaimed, clapping his hands. His voice lowered and he winked at Aiden. "Have to love having the girl next door, literally next door. If you know what I mean."

He went rigid beside me. "Living together?"

"Did Lacey not tell you?" he asked dramatically, his mouth falling open in mock-horror. "Oh! I'm sorry!"

"No you're not." I hissed, my fingers literally twitching in desire to strangle him.

The 'new leaf' facade was fading pretty damn quickly. How did I think I could ever get along with this imbosile?

"Well, this is just a tad too awkward for me. See you at home, roomie!" he grinned, giving me a wave over his shoulder. He trotted away, positively glowing with happiness. The temptation to rearrange his facial features was growing with more intensity every moment I thought about what just happened.

Speaking of...

I gulped, swivelling my head to Aiden. He didn't look mad and he didn't look curious. He just stared at me with disappointment. And that, was probably the worse look I could have gotten. I dropped my head in shame. Why I hadn't just told him when I found out, was beyond me. I think not saying it out loud would mean it wasn't true. But clearly, it was.

"You're living with him?"

"Yes."

"It's been a week?"

"Yes."

He slowly rolled his tongue across his teeth. "Okay."

"Okay?"

"Okay."

I bit my lip as he continued to stare at me, his eyes shadowing disappointment. I sighed, rubbing my hands across my face.

"I wanted to tell you but I didn't and then I just avoided it and I don't know. I didn't want to say it out loud."

"You know you can tell me anything. You had so many opportunities to."

"I know."

"And you didn't even try."

"I know."

"Well, it know explains why you've been so moody." he sighed, pulling his arm from me.

"Yep..." I trailed off, playing with the hem of my skirt.

"It's making sense now. Why the lights are always off at your house. Why you've been travelling together to school with him."

"I should have told you."

"That you were staying with your ex bestfriend/boyfriend of sixteen years who you secretly still really care about? Yeah. You should have."

"You're mad."

"Yeah. I am a little bit." he said, gently pushing me from him. "I'm going to go. I'll... talk to you later."

I watched him walk away from me. I lent back onto the tree, suddenly feeling exhausted. The lies had caught up to me, over took me and tripped me along the way. Okay so Carter had managed to destroy the only relationship I cared about at the moment. Awesome. I clambered to my feet and took off towards school. I only managed about five steps before my eyes met Mercedes and Aiden, in full embrace.

My mouth fell open slightly. I didn't move as I watched them. Was I being selfish trying desperately to cling onto a relationship that will never work? Why couldn't I let my best friend be happy? I'm sure Mercedes would probably get more out of a relationship with him then I ever would. I do generally like him, I do, but was I being selfish?

"I didn't think it was true you actually hadn't told your pet we were living together." Carter said, materialising beside me. "But I do admit I did get some satisfaction from it."

I hardly even processed his words. I was too absorbed in the image in front of me, where my boyfriend and best friend were still hugging each other as if the world was about to end. My stomach whirled restlessly in my stomach as I looked away, slightly disgusted. I know she really liked him, but so did I. I just didn't know what to do. I was horrible to him. Should I sacrifice my own happiness for hers? And possibly his? Would he be happier with a better girlfriend like her? Or what if I did break it off with him and they didn't end up together anyway? God, this was getting more and more complicated by the minute.

Carter watched me, tilting his head to the side. "Sucks doesn't it? Seeing the person you like, happy with someone else."

My eyes began to sting. I turned and barged Carter out of the way. Of course today would be the day I just can't leave. Stupid after school detention with my stupid teacher and stupid ex-best friend/boyfriend/current roommate.

I sunk onto a bench and buried my head into my hands. I just don't know what to do. First world problems or what. I tried to imagine other people around in a lot worse situations than my petty, high school drama but not even that could damper my pity parade.

The rest of the day I went through blankly, hardly speaking a word to anyone. I ignored Carter's offer to go home and slowly dawdled, feeling exhausted. No running for me today. Eventually I went home and fell face first onto my bed. I stayed there for about an hour before I was rudely interrupted.

I glanced up, through my mop of blonde hair covering my face to see him smartly dressed in a button up shirt. I let my eyes roam fleetingly, enjoying the view.

"Where are you going?"

"Dinner. Remember?"

"Right." I rolled my eyes and continued to have an intimate face plant with my bed.

"No seriously, there is no food. We actually are going out to dinner."

"Can't we just order in?" I groaned.

"No, Kim has just come back and she's on a spring cleaning frenzie. I'm staying away from her and over-whelming amount of sanitiser."

"Okay, well I'll order in then."

"Going out will get your mind off of things." he offered, sitting beside me. The bed automatically dipped causing me to, annoyingly, roll into him. I frowned into my mattress. "It'd probably do you some good."

"I'm good, thanks."

"Seriously."

"My mind wouldn't be on anything if it wasn't for you anyway! So why would I want to spend the evening with you to get my mind away from thinking about the mess you caused?"

"I actually only told the truth. Which you should have done in the first place. You can't actually be mad at me for that? You didn't think he was going to realise eventually?"

He brought up some valid points, but that still didn't make the whole situation okay. As if on cue, my stomach growled. I actually was pretty hungry. I sighed, rubbing my eyes.

"Fine."

A genuine smile lit up his face and I paused momentarily, in a daze. I very rarely saw that smile anymore. His trademark smirk seemingly was indented in his skin. It was refreshing and comforting to see his smile again.

"Let a girl get dressed!" I laughed, pressing my hands on his chest, gently pushing him out. I ignored how nice his chest felt underneath my fingertips and shut the door. The idea of getting out of the house was actually appealing. It made me feel better already.

Although I was still annoyed at him, I wanted to impress him. I grabbed out one of my nice black dresses. I sunk to my knees and rummaged through my jewellery box, attempting to find some that matched my dress. My hands paused when my finger scooped up the diamond ring Carter bought me for my sixteenth birthday. It was still breath-taking and the most beautiful ring I had ever seen.

I hadn't worn it since our falling out. It pained me because it was so amazing. Swallowing my pride, I slipped it on my finger. It felt as though I had never taken it off. I bit my lip softly and let myself observe it. A small smile crept onto my face. My sixteenth birthday had been the best day of my life. It was well spent with my family, best friends and (at the time) the most amazing boyfriend I could ever ask for.

The day after, however, was the day that had my perfect world crumbling all around me. I still hadn't picked up the pieces.

After making sure I was presentable, I wandered out to the lounge room where Carter was lazily sprawled out. He cleared his throat uneasily when he saw me.

"Wow Lace, you look great." he said, his eyebrows raised, impressed.

"Why thank you," I smiled, secretly basking in his compliment, my previous bad mood having evaporated the moment I slipped the smooth material of my dress onto my body. It's surprising how fulfilling getting ready for a night out can be.

His eyes stopped and his body froze when they landed on my hand. I looked down and into the dazzling diamond perched on my finger.

"You haven't worn that since your sixteenth birthday."

"No." I said softly, biting my lip. "I haven't."

He ran his hand through his hair, not making eye contact with me. "We better go."

"Sure."

I followed him out wordlessly. Nervously, I played with the ring, as I sat uncomfortably in his car. Awkwardness hung between us. It was like we had moved on with our relationship. Towards a better and more comforting place although it was almost like we weren't ready for it? That sounds weird since I was really annoyed at him ten minutes ago, but Carter had a way of completely changing my mind and mood with only a word, a look or even a smile. It was kind of scary.

It was a difficult feeling to describe.

The ride to the restaurant was silent. I let out an uneasy breath when the lights of the restaurant appeared in the window. As we walked in, Carter's hand rested on the small of my back, which had tingles shooting down my legs. I tried my hardest to act as casual as possible.

As soon as I entered, my eyes swept over to a table where a very familiar looking boy and his family were placed. My heart stuttered to a stop. His eyes met mine. They flickered to my right, where Carter's body was brushing up against mine. His face mirrored the expression I wore upon seeing Mercedes and him earlier today.

Aiden's lips spread into a thin line. We still hadn't talked since our blow up at school today. Seeing me with Carter was probably not going to help the situation. Aiden's mother looked up and frowned. I watched her lean over. Her lips were as easy to read as a newspaper headline.

"Who is that she's with?"

I gulped, looking at Carter, who as silently watching the scene unfold. He gave me a smirk as he leaned confidently onto the booth where the man was waiting patiently. He turned and gave me a wink, rubbing my arm softly.

"Table for two."

Other than awkward eye contact, uncomfortably loud conversations and a dry salad, dinner went quite smoothly.

It was afterwards, where it got interesting.

Apparently Carter's dad saved the bartender's wife's life once (as he is a doctor), so we got served an unlimited amount of alcoholic beverages, (even being under aged. I didn't ask, it wasn't like I was complaining). I stumbled out of the restaurant, hand in hand with Carter, giggling at something he said.

Aiden and his family had left the restaurant and honestly, I hadn't thought about him for the last hour.

"You can't drive!" I said, a little too loudly, as he began fumbling for his keys.

"Yeah I can."

"Are you crazy?" I exclaimed, pulling him roughly. "You'll die!"

"Like you would care."

"Of course I would care. Stop it!" I grabbed his keys and laughed maliciously, swinging the chunky key ring loosely around my finger.

"Give them back!"

"Gotta catch me first." I taunted, before legging it towards his car.

Which kind of contradicts the point of taking his keys but I was semi-drunk and thinking rationally wasn't an option. He effortlessly caught up to me pretty quick. He wrapped his arms around me and I felt the oxygen leave my lungs. Without thinking, I turned and wrapped my arms around him as tight as I could. I buried my face into chest and inhaled, loving his intoxicating smell.

"Are you okay?" he mumbled, surprised at my sudden change of pace.

I didn't reply and he hugged me back. He gently pressed me against the side of the car and cupped my face in his palms. He lent down, his breath fanning across my face. His lips inched towards mine and I pulled away immediately, the warning alarms inside my head on full alert.

It was wrong.

I couldn't do that to Aiden. Not after everything else I've already put him through.

"I'll call a Taxi." I murmured, my voice unable to go any louder, as I pulled away from him.

Although we didn't speak a word with each other on the way home, we didn't need to. He held my hand and I didn't stop him. In fact, it felt nice. I was so sick of hating him. I just wanted, for one night, let myself enjoy his presence. I'm not sure if the ring was making me sentimental, or if I was just fed up of fighting with him. Whatever it was, I was just going with it. I was too fuzzy and alcohol-influenced to do anything about it.

The Taxi came to a halt, Carter slapped the money into his waiting palm and we were stumbling up his porch, laughing at I don't even know what. I just seemed to find everything funny and couldn't stop laughing once I started. Once the door was shut, I turned to take my shoes off and he was there. He gripped my wrists with his hands, steadying me.

Licking my lips, I looked up. This time, when he lent down, I didn't stop him. Our lips met and all my suppressed memories rushed back into my body, leaving me breathless. I kissed him as hard as I could back. He lifted me, as if I was weightless. To him, I probably was. His fingers felt amazing running through my hair. I let myself enjoy the moment as much as I could. We stayed like that, for what felt like an eon. Electricity spiked through my veins and rippled through my body. My legs which were firmly wrapped around him, felt weak. We didn't go further than this, but it still had my heart plummeting into my stomach. I could not get enough of him. I couldn't deny it anymore.

I will always and forever love Carter Williams.

Yes, he drove me absolutely insane and 99% of the time I wanted to murder him, but God, I love him. I loved him so much it hurt. Pretending to hate him to cover my true feelings was beginning to take its toll on me. I just couldn't resist any longer.

We finally broke a part and my legs felt like jelly. He gently lowered me to the ground and I fell back onto the stairs, panting. It was like our lips were magnets, just drawn to each other. I couldn't stop kissing him. Brush my hair, kiss. Put on my pajamas, kiss. Shower, kiss. Scrub my teeth, kiss. It was like there was a drug in the air affecting the way our bodies moved and our brains functioned.

I felt so alive and electric. How could I sleep when I felt so amazing? I didn't want this night to end. I just wanted to be with him.

His fingers gently caressed my chin. He left a trail of soft kisses across my jawline and onto my neck, making tingles shoot down my body. He tilted my head back and pressed his lips to my ear.

"You're the only one who can make me feel alive."

An uncontrollable shiver rolled down my spine. I collapsed into bed and snuggled against him, loving every second of it. Eventually, I fell into a comfortable and deep sleep, my thoughts on Carter the entire time.

Tonight, would have to be the second most amazing night of my life.

I was dreading returning back to reality in the morning.

Chapter 10

After spending longer than I should have gazing at his peaceful, sleeping face with a love-sick smile on my face, I bailed. I must admit, I most likely broke my record in getting ready, as I was up and out of the house within twenty minutes. Once I had put a safe distance between me and the house, I sunk to the ground and buried my face into my thighs.

Last night was stupid.

Okay, so it was the best night I have had since my sixteenth birthday and I still felt giddy when I thought about his lips against mine, but it was still stupid. I was not the type of person to cheat on my boyfriend, and yet, I went ahead and did it. Even though I had the same thing happen to me a year ago and it had crushed my heart and ruined the best thing I had in my life.

I was a stupid, stupid girl.

I realise I'm over-using the word stupid, but that's the only word that feels adequate enough to describe myself right now. The headache, sore throat and exhaustion probably didn't help brain processing either.

Guilt hung heavily in my chest as I took a moment to be ashamed of myself. I had to tell Aiden and I had to tell him today. I had to tell the boy who loved me and would do anything for me, that I had such little respect towards him that I cheated on him. Not just one little kiss that meant nothing, either.

I was a horrible human being.

School loomed over me and a feeling of dread spread through my veins, the closer I got. I was never particularly thrilled to be here, but today even more than usual. Slowly, my body came to a stop as I took a moment to mentally prepare myself for what I had to do. I didn't have a speech prepared. I was just going to tell him what happened and I was sorry. What's done is done and there was no going back.

With my mouth dry, eyes stinging and head hanging, I dragged my feet through the entrance. I wandered over to our usual spot and he wasn't there. Sweeping my eyes through the area, I realised he mustn't be here yet. I fumbled for my phone and retrieved it from my pocket. My heart felt as though it dropped into my stomach.

'Hey, I'm going camping for a few days and won't have reception. Sorry about the short notice, I wasn't going to go but decided to last minute. Talk when we get back? Love you. X'

Well that's just great.

Reluctantly, I dialled his number, hoping he hadn't left already. Straight to voice mail. The same thing happened the second time. Sighing, I ran my fingers through my hair. Of course this would happen to me.

"He's gone camping." a voice said behind me.

My head whipped to the right, so fast I may have got whiplash, upon hearing Mercedes' voice.

"Oh really? I didn't realise my boyfriend had gone camping. But I know I can always rely on you to fill me in on everything he's doing. Thanks for keeping such a close eye on him." I spat, sarcasm dripping from my voice.

She stared at me, startled. "I didn't mean to-"

"Save it." I pushed around her and strode towards school. I only made it a step in before the bell signalled loudly, thank God.

Now I was more confused than ever with what to do. In one way, I want Aiden to break up with me, so I don't hurt his feelings (more than I already have), so I can move on with Carter. But then again, Aiden does make me happy and I sort of don't want to break up? Also, I have the nagging voice of letting Mercedes be with him but she really gets under my skin. Seeing them together infuriates me so I don't want to do that either.

This was way more drama then I wanted right now.

My phone vibrated and I hastily grabbed it out again. Unfortunately, it wasn't Aiden. It was mum just asking me how everything was going and to ring her when I got the chance. It was nice, but I still hoped it was Aiden, telling me we needed to talk. Or that he loved me no matter what and nothing could break us.

It's sad that I don't even know what I want anymore.

"You do realise the bell rang about three minutes ago?" his smooth voice cut through my mental debate.

I jumped in surprise, not noticing he had crept up on me. I tried to avoid staring at him, but the brief second I had, his appearance made my throat go dry. He looked amazing, as always. Last night's memories burned my mind and made me suddenly flustered.

"Crap."

"About last night..." he trailed off, almost nervously.

Carter, nervous? That's new.

"I'll talk to you about it later."

I doubted that I would, but it was a solid excuse not to undergo the conversation now. If we got into it, I wouldn't be making it to class anytime soon.

"I just-"

Again, I walked away as someone was trying to tell me something. I made it to English without a detention, which was the only good thing that's happened today.

Was the universe trying to let me know I shouldn't break up with Aiden? This camping trip came at an extremely inappropriate time. Or maybe it was appropriate? Should I think everything through before I break it off with him? Should I just tell him everything and let him decide? Surely he would have to get rid of me after this, right?

I rubbed my hands over my face, groaning.

"Oh, I'm sorry, am I disturbing you Ms Adams?"

"What?" I asked, blinking back into reality. I then realised that my groan was very load, causing heads to swivel my way.

"I beg your pardon." she corrected.

"What?" I repeated more slowly this time.

"I'm not in the mood for your rudeness today, Lacey." she said, irritated. "Pay attention or leave. I don't care which one."

Sighing deeply through my nose, I dropped my gaze and continued reading along with the class. I needed to focus on my school work, not my teenage drama. Soon enough, my mind wandered and I was gazing out the window, pondering about my life once more. I vacantly stared at the large tree which was perched in the centre of the ground. Aiden and I often lounged underneath it, seeking its shade. If I did break it off with him, I would miss our lazy hangouts there. I would miss him running his hand through my hair...

"Lacey, could you read the next paragraph?"

"No, I'm good." I replied automatically, not even processing what I said, unable to drag my eyes from the tree.

"Grow up Lacey, you're a senior now. If you don't want to learn, then just go. Stop disrupting everyone else."

Grow up Lacey. Her words stuck to me, although I'm unsure why.

"Saying no to reading something, which doesn't have any relevance by the way, is not disrupting the class. You stopping and making that comment is what has disrupted the class." I snapped. I blinked and sat still for a second, not having expected those words to come out of my mouth. By the look on Mrs Caden's face, she didn't expect it either.

She stared at me for a moment, irritation evident on her face. She sighed and clicked her fingers at the door.

"Just go."

"Gladly." I retorted, suddenly annoyed at this whole situation. School sucks.

Snatching up my stuff, I stormed out. My cheeks were flushed from anger as I jammed my things into my bag. I muttered some profanities under my breath. Without bothering to wait for her to come out and lecture me, I just left. I didn't need to deal with this today. My mind was too preoccupied.

Okay, so my attendance level is beginning to dwell, but until my parents come home and I put much-needed distance between Carter, I couldn't really care less. My world will settle back into its usual routine soon and I will be fine.

I hope.

So, I ran. I ran hard and I ran fast. My sides were aching, my legs burning. I only stopped when I found it difficult to breathe. Leaning over, I rested my hands on my knees, my chest heaving. Right here, right now, I wish I could dig myself a hole and bury myself into it.

Running was my escape from life. It was only temporary, but it helped me feel as though I was somewhat sane. Although anyone watching me would probably think otherwise.

My old, favourite song 'Wake me up, when September ends' by Green-day suddenly had some relevance in my life.

This was going to be a long few days.

A long few days was an exaggeration. The amount of time I have spent couped up in my room, repeating Prison Break over and over again was ridiculous. My eyes just had to rest on Carter and tingles began in my toes. And spread through my entire body like I had been lit on fire.

Groaning with frustration, I ran my fingers through my hair. This much stress, would not be good for my cardiac system. I need fresh air. Emerging from underneath my blankets, I scrambled to my feet. I listened for Carter, but was only met with his blaring music. I wasn't going to be able to hear his footsteps over that.

Edging out of my room silently, I padded across the hall towards the stairs. I smirked when I thought I had made it. Too soon.

"Lacey-"

As if his voice triggered my feet, I bolted down the stairs and slammed the door behind me. I pressed my forehead to it, wanting nothing else to do except punch a hole through it. While my mind was processing ways to inflict damage on myself, I didn't realise someone was behind me.

"Er- Lace?"

I jumped about a metre in the air, whirling around, coming face to face with my boyfriend. I sighed in relief and pulled him to me. I buried my face into his chest and wrapped my arms securely around him. I had never been so glad to see him. Except, I had to tell him the worst possible news and I may never see him after this.

Oh, the irony.

"Hey," he laughed, hugging me back. He removed his arms and gave me a lope-sided smile. "What's up?"

His kind voice put me over the edge. Suddenly, I burst into tears. Not just silent tears rolling down my cheeks. Giant, chest-wracking sobs violently bursting through my body.

"Woah," he exclaimed, cupping my face with his palms. He bent so he was eye level with me. "What's wrong?"

"I am a horrible human being and the worst girlfriend you could possibly ever ask. You deserve s-so much better. I-I-I'm so sorry." I stammered like an idiot. I pulled my face from him and cried harder, if even possible.

"No you're not?"

"I am. Honestly. You don't understand."

"Help me to." he said softly, making things even worse.

I wanted him to be mad. Angry. Throw things. His soft, gentle nature was making this much harder than it already was. I grabbed his hand and pulled him after to me. I sat on the steps, hastily wiping at my cheeks. He was silent as he waited for me to speak.

"I don't know how to say this, so I'm going to say it straight-forward. Okay?"

"Okay..." he trailed off, nervously rubbing the back of his neck.

"I cheated on you." I stated bluntly.

Silence.

It was deafening. I gulped, burying my face into my hands.

"Carter?" he asked in a quiet voice.

"Yes."

"Was it just a kiss?" he asked even more quietly.

It was my turn to be silent.

He raised his hand to his face. I didn't dare look at him. I couldn't bring myself to. We sat in silence for a long time. Eventually, I peeked a glance at him.

For the love of God, he was crying. I lost it.

I cried. He cried. We cried together. Over what I did.

"My God, will you shut up!?" Carter yelled, banging the door open. "It is a bloody sob fest out here. This isn't a charity house. This isn't a home for the lost and deprived. This is my house. Get the bloody hell out or shut up before I-"

Aiden was up like a strike of lightening had struck him. His fist was projected into his face before I could blink. Carter cried out in shock. Aiden pulled him towards us before slamming his back into the wall. He kneed him in the stomach, before Carter fought back.

Carter grabbed fistfuls of his shirt and threw him, literally threw him off the porch. A strangled cry tore from my throat as Aiden landed in a painful sprawl on the cement. Carter pushed past me to go at him again but I reefed him back. He shoved me away and I slapped him. My hand stung and his face was red. He staggered to the side and I pushed him. He fell hard backwards and I didn't stop to watch. I jumped down and frantically ran my hands over Aiden.

"Are you hurt? Are you okay?" I asked in blind panic, my hands hastily prodding his body.

His hands were red raw and his knuckle split. He jerked his hands away. Hurt washed over me. I deserved it. Instantly, I stopped and pulled back. Of course he wouldn't want me touch him. Not after what I did.

He leapt to his feet and I followed, at a much slower rate.

"I hate you."

At first, I thought his venomous words were directed at me and I almost crumbled. But his gaze was locked on Carter, who was still sitting, hastily wiping at his blood-soaked face.

"I hate you so fucking much," his sentence didn't finish as he screamed in rage. This was the first time in my life I had heard Aiden swear. "You toy with her like you toy with every other girl at school. You're such a jerk. I hate you. I hate you so damn much. I can't stand to even look at you."

Carter glared back, but didn't utter a word. Which I was thankful for. Aiden's eyes then swivelled towards me. I took a step back.

"And you." he said, his voice level and low. "I thought you were better than this."

A strange sound left my lips. I can't quite describe what it was, but embarrassingly enough, it happened. He turned and walked away from me. He could have said anything to me, and I would have taken it head on. Those seven words, were enough to undo me.

If only he had said anything else. Because he was absolutely right.

Without looking back at Carter, I took off towards my car. I was in no position to drive but I had to get away. Anywhere, away from him. So, I went to the only place I could think of.

Our cubby.

It had been a long time since I felt the need to come here.

I sat on the front, leaning back on one of the railings. Just being here, I instantly felt an overwhelming sense of security and comfort. The amazing memories I had here was enough to keep me sane. Although the memories were with the person I was trying to get away from.

I had no Mercedes.

No Carter.

No Aiden.

Sure, I had other friends, but they were just people I hung out at school and parties. We were friends because we went to school together. Not because we're all that compatible. For so long, I've been wrapped and consumed in Carter Williams, I've ignored everyone else.

I was able to break free from that and socialise amongst a new group. Aiden and his friends. They were great. Not the most fun people, but they were nice and I got along with them fine. I guess I won't be spending much time with them anymore.

I literally had no one. Not even my parents were here.

Although this sounds sad, I didn't actually care all that much. I made the decision long ago that I didn't need many friends and I now had to stick with it. I had myself, my sanity (kind of), and a long life ahead of me.

I need to get out of this town and away from Carter. That is the only hope I have, to becoming normal. To live a normal and healthy life, without him.

Even after everything, the thought of being away from him brought a dull ache to my chest. I sighed and closed my eyes. I was exhausted. I have a good life, don't get me wrong, but the people in it aren't so good. Or the decisions I made with these people, rather.

I sat there, pondering about my life. I was tempted to hop in my car, drive until I had no petrol and let myself be away for a while. But no. I let myself come back to the very place I should be avoiding. Anything to do with Carter was trouble.

Lying back, I let my eyelids close. I focused on breathing in the fresh air. I'm not sure how much time passed, but I didn't remain alone. His footsteps could be heard but I didn't move. It remained silent for a while before I eventually peered up at Carter who sat at my feet. The blood was gone from his face, but his eye had a tinge of purple around it already.

However, he didn't seem as calm and collected as he usually was. I stared at the mark on his face that was already beginning to swell.

Must have been a good hit.

"I'm sorry."

Reluctantly, I sat up. I didn't respond.

"For everything. Not just today."

My heart rate began to pick up. For so long, I have wanted him to say sorry. And mean it. Was he really about to, after all this time? I sucked in a breath as he ran his hand restlessly through his hair. He actually looked nervous. For the second time today, I made him nervous.

He turned and looked at me dead in the eyes. "I am honestly sorry for everything. You're the most beautiful and amazing girl in the world. I let you slip through my fingers. There are things about that night that you do not know, or understand. And when you're ready, I will tell you. God, I'm so sorry Lacey. For that night. For this past year. I have gone out of my way to cover the hurt I feel from not being close to you. To cover the guilt I feel over what has happened. I love you. I always have loved you and I always will. I screwed things up, I know. I honestly can't tell you how sorry I am. I hope one day, we can move on and you can forgive me, for all that I have done. I have wanted to say this for so long, but have been afraid. It scares me to think you actually hate me. That deep inside, you actually will never forgive me. That things will really never be the same. You don't understand how much it hurts, to see you with him. With Aiden. Every day I had to see that. To see you with him. It was like I didn't even matter. That's why I am with so many girls. They're all attempts to get me over you. To distract me. No one will ever be able to replace you. No one, will ever mean as much to me, as you do."

My mouth was open as I gazed at him.

I was expecting a, 'Sorry I screwed you, kissed your best friend and ditched you on your birthday,' type thing. But no. I actually a received a heartfelt apology, filled with many of the things I have spent the last year thinking. Wondering. Asking. My mind was still processing the fact that all my hopes were in fact true. How could I deserve the love I have craved for so long, after what I just did the Aiden? How was that fair? How could I let myself move on with Carter, after I know what I did?

Tears were in his eyes and his nose slightly red. My chest ached and I actually rubbed it with my hand, to attempt to soothe the throb that was accumulating. I rolled my lips into my mouth, wanting to cry again too.

It has been an emotional afternoon.

"I have imagined you saying that a thousand times in my head." I whispered, my voice hoarse. Tears burned at my eyes and my hands were trembling. "I never thought you would say it, let alone feel it."

"I know."

He understood me completely because he clearly had been through the same as me. A tear slid down my cheek and he hesitantly wiped it off. I inched closer and rested my head on his shoulder. He wrapped an arm around me. It was nice. Just being with him. He was like a drug that I needed in my daily life, to keep me sane. Although he is the very thing that also sends me insane.

Oh how things can change in mere moments, from just a few words.

"That Aiden guy was never going to stand a chance." he said. I swear I could almost hear the sympathy in his voice.

I squeezed my eyes shut.

Were Aiden and I broken up? Surely we were.

Did this mean Carter wanted to get back together? As in actual together, together?

Not one of us could be without the other. But recently, together, we were like two natural disasters.

Chapter 11

The sun soaked into my skin as I sighed, reclining further back onto my chair. The best thing about staying at Carter's house, was his gigantic, amazing pool that I got to paddle in and lay around whenever I felt like.

I had my sunglasses perched on my nose, and a cup of lemon lime and bitters placed firmly by my side. Life was bliss. Well, if you didn't count that I cheated on my boyfriend with my ex-bestfriend/boyfriend and now everything was messed up.

It had been three days, since Aiden threw his fist into Carter's face, upon hearing the news of our... incident.

Aiden wasn't at school the first day, avoided me the second and now it was a beautiful Saturday morning. I hadn't seen either of the boys and it was great. I was spending the morning with me, myself and I.

I'm not sure if Aiden and I had officially broken up, so I was attempting to avoid Carter. But seeing as we live in the same house and go to the same school, with half of our classes together, you can see how this may be an unsuccessful endeavour. Although I had tried to avoid him, I ended up spending most of my time with him.

It was actually nice.

We just lazed around, watching movies, cooking delicious baked goods and just talking like we hadn't in what felt like a life time. I had made sure there were no 'incidents' again, however. Was not going to go down the possible cheat road again.

We weren't animals. We could hang out without throwing ourselves at each other. Or... so I hope. I sighed, running my fingers through my long, blonde hair. Just spending time with him had been amazing.

If things weren't already over with Aiden, they needed to be. Even if I still felt some attraction towards him, it was like nothing to what I felt for Carter. Like comparing a flea to an elephant. Harsh, but I'm being truthful here.

Therefore, I was attempting to spend my day without either of the boys in my life and enjoy my own company for a few hours.

This lasted about twenty minutes.

"CANNON BALL!" a voice boomed, causing my body to jolt in alarm.

And that's when the ice, cold water splashed across my naked flesh. A scream tore from my lips as I scrambled away from the water. Carter emerged, flicking his hair, sending a shower of water droplets around him.

I folded my arms defensively across my chest and frowned at him.

"Was that necessary?"

He took a moment to think of a response. "Yes."

I sighed, puffing out my cheeks. Well my personal day had come to a sudden end. I drained my lemon lime and bitters in one mouthful. By the time I placed it down, his arms were wrapping around my abdomen, sending an automatic flare of heat underneath my skin.

"Don't you dare-" I began to warn but it was too late.

My body flew in mid-air and I had about two seconds of shock, before my body was submerged into the sickenly cold water. I sucked in a breath automatically, my mouth filling with water. I flailed to the top and began chocking and coughing.

Once recovering from my near-drown, I swivelled my eyes to his. "That's it."

He smirked playfully. "Catch me. If you can."

He didn't need to say it twice. I pulled myself from the pool and took after him, not caring that I was running across slippery cement with wet feet. I was fast, but I didn't play football like he did. I had nothing on him.

He sprinted like Usain Bolt away from me. Soon, I was breathless. Hiding, was my best option. I darted away quickly, before he turned around. I heard his footsteps come to a halt. I smirked, getting exactly what I had planned.

In running games, I hardly ever stood a chance. (Except that one time at the river and still now, it was one of the proudest moments of my life). But hiding games? Well, that was my expertise.

He slowly began walking back to the pool and I followed, finding new hiding places along the way. When he was close enough, I grinned. I launched myself after him and body slammed him into the pool. I ignored the stab of the cold water the flooded around my body. It was worth it though, having caught him off guard. He roared underneath the water and grabbed me.

Uh oh.

He pushed down my shoulders and held my under. I thrashed and flailed at him, but he was too strong. After about five seconds, he pulled me up and I laughed, almost hysterically. He literally could have killed me. With ease.

"Truce." I panted, raising my hands in somewhat of a peace signal. "I call truce."

"Wuss." he smirked.

"Takes one to know one."

"Touche." he laughed.

He wrapped an arm around my shoulder and pulled me to him. "Okay. Truce."

I ignored the fact that my cheek was pressed against the defined muscles of his chest. I also ignored the fact that my heart soared and my fingers slowly ran across his stomach. He released his hold on me. I stared up at him.

I had to say, my self-control had been impeccable. Three days with him and not giving in to his constant attempts to hook up, could be a considered a world record. Honestly, if you saw this God sculpted man before me, you would have trouble controlling yourself as well.

One kiss... just one...

"I should learn to knock." a voice said, effectively snapping me out of my Carter trance. "Oh wait. I did."

I jerked my body away from Carter and stared at Aiden. His lips were spread in a thin line. I realised, our position did not look too good. I gulped, moving further and further away from Carter. I pulled myself out with ease and stood there, unsure of what to do.

Aiden's eyes dipped as he took in my body. I took this moment to stare at him as well. He was dressed in a casual shirt and loose shorts. His hair looked slightly windblown, as if he had had the window down in his car when driving over here.

His sunglasses were mounted on top of his head, further pushing his hair back. He looked nice. He was a typical cute school boy, who girls would openly fond over. I glanced at Carter, who was still in the pool, water glistening from his defined chest.

There was a definite difference between them.

"We weren't." I felt the need to say, pulling myself out of my internal comparison. I felt as though I had to clarify to him that nothing was going on. "Doing anything... he pushed me in."

"Of course." he said, sarcasm hinting in his voice. "I get it."

I swallowed nervously. Without looking back at Carter, I fetched my towel and wrapped it around my body.

"Let's for a walk," I suggested, inclining my head.

With a curt nod, I followed him out to the side of the house. We sat on a pair of lawn chairs and stared at each other for a few moments. Clearly, I was going to have to break the silence.

"I promise you we weren't doing anything. Nor have we, in the past few days."

"I suppose it isn't really any of my business anyway." he said, clearing his throat. "I'm assuming we're not together any more. Even if I still don't want to end it."

After everything, he still wanted to be with me? The idea seemed incredulous to me. If I were in his position, I would want to punch me in the face, after being such a jerk. But no. Aiden was just a nice guy and tried to see the best in people.

I never realised that that could be a bad thing.

"So whipped," a heard a voice mutter.

Clearly someone was eavesdropping.

"Carter, I'm going to kick you in the throat with my foot bone if you do not leave us alone." I growled. I threw my chair back to emphasise my point. "Just piss off for five seconds!"

I was met with silence and I let out a puff of air, flustered. Picking up my chair, I re-sat, fiddling with my hands.

"Aiden, I want to be with you, but I think I will hurt you again. And that is something I do not want to do."

My hands were shaking, so I clamped them together. This was going to hurt him, but I had to be honest. I had to be firm with him, so I wouldn't continue to keep hurting him. This slap on the face would be better than the continual punches I will be throwing in our relationship. If that even makes sense.

"I'm too in love with him." I whispered, but loud enough for him to hear, squeezing my eyes shut. "I am so sorry Aiden. For everything. I really am."

He let out a deep sigh, his eyes tinged red. "Well then... I guess this is it."

I grimaced as I could see he was trying to hold himself together. "Yeah..."

He rubbed the back of his neck uneasily. "Believe it or not and I know this hardly ever works, but I still hope we can be friends. And to hang out. It will be hard, but I still want you in my life Lacey. I couldn't imagine you not in it."

My heart twitched in my chest. I smiled through my tears and reached over, holding his hand.

"I honestly feel the exact same way. We will remain friends. I promise."

He gave me a tight lipped smile. "Good. That's... that's good. Thanks."

I reclined back and we sat in silence. I wasn't sure where we should go from here. I fiddled with my fingers nervously, biting back tears. If I lost it, so would he. I focused on my breathing until I had myself calm.

Images of Mercedes bounced around in my head. Mercedes and Aiden. I blinked, forcing them out of my head. I had to stop thinking about this. If we were over, I couldn't do that to him or myself.

But the words tumbled out before I could control myself.

"I guess you can go with Mercedes now." my voice came out harsher then I intended. "That's what she has wanted all along."

"Don't." he barked, making my flick my eyes towards him. I swallowed, knowing I shouldn't have said anything. It was selfish. He had a strange expression on his face, which if I were to analyse, almost seemed like guilt. "Don't you dare act like the jealous girlfriend now."

He was right. Aiden deserved to be happy. If it was with Mercedes, fine. I would prefer someone different, but I would learn to deal with it.

I stood up and so did Aiden. I rounded the table and softly hugged him. I let myself enjoy the moment, as it may be one of the last times I ever hold this boy. The thought made me sad, but it was what needed to be done. I couldn't keep holding him back, when truthfully, I would always love Carter.

"I'm sorry."

He pulled away from me and without another word, strode to his car. I rolled my lips into my mouth and watched him go. After everything, he still wanted to be friends? I honestly think I underestimated how much he cared for me.

Hugging the towel closer to me, I made my way back inside at a painfully slow rate. I let myself just process the last few moments. Carter stared at me when I entered the glass doors, with a thoughtful expression on his face. I don't doubt for a second he heard every word that was exchanged between Aiden and I.

Especially the part about me declaring my undying love for him.

"Lace-" he began but I just shook my head.

"Not now."

I shouldered past him and headed for my room, feeling like a complete jerk. I hated myself for hurting Aiden, but what's done is done. The best thing to do was to move forward with my life and attempt to redeem all things I have done wrong.

I fell face first onto my bed, where I cried until the world went black and I fell asleep.

Since my break up with Aiden, I seemed to want to gain ten kilos.

Nutella, cookies and caramello chocolate, had been my best friend for the last week. At the time, it seemed as though it would help.

I tried to convince myself to go running, but I didn't have the energy. I was hardly even motivated to go to school. I even fell asleep in one of my study periods, resulting in being twenty three minutes late to class and another detention on my record. I don't know what was wrong with me. I wasn't sick, but I just felt so tired.

Aiden hadn't moved on with Mercedes, much to my guilty relief, but she had been talking to me. I was being nicer to her, but I couldn't stand to be around her very long. I was a terrible best friend, but I am tired, angry and alone, sue me.

Miranda had been home as well, so that was good. I wasn't alone with Carter all the time and someone was making my meals, so double win there. We still spent time together obviously, but he wasn't as full on and sexual when she was there.

We just ate junk food, or well, I ate the junk food while he stuck to his protein shakes and whatnot. We watched old movies and I enjoyed just spending time with him, while he wasn't being sleazy. I think he realised I needed time to heal and move past the whole Aiden thing, so he was just there for me and I was really grateful for it.

I had been spending a lot of time at the cubby too. Almost every afternoon I would just go there and let myself sit in my own silence. Mercedes still wore a guilty look, which was forever plastered on her face, but wouldn't fess up to whatever she had done. I'm assuming it had something to do with Aiden, so I really don't want to know what it is. I'm trying to move on, not dwell on 'what if's'.

Carter's fingers began making circular patterns on my scalp and I sighed into it. My dad used to do this to me all the time when I was little. I fell asleep instantly every time.

"That feels nice." I murmured, my eyes automatically feeling heavy.

"I remember your father used to always do this." he said, basically speaking my previous thoughts.

My smile grew. I loved when he talked about things we used to do together. It made me happy that I wasn't the only one who reminisced our past.

I didn't want to admit that dad still does this sometimes. I snuggled into him and rested my head on his stomach. I was borderline asleep, when his fingers stopped. I wanted to protest, but I didn't get a chance.

His lips softly kissed my forehead. "I love you."

My breath hitched into my throat. My eyes snapped open. I gazed up at his beautiful face and a genuine smile (I felt like I hadn't smiled in a long time) spread across my face. My eyes wandered over his straight jawline and amazingly tanned skin.

"I love you more."

"Impossible." he whispered.

I sighed, closing my eyes again. For so long, I couldn't force the words 'I love you' to Aiden, although we had been dating a pretty long time. I wasn't even back with Carter, physically anyway, and the words felt natural on my lips.

I didn't hesitate saying it back to him because it was true.

Ever since we hooked up, I literally had not seen Carter hardly look at another girl. Usually they were hanging off his shoulders or leaving his bedroom. I had not seen one girl in this house or one with him at school.

This also made me selfishly happy.

It feels as though it is for real this time. That he is willing to be back with me. Ignore all the flirtatious girls that throw themselves at him. For me. Boring, old, plain me.

I pushed myself up and gently kissed underneath his jaw. I trailed kissed across his chin until I reached the corner of his mouth. I was going to stop there, but he held my face and kissed me.

With all he had apparently.

Tingles erupted underneath my skin and rolled in waves throughout my entire body. I reached up eagerly, kissing him back. I was breathless and my heart rate had tripled. I pulled back, panting, my eyes half closed.

I had missed that so much.

Sighing, I leant back into him and closed my eyes.

I never thought it was possible to love someone so much.

"Let's do something fun!" Carter exclaimed, sounding like an excited child. His eyes twinkled with something I wasn't quite sure of, but it was enough to make me smile.

"Like what?"

He suddenly stopped, a slow smile stretching across his face. "I'll surprise you."

His excited behaviour was contagious. I soon found myself beaming back at him. It would be nice to actually get out of the house, other than for school. As I was already in my snug jeans and three quarter top, all I needed was my bag and jacket.

"After you, m'lady." he said, attempting a posh accent.

I grinned back at him. "Why thank you."

As we walked to the car, his fingers entwined with mine. I stared up at him and gave him a genuine smile. My cheeks were beginning to hurt, as I had been smiling so much around him lately. He just made me feel so ridiculously happy.

"Where are we going?" I asked, enjoying holding his hand. Even if it was only for a few steps.

He opened the passenger door and let me in. I slid smoothly into the seat. He leaned over and buckled me in, his cool breath fanning my face.

"You'll see."

I hardly registered what he said as my eyes were trained on his lips, which were mere inches away from my own. All I wanted was to lean forward and let them meet, but he pulled back and shut the door.

It took twenty minutes, before I realised where we were going. A full-blown grin lit up my face as I automatically slapped him repeatedly on the arm.

"Yay, yay, yay!"

He smiled and we both leaped out of the car, eager to get in. We hadn't done this for a long time.

Bowling.

Bowling was one of my most favourite activities to do and Carter and I used to spend almost every weekend here. We loved it. Oh and we also got extremely competitive which one time lead to a wrestle fight. We got kicked out and were banned for a month.

Oh, what a long month that was. I don't think I had been back with him since, although I still went a couple of times with dad. He threw his arm lazily around my shoulders and I threw my head back with laughter, thinking back to our last memory here.

"Are you thinking back to when we got kicked out?" he said, breathing a laugh of his own.

"No?"

"Don't lie to me girl, I can read you like a book."

"You wish." I laughed back, although we both knew it was true.

We pushed the doors open and tumbled in. Straight away the counter guy recognised us and visibly sighed.

"Not you two again."

I was impressed. The guy must have a good memory, since we hadn't been here, together, for a long time.

Carter gave him his trademark smirk and leaned confidently on the counter. Arrogance rolled off of him in waves.

"One month is truly over, my friend." he said smoothly sounding quite pretentious. "So, which lane are we at?"

Once we finally got sorted with our shoes and whatnot, I was sending my fluero pink bowling ball down the lane. I watched in anticipation as it rolled down. Slowly, it began veering to the right.

Right into the gutter.

"Ah man."

Carter snorted behind me much to my annoyance. "Good start."

"Like you can do any better."

I gave him a cool stare as he smirked at me. As confidently as possible, he picking his ball up, tantalisingly slow and strolled to the lane. He turned back, just to smirk once more, confidence oozing from him, before sending his ball barrelling down the lane.

Which resulted in a strike. I let out a puff of air, not impressed.

He strode back, pretending to flick dust from his shoulder. "That's how the professionals do it, babe."

Like always, the competitive nature stirred inside me.

"Oh, it's so on."

Despite my greatest efforts, Carter well and truly destroyed me.

Like he always did. I didn't even make it into the 100s. Carter literally beat me, doubling my score. Which infuriated me to no end.

I growled in frustration as I angrily undid my laces. "Stupid game."

Carter laughed and covered it with a cough, once I glared at him. However, he couldn't wipe the grin from his face which was just as bad as him laughing. He loved beating me at anything he could because he knew it ticked me off greatly.

"You know it always ends this way."

"Does not." I felt the need to protest and protect my pride. "Not always..."

"Yes always." he rolled his eyes. "It's okay. I kind of enjoy watching you suck-oomph!"

I punched him hard in the stomach and he gasped in surprise, buckling over. I grinned down at him, patting him roughly on the shoulder. I enjoyed doing that way too much.

"Sorry babe. You know how it always ends like this."

"Yep." he gasped, trying to straighten. "I see. Sorry."

We handed in our shoes and Carter grinned at guy, who had been watching us like a hawk ever since we stepped foot in the bowling alley.

"Adios amigo, see you tomorrow. And the day after that, and the day after that..." he trailed off, grinning with all he had.

The guy gave us a pained expression and turned, obviously trying to contain his anger. I laughed, following Carter out. He always knew how to stir people up. And when it wasn't directed at me, I found it pretty entertaining.

This time, I was the one reaching for his hand. I tugged him back to me and he stared down at me in surprise. I stood on my tip-toes and planted a soft kiss on his lips.

"Thank you."

He smiled and kissed me once more, before stepping away. "Any time."

I smiled, enjoying this. But then I heard her and my good mood evaporated into the cool night air. Of course she would be here, to dampen on my parade. I finally leave the house and do something fun, and she's here.

"Oh, look who it is, the happy couple."

I pivoted slowly, my eyes landing on Mercedes. She gave us a tight lipped smile, her eyes flashing with red hot anger. I quirked an eyebrow, surprised. We weren't seeing eye to eye, on well, anything really, but this anger was new to me.

I would have thought she would be ecstatic about Aiden and I's break up. But for some reason, she looked angrier than ever.

"Lacey," she started, a cocky smirk plastered on her face. "I have something to tell you."

Chapter 12

I'm not sure whether I wanted to cry or punch them both in the throat.

I decided on doing something similar to option two. Lunging forward, my palm slashed across her face. Mercedes cried out, staggering to the side. She clutched her head in hers hands, her right cheek instantly turning red.

If the news had been any different, I would have kneed her in the stomach.

Her mouth opened, but I swivelled my eyes to her. I death stared her so hard I thought they were going to pop out of their sockets. I knew I had been a bad best friend, but I would never, do anything like this to her.

"If you open your mouth and speak to me again, I'm going to rip your tongue out with my bare hands." I stepped towards her, my eyes turning into slits. "In fact, I don't think I can't even wait for you to talk. I want to do it right now."

She swallowed, taking a few steps back. "Lace-"

An enraged growl tore from my throat. My hand circled around the end of her hair and I yanked it as hard as I could. A scream pierced my ears, but it only egged me on. I wanted her blood on my hands. My vision was turning red.

I needed to hit her.

Carter's strong arms wrenched me back. I swung my elbow into his side. He hardly even flinched. He wrapped his arms around me, in attempt to stop me flailing. I felt like a criminal who had just been caught. Or maybe someone who had just escaped a psych ward. Either way, my chest was rising rapidly and my breathing sounded like I smoked three packs a day.

My hair was messy, my eyes were tinged and my entire body trembling with fury. I probably looked insane. I felt insane.

"I know you're mad and I know we have a lot to talk about, but you need to stop."

"Are you guys serious?" the guy working at the bowling alley asked furiously, before I had a chance to bite back. "First time back together after your ban and you start a fight?"

No one replied, we all just shot daggers at him for interrupting.

He sighed in frustration, rubbing his fingers over his temples. "Get out and don't come back."

He turned his back to us and stormed towards his counter, his back rigid. His words had no effect on me. Nothing had much effect on me after what I just heard. I stopped struggling. I stopped my attempt to break from his arms. I stood perfectly still and focused on my breathing, trying to regain normality.

After a few moments Carter's grip went slack as he stepped away from me wearily. He was looking at me like I was a ticking time bomb, seconds away from exploding. He was right to look at me like that because that's precisely how I was feeling.

"You think I'm mad?" I asked, my voice so low and even, I surprised myself. It held so much anger, it was startling.

He rubbed the back of his neck, looking nervous.

"You think we have a 'lot to talk about'?" I asked calmly, although my body was shaky with fury.

He swallowed, glancing at Mercedes.

"I don't ever want you to speak to me again. I'll be gone by the time you get home. I'd rather live on streets than be anywhere near you."

I turned from him before he could say anything. My eyes were stinging. I wasn't sure if I wanted to cry out of depression, or anger. Maybe a bit of both.

"And you." Mercedes looked at me in the eye. She knew she would get a reaction from me. She wanted me to be mad. To be hurt. But I think she underestimated exactly how hurt I was. "You are dead to me."

Her mouth popped open. She looked shocked. Is she serious? Our friendship was already in dangerous waters, it couldn't possibly handle anything like this.

Tantalisingly slow, I ran my eyes over her. My face was a mirror of complete and utter disgust. With that, I stormed out of the bowling alley. I walked over to Carter's car and kicked it. I began beating at the windows, the tyres, anything I could touch. It was a way to let some of my pent up anger out, since I can't hit the target I actually want to. I heard him yell after me. His footsteps began to thunder on the path. Hurting his car was the way to hurting his heart. He loved this thing.

With one final punch, I struck my fist onto the front screen. A crack formed underneath my knuckles. My hands burned and stung, blood forming on them, but I didn't care. I hardly even felt the pain. Calmly, I walked from him car, as if nothing had happened.

I didn't stop walking until my feet hurt, my back was sore and my head was hanging. Carter kept calling out to me, but soon, his voice died away with everything else. He knew coming after me would be no use, so I assume he's going to let me 'cool off'.

I hadn't kept track of where I was going. I was planning to go get my stuff from Carter's, but that would be the first place he would go, before coming to search for me. So, I stayed on the streets. Walking over to a park that no one really goes to anymore, I perched myself on one of the swings. The harsh wind slapped my face roughly, making me wish I had brought a thicker jacket with me.

Only then, I let myself cry.

I hated crying. But I needed to. My body couldn't handle this being bottled up.

Chest-wracking sobs rolled through my body. I was crying so hard that it hurt. My chest ached. I clawed through my clothes, as if that would ease the pain my heart was feeling. I wanted to die. I struggled to breathe as I rocked back and forth.

I felt completely ruined.

I don't care if I'm being dramatic. If you were completely in love (maybe even obsessed) with someone, only to have them toy with you and break your heart over and over again, you would probably feel this way as well.

But what I didn't expect, was my best friend not only want to ruin one of my relationships, but my next one as well.

I hated her so much. But not as much as I hated him.

Or myself, for letting myself get close to Carter Williams again.

Carter's P.O.V:

I felt sick to my stomach.

Sleep was a distant concept to me. It had been two days and I have heard nothing from Lacey. No one has. I can't sleep. I can't eat. I vomit randomly, I cry and there's this numb, empty feeling in my chest. I have never experienced anything like this before.

I was a complete jerk and deserve this.

The amount of times I had attempted to call or text her is ridiculous. I don't even care if she doesn't want to talk to me. I just need to know she is okay.

That she is alive.

I ran my hands roughly over my face. I hated myself for what I did to her. How am I ever going to regain her trust after this? I was a stupid, young boy who didn't think. I regret everything I have done which has hurt her. She doesn't deserve it. The only time she is ever angry or upset, is when I have done something stupid.

Her life would be better without me. But I was too selfish to let her go. I couldn't stand to be away with her. Obviously. Otherwise I wouldn't have been with so many other girls, in attempt to forget about her. Ironically enough, this is what got me into this situation in the first place.

Seeing her every day, with that tool, made me so insane with jealously. I can't even describe how jealous I was. I was so in love with her, it was dangerous. I am in love with her. It made me do stupid things that I'm not proud of.

I guess love changes you.

Slowly, I stood, before stumbling towards the bathroom. I spent so many hours, driving everywhere and anywhere I could think of. It was like she had disappeared from the face of the earth. I continuously checked the cubby. It looked well-kept as usual and no one was ever there. I thought, just maybe, she went there as all her clothes and belongings are still at my house. But there was no sign of her anywhere.

After not hearing from her, for the second night in a row, I decided to get so drunk I forgot my own name. I drank entire bottle of vodka within half an hour and some other shots I can't even remember. To say I was slightly hung over would be erroneous.

The sick sensation I have had in my stomach, is not only worry, but a literal sickness. I have thrown up my entire food intake. I must have. No one should be able to produce as much vomit as I did. Not only was I sick and worried about her, I was afraid of her parents. Of them finding out what has happened.

Imagine if Elizabeth and Ben came home right now.

"Oh hey guys. We lost your kid, but other than that, we're going fine."

Yeah. That would go down well.

I stared at the person who was reflecting back at me. His hair was sticking up in odd angles. Deep, purple bags that have never existed before, hung beneath his eyes. Dried up vomit was smudged across his chin.

I didn't even recognise myself.

Splashing warm water on my face felt good. I began furiously scrubbing at my skin. I needed to remove the filth, aka Mercedes touch, from my skin. It was weeks if not months ago since, but I could still feel her on me.

The thought made me even sicker.

"Are you attempting to skin yourself alive?" a voice asked.

I jumped about a metre in the air, slamming my head on the cabinet. Black dots erupted across my vision. The egg that will probably form on my head, will not help the already hammering headache that has gathered behind my eyes. Wincing, I took a step back, rubbing my head.

"What are you doing here and how the hell did you get in?"

"Is that the way you really should be speaking to the mother of your child?" she asked, a cruel smile stretching across her face. Her eyes held glee that looked as though she was controlling a game. A game which controlled my life and I was just her pawn.

"I wore protection. Didn't think that one through, did you?" I spat.

"They don't always work."

"They have always for me. You are not special. You are no exception."

She sighed, leaning against the door frame nonchalantly. "And here I was thinking we would have a June wedding."

I wanted to choke her.

"You are not pregnant."

"Yes I am."

"No. You're not."

"I can stand here all day and argue with you Carter, but you need to face the facts. I am pregnant. You're the father. The quicker you get your mind around it, the better."

"Prove it." I growled.

"I have an ultrasound booked next week. You can come with me."

"Like hell I would go anywhere with you."

"Carter, underneath your whole 'player and jerk' facade, you're genuinely a good guy. Sometimes, anyway. I know you will do whatever possible for your child. You will be a good father. I may not be the person you want me to be, but you can't deny your child of the life it deserves."

"I would be the best father in the entire world." I ground out. Those were some of the truest words that have ever come out of her mouth. "If only yours was mine."

She sighed in annoyance. "Why not come with me to the ultrasound if you don't believe me?"

"Going to an ultrasound and proving that you're pregnant, won't tell me if I'm the father."

"A DNA test would."

My mouth snapped shut pretty quickly. I didn't have anything to say back to that.

"Exactly. Pick me on Tuesday morning. The appointment is at nine a.m." she said, with a wide smile spread across her face. "I'll show myself out."

"You do realise Lacy is an official missing person now?" I yelled at her, wanting her to feel exactly how I did. I want her to suffer and understand the damage she has caused. "I'm about to head to the police station and tell them it has been the mandatory forty eight hours. An official search can be conducted now."

The colour drained a little from her face. "You haven't heard from her in two days?"

"No one has."

She grew silent, which only annoyed me further.

"It's all because of you." I said, seething. I could feel my face growing hot. A deep flush ran down the back of my neck.

"Don't act like you're a saint!" She suddenly screeched, taking me by surprise. She strode over to me and punched me square in the chest. I hardly even felt it, but I still took a step back. My lower back hit the edge of the sink, making me realise I had nowhere else to go. "Don't act like you're innocent in this! If you hadn't seduced me, like you do to so many other girls, we wouldn't be in this situation in the first place!"

"It was a stupid move, I know. One that I regret whole heartedly." I saw her face fall slightly as I said that, but I kept going. "I hate myself every day, for even touching you. But what's done is done. I wasn't the one who dropped the bomb on her like that. I wasn't the one to make her run away. I actually care for Lacey."

We shared a heated stare for several minutes, both of us too angry to speak. Finally, she was the one who broke the ice.

"I hate you."

"Don't worry, the feeling is mutual."

Her face turned a dark shade of red. Her mouth opened and closed a few times as she struggled to say something back. After spluttering a few painful, incoherent words and watching her gape like a fish, she turned and took off from my bathroom. Angrily, I projected my foot into the shower door. Glass shattered around me and struck my foot.

Apparently when either Lacey or I got mad, we liked to break glass. I hardly even felt the pain of the glass shards. I didn't care. There were bigger problems I needed to face.

I was about to tell the police that my almost girlfriend is a missing person because I mistakenly slept with her best friend and got her knocked up.

I hate my life.

Lacey's P.O.V:

I am so glad I have the cubby.

This has been my hide-away for the last two days. Carter pops by, at least once every hour, but I always manage to make a run for it. I don't want him to know where I am. I keep the place tidy, as if no one has been here for days.

Except, that I had been. And I wasn't alone.

"How are you feeling?" he asked me, plopping down on the steps and handing me a warm cup of tea. I smiled at him, grateful he was here.

"Shattered. Broken. Miserable." I replied, taking a tentative sip.

He gave me a sad smile. "You'll be okay."

"Is that how I made you feel?" I asked quietly, not looking at him. "When you found out I cheated on you with Carter, is this how you felt?"

Aiden fell quiet for a moment. "Yes and no."

I drew my legs up to my chest, feeling like a terrible person. Absently, I slipped one of my fingers behind my bandage and scratched. After stupidly punching Carter's car window, it left me with bruised knuckles and a swollen hand. The swelling still hasn't gone down, much to my annoyance. Hopefully I haven't done any other damage. That's going to be embarrassing to explain to the doctor.

"Nothing big, just had a fight with my best friend and almost boyfriend, got angry and punched his car window. But no, I don't have anger management issues or anything."

"Yes, I felt miserable for a while because I loved you. No, I did not feel broken. I knew I would be okay, because I expected this from the start. Not you cheating, of course. But the fact that I was getting involved with you, when I knew your history with Carter. I took the risk anyway because I wanted to be with you. It was good... amazing while it lasted. But I don't regret, for one second, ever being involved with you."

I stared at him for a moment, shocked at his words. He was so amazing. Why could I not return his love? Why did I have to always make the wrong decisions and be with the wrong boys? Boy, anyway.

"You are too good for me." I sighed. "I don't deserve someone like you."

"You deserve the world at your fingertips." he whispered, almost bringing me to tears, which felt like the thousandth time this year. I had never cried so much in my life, than I had this past few months.

I glanced up and he was staring right into my eyes, as if he knew me better than I knew myself. Something inside my chest swelled. He wasn't Carter, but he was a nice, caring guy who loved me. Why couldn't I have stayed with him?

Although Carter has hurt you, you will never stop loving him. A voice whispered in my head. The way you feel when you're with him, the way you are just from hearing his voice... No one, will ever live up to his standards. You will never be able to be with someone else again. And this scares the hell out of you.

I sighed deeply through my nose, my eyes drifting closed.

"So do you."

He slid an arm around my shoulders and hugged me close to him. I nuzzled my face into his chest, seeking his warmth. Although it had been sunny out, my body had remained cold. I was beginning to question whether I would ever feel warm again.

"I was wrong about Mercedes." he suddenly said, his voice low. "I genuinely thought she was a good person. Fills me with regret."

Why did he feel regret?

I didn't reply. My lip twitched upon hearing her name. I swallowed down my anger and stayed silent. I didn't want to waste any more time and energy crying about her.

"You know how she spoke to me a lot, when I was with you?"

"Yes?" I ground out, trying to keep my anger in check.

"She was hooking up with someone. That's why I didn't understand why you thought she was trying to hit on me all the time. I assumed you knew. But now that I think about it, it was obvious you didn't."

"What?" I asked, pulling back. Mercedes has been with someone else? So much for being whole heartedly in love with Aiden. Unless this guy was a distraction, or a replacement of the real thing. "Who?"

"Thomas someone. She never told me his last name."

"That sneaky, little, bitch."

He let out a soft laugh, jostling my hair. "Don't worry about her. You don't need someone like that in your life."

"But she is in my life. I can't get away from her."

He rolled his lips into his mouth. "You'll just have- uh oh."

"What?" I asked, instantly straightening up, alarm shooting through my veins. "Uh oh what?"

"Carter..." he trailed off and that's when I heard the footsteps.

I clambered to my feet, in attempt to run before he saw me, but it was too late. Our eyes met and the wind was knocked out of me. Like it always was when I saw him. Even when I hated him, more than now anyway (if possible), he still had this effect on me. I don't think the tingly feeling in my toes or the way my heart skipped a beat when I was around him will ever go away. This idea would be exciting if we weren't in the situation we're in now.

He looked terrible. Which was weird, because Carter was like a sculpture hand made from God himself. Even when he had the flu really bad and was off school for a week two years ago, he looked amazing the entire time. Although he had a fever and was drenched in cold sweat, with drool on his chin.

Seeing him look bad, well, it was startling.

His usually tanned skin, was as pale as I've ever seen it. It was off colour and his face looked haggard, as though he hadn't been eating. His eyes were blood shot, from what I'm assuming it lack of sleep and his eyes were so purple it looked like he had been in a fight.

"Nice to see you alive." he choked out, his voice hoarse.

I had nothing to say back.

"Nice to also see you Aiden. Didn't find the time to reply back to one of my million messages?"

"He messaged you?" I asked Aiden in surprise, whipping my head towards him. Guilt flashed across his face.

I hadn't known that.

"And called and left voice mails." Carter continued, looking extremely annoyed. "I get that you don't want to speak to me, but hell, my mother has been trusted to look after you. You couldn't find it in your heart to call her and say you're alive? That you're okay? She has been worried sick. The police were notified and about to send out a search party, before someone said they saw someone fitting your description in this area. I just knew it had to be here. Our place. Our special place and you brought him here?"

Everything he said was right. I was miserable, angry and upset, but that didn't give me a right to run off and make everyone so worried. I didn't even think of Miranda. I was too focused on myself to even acknowledge her.

"Maybe I should go..." Aiden muttered awkwardly, scratching his forehead.

"No!"

"Yes, I think that's an excellent idea." Carter snapped.

Aiden stared at me, looking apologetic. "I'll call you later."

"Like hell you will!" Carter yelled out, his fists clenched. If this situation wasn't so serious, I would laugh at him.

Hell was his favourite word of the month apparently.

"Like you have any right to dictate who can and cannot call me!" I yelled back, equally as frustrated now. "Don't act like you care about me now. The continuous amount of times you've gone out of your way to hurt me, shows that you don't!"

I hardly even registered that Aiden left. I was too pent up, thinking about the whole situation that got us here in the first place. This was exactly why Aiden and I will never work. He was a nice, amazing guy, who any girl would die to be with. But when Carter comes into the picture, I'm so absorbed in his presence, that nothing else matters. The whole world could be in flames around me for all I know.

I was in way over my head with this boy.

"There's so much about the night of your sixteenth birthday that you don't know!" he cried out desperately. He limped, as if in physical pain, to the bottom of the stairs, his eyes pleading for me to understand. It wasn't just the whole 'sleeping with my best friend and getting her pregnant thing' that had me so annoyed. It contributed greatly of course, but it was the fact that every time I got close to him, he would do something to push me away. I paused and stared into those eyes I love so much.

Is it true?

Is there really something I don't know about the night that ruined us?

Did I even want to know?

"I didn't want to leave you that night. I could have stayed like that for the rest of my life! I promise you. But I needed to leave."

The anger inside me fizzled out. I felt exhausted. I sagged down and collapsed onto the top step, unable to support my own weight anymore. He sat on the bottom step and looked up at me. I felt empty. I stared coolly down towards him, giving up on being sad and angry. I was just tired of all my emotions and feelings. With a sigh, I rubbed my face roughly.

"Tell me everything."

Chapter 13

I was finally doing it.

After so long of holding back being afraid to, I finally was.

Running my tongue across my lips, I let myself pause for a moment. I knew this wasn't a good idea, but I felt so messed up inside. I didn't have anywhere else to go or anyone else to be with. I literally had no one.

My fingers trailed down his chest, my lips making a track across his stomach. His finger slid underneath my chin, so that I was looking into his beautiful eyes. I took a moment to just appreciate him. He was not only gorgeous but had the biggest heart I had ever known.

He had been good to me when I didn't deserve it.

"Are you sure?" he asked me softly, giving me an escape clause if I needed it.

I didn't reply, but slammed my lips to his instead. This answer must have been sufficient enough, because my top was ripped from my body with seconds. This was going very fast paced since only an hour ago I was almost suicidal.

I suppose we've waited long enough, that now it feels like we're running out of time.

My heart was beating rapidly inside my chest. My fingers began trembling. Noticing this, he entwined his fingers with mine, giving me a look of certainty. He slowly raised my hand to his lips and softly kissed it, making my stomach do a flip.

Was I ready to do this again?

"I love you so much, Lacey." he whispered onto my lips, running his hands through my hair. "You don't not know how long I have wanted to do this."

"I know, Aiden. I know."

Six Hours Earlier

I silently stared into Carter's electric eyes.

Okay, so his story made sense and did change things. But how much did it really change? It took him over a year to tell me that? Could have saved us a lot of time and anger management courses. This is why I am not sure if he is telling the truth.

"Do you understand now?" he asked me quietly, rubbing his foot absently. Oh yeah, he kicked his foot through his shower door. Guess he will be sharing mine now! Yay...

"Yeah, totally, we can get back together now." I said sweetly. "It changes the fact that you slept with my best friend and got her pregnant. I can forgive you now and move on."

"Lace-" he started, rubbing the back of his neck as a flush crept over his skin.

"Look Carter, yeah, you may not have been the jerk I thought you were that night, but it still doesn't change the fact that you've been a jerk recently. I'm going to need time to come to terms with the whole pregnancy thing. It's not really like we can be together anyway, when you will be at Mercedes beck and call for everything."

He literally shuddered at the thought. A grimace formed on his face as if he was deeply disturbed by the idea. I was also slightly disgusted at the thought. She was no best friend of mine anymore. I could finally accept the fact that I never really liked her all along.

"I really screwed up."

"Literally."

I couldn't help add that last bit.

He pursed his lips at me and frowned. "I know it will take time, a long time, to move past this but I wanted you to know about that night, I was literally drugged. I have no idea what was going on. It was so messed up."

I couldn't help feel a little sorry for him after the way I acted. He tried to do the right thing by stopping Andrew and got drugged in the process. So what do I do? Jump to the worst conclusions without hearing his side of the story. Good girlfriend I was.

"Why did you sleep with her?" I asked softly. "You knew it would destroy me if I found out."

He sighed wearily, his hands covering his eyes. "You're the only girl who doesn't willingly drop everything for me. You put up a fight to my constant flirt, my compliments and my actions. No girl has ever done that to me. And the fact that you paraded Aiden in front of me drove me insane. Mercedes came to my front door, wearing her tight little skirt and I wanted to hurt you like the way you hurt me. Every single day. So, without thinking of the consequences..."

I never realised how much he was affected by me being with Aiden.

"I thought you hated me as much as I hated you. I had no idea you would be jealous over Aiden. The idea seems incredulous to me."

"I wanted to rip his throat out with my bare teeth and shove it-" he began but again, I cut him off.

"Please don't go there. He's a good guy. He doesn't deserve the hate you're throwing towards him. He was there for me when you weren't."

Carter's jaw clenched angrily. "He should never have been anywhere near you."

"Look, I'm tired, hungry and I just want to go home." I sighed, exhausted. "To your home, I mean."

"Let's go then." he said, helping me up. He stared distastefully down at my hand and I couldn't stop the guilt from bubbling in the pit of my stomach. "I can't believe you punched Meredith."

I rolled my eyes at the name of his car. "You deserved it to be in your face, but I thought I'd take a different path of violence."

Carter had named his car Meredith when he first got it. We had both been obsessed with Grey's Anatomy. Carter used to say he wanted to be a surgeon but I always just laughed at him. He was the football kind of guy, not the type to study years of medicine.

He gritted his teeth, clearly annoyed, but didn't want to push his luck. I entered the cabin and collected all my stuff, ignoring Carter's looming presence. He still hung close to me, as if nothing had happened. But it had. And it was going to take me a while to get back to the way we were. If we would ever get back there.

Following him out of the cabin, I peered wearily over my shoulder. I was going to miss hanging here, just with Aiden, trying to forget Carter. I sighed and increased my pace, the desire to go sleep in my bed (temporary bed anyway) was becoming overwhelming.

I never thought I'd be so glad to go to Carter's house again.

My guilt doubled by the time I stepped into Carter's mansion. I hadn't spoken to Miranda for several days. I couldn't imagine the trauma and trouble I had put her through. Selfish. That was the one word that could sum up my personality in a nutshell. I can't believe I didn't bother to call her and let her know I was alright.

I stepped into the kitchen and faced her, my heart rate beginning to increase. She was sitting at the dining room table, her legs neatly folded across her lap, her hands interlaced on top of the table. Her face was calm and steady, however, her eyes were icy cold.

"Nice to see you Lacey." her voice was low and riled with sarcasm. "It's really nice that you called and told me you were okay. I'm especially glad that you ran away when I am supposed to be taking care of you."

I could feel Carter's eyes burning into my skull. My eyes stung but I refused to show any emotion. I straightened my spine, looking at her levelly.

"I'm sorry."

A bitter laugh escaped her mouth. She threw her hands up in exasperation. "That's good. I'm sure that will make everything okay."

I physically bit my tongue, to stop myself saying anything I would regret. Miranda was like a second mum to me. I could not put her through that and then be rude to her. Not when she had provided me a place to stay and food for me to eat.

"I could not be near Carter or I would have done something worse than run away." My voice was cold.

Her face twitched slightly. She was probably thinking back to one of the times I've self-harmed.

"What's going on?" her eyes darted between Carter and myself.

"Would you like to tell her Carter, or should I?" I asked sweetly. "I'm sure you tell the story better than I do anyway."

He remained silent, however his eyes bored into mine. I knew I was crossing the line, but I did it anyway. A vicious smile tugged onto my face as words seemed to have escaped him. I could feel myself getting angry and worked up about the whole situation all over again.

"Nothing?" I questioned.

Folding my arms across my chest, I swivelled to face Miranda again. The anger I have been trying to squash down began bubbling to the surface.

"He slept with my best friend and got her pregnant. Congratulations, you're a grandmother."

And with that verbal slap in the face, I stalked into my room and slammed the door shut as hard as I could.

Okay, Miranda didn't deserve the bomb to be dropped on her like that but I was mad and wanted to get back at Carter. She was going to find out either way, I just beat him to it. He probably wouldn't have told her for another month if it was up to him.

May as well get it out in the open.

I threw my stuff onto the floor and collapsed onto the bed. I curled up into foetal position, resting my forehead on my knees. The more I thought about Carter right now, the more I wanted to be with Aiden. He was just so nice and understanding.

He has never done anything to hurt me, as far as I'm aware.

I stayed like this, curled up in a ball for about an hour. My body felt cramped and I had grown uncomfortable a while ago now, but I didn't have the energy to move. First thing in the morning, I was going for a run. I really need the numbing feeling that generates under my skin.

Suddenly, my door busted open. I flinched, causing my muscles to wince. I stretched out, rolling my head around. Carter stood there, looking extremely furious. His skin was slightly off colour, his eyes watery and his cheeks tinged red. I gulped uneasily, suddenly filled with regret.

"Do you feel better now?"

"What?" I asked, my voice coming out hoarse.

"Telling my mother after everything she has been through with you? A + effort on helping my life fall to pieces."

"I'm making your life fall to pieces?" I snapped, leaping to my feet, ignoring the complaints from my muscles. Suddenly, I wasn't feeling so guilty. He deserved everything he got. "You have got to be joking."

"I should have been the one to tell her this." he growled, his jaw ticking.

"Maybe you shouldn't have done it in the first place!" I screeched, fuming. "When you're mad, you don't just have to sleep with people to make yourself feel better! Consider how the other people in the situation feel! It's not just about you."

"You know what?" he asked, his voice dropping down low. He took a step towards me, his eyes in slits. "I don't regret it. In fact, I'd do it again."

I feel as though I have been punched in the stomach. The wind knocked out of me. I took a step back, hurt flooding into my chest. His face twitched and I thought I saw a flash of regret in his eyes, but his mask was back in place within mere seconds. This made me question whether I had seen anything at all. I felt breathless, as though there suddenly wasn't enough oxygen in the room.

I took a step back, my eyes burning. I can't believe he said that.

"Get out." I whispered. The burning desire to run away swelled in my chest, but I ignored it. Clearly that was not a good idea last time. I cleared my throat, my voice coming out stronger. "Get the hell out of my room and the hell out of my life. I hate you."

Without another word, he stalked from my room, slamming the door behind him. I sunk to my knees, the hurt inside me was indescribable. How could I love such a monster? I could not go back to him. I know I shouldn't. Maybe we were just two people who weren't compatible, despite our chemistry. Clearly we can't work out since it always ends in disaster.

Before I let myself have a full-blown break down, my phone began blaring beside me. With sniff hands, I raised the phone to my ear.

"Oh Lacey," my mother's voice whispered. "Are you okay? I have been so worried. I got the phone call last night that you had run away. I was organising a flight back when Miranda rang back saying there was a sighting of you."

"Long story." I croaked out, glad I could even string a sentence together right now. "I'll tell you about it when you get home."

"Are you okay?"

'Okay' was not even in my vocabulary anymore.

"Yep." I forced out, the words causing my physical pain. "What's up?"

"Your grandmother." mum said, her voice filled with sadness. "She died this morning."

I'm honestly not sure I could feel any worse.

How could so many things go wrong in such a short amount of time?

I'm not sure if mum said anything else because the phone slipped from my fingers. I was numb. After sitting in silence for a ridiculous amount of time, I got up. Almost robotically, I walked from my room, and down the stairs towards my car.

I didn't stop to talk to anyone on my way out. I think I, and that family, have caused each other enough damage for one day.

Coldness seeped through my veins and I felt void of emotion. I started my car, hardly registering the fact that I should not be in a car whilst in this state. I wasn't sure of where I was going until the car had stopped.

I looked at the front door and sighed. I felt nothing. Robotically, I removed myself from the car. Dragging my feet with my head hanging, I stepped onto his porch. It wasn't long before he answered, giving me the beautiful smile I loved.

"Lacey?" he asked, his smile instantly dropping. "What's wrong?"

I grabbed his shirt with my hand and tugged him towards me, my lips crushing against his. We stepped apart, breathless. My eyes stared into his confused ones. I stepped closer, so there was no space left between us.

"Aiden, I love you, too."

Chapter 14

Well, you could say I was a hypocrite.

It had been exactly three hours, twelve minutes and twenty four seconds since I had gone to Aiden's. Well, if Carter gets to run off with Mercedes, why can't I do the same with my own Prince Charming?

Sighing, I stared tiredly at the ceiling. Although my eyes were stinging from exhaustion, I couldn't rest. Every little thing that happened today was racing through my wired brain.

Carter saying he would sleep with my best friend again.

My grandmother dying.

Sleeping with Aiden.

I sighed, rolling to my side. I stared at his defined back. Absently, I reached out and ran my fingers down his skin. At my touch, he jolted awake. As he turned, his eyes widened. It was as though he was expecting me not to be there. My eyes darted low. I felt guilty that he thought that low of me.

What type of person was I?

"Hey," he breathed. "Are you okay?"

"No. Not really."

He wrapped an arm around my neck and drew me towards him. He pressed his lips against my forehead soothingly. I exhaled into him, relaxing at his touch.

"You don't regret it, do you?" he asked tentatively.

"No," I said softly, some of my cold exterior melting as my eyes took in his face. I reached up and ran my fingertips across his jaw. "I just regret what drove me to do it. I wish we had done it under different circumstances."

He looked guilty for a moment. He probably thought he took disadvantage of me when I was emotionally unstable. Which was kind of true, but I wanted to do it. I don't regret the action itself, because it was great. Just that I had to be hurt beyond repair to want to be with him.

"When's the funeral?"

"Two days," I replied, thinking back to the text mum sent me since I refused to answer her persistent calls. Other than Aiden, I really did not want to speak to anyone right now. I would be happy if I could cocoon myself into the blanket and wake up when this was all over.

Feelings of dread and pain filtered through my veins. I blinked, trying to hold back the tears that were threatening to be unleashed. The thought of being around people right now was enough to make me feel physically ill, let alone being at my own grandmother's funeral. I was going to lose it, I could tell.

"That's soon." his voice pulled me back to reality.

"I know," I sighed, drawing back from him to rub my eyes wearily. I hastily wiped away the tears that fell, hoping he didn't notice. I was sick of crying. I was sick of people feeling sorry for me. I just wanted it all to be over. "I'm flying there Thursday."

"How long are you staying?"

I jerked my shoulder up. "I don't know. I suppose until mum and dad come home. There will be things to sort out."

"Well I hope you're not gone too long." he said, rolling me onto my back. He propped himself onto his elbow so that his face hovered over mine. "I don't think I could stand not being with you again."

I decided against stating that we haven't really "been together" lately anyway, but his words were too sweet to squander. I exhaled, taking a moment to gaze at him. For too long, I have taken this gorgeous and sweet boy for granted. I needed to start appreciating what I had, before I lost it all again.

"Lace," he began, his eyes boring into mine, effectively pulling me out of my emotional dilemma. "I know things are complicated and you're not really in a good head space right now, but I want to be with you. I love you. I just hope that you can feel the same way about me again. What we had was great until Carter began messing with you again. God, the things I want to do to him for what he has done to you."

"I love you too." I replied, the words not actually that hard to get out, as they usually were. "I do want to be with you. I just don't want to promise you anything right now and let you be hurt again. But I do want to try. Just maybe give me some time. But I still want to spend time with you. Does that make sense?"

"You want to be with me, but not make anything official yet?" He clarified more simply.

"Well, you said it a lot more clearly."

"I'm cool with that." he said, giving me a lazy smile, which I was grateful for. Again, I felt an overwhelming sense of gratefulness for his understanding nature. "Now get some sleep. You look exhausted."

"I feel it," I breathed, attempting to blink away the stinging sensation in my eyes. I arched my neck and brushed my lips against his. I placed my palm against his cheek and rubbed against his jaw with my thumb. "Thank you."

His arm wrapped securely around me and I nuzzled my head into his chest. I was surprised at how comfortable and safe I felt in his arms. After kind-of-being-with-Carter again, I didn't think I would be this comfortable with anyone else.

Turns out, I liked Aiden a lot more than I realised.

Sobs wracked my body violently. I trembled, my teeth biting down into my clenched fist as I tried to limit the sounds that were clawing at my throat. Images upon images of her casket getting lowered into the ground whirled around inside my head.

Bodies and bodies of people coming towards me. Their 'comforting' words bouncing around inside my brain. Black was everywhere and I could not rid it from my aching mind. I felt the urge to be sick but somehow kept it down.

I was tired of crying. So sick of feeling terrible all the time. I just wanted this emotional roller coaster to stop.

"Shh baby," mum said, rubbing her hand soothingly over my back. "Shh."

She was not much help seeing as her eyes were just as bad as mine. Both of us were bawling, one step away from having a full blown Britney moment. Okay, I will never shave my hair but I could go 'crazy'.

I ignored the continuous stares I was receiving on the plane. Everyone was watching me wearily, in case I was about to snap and start sending punches or something. If I wasn't so hysterical, I would have laughed at their expressions.

It was amazing being back with my parents. I've been so busy with the mess at home, I hadn't realised how much I had needed them here with me. Miranda was practically family, but ever since my 16th birthday, things had never been the same. Whether they realised or not, they were not considered the family they once were to me.

Since the funeral, I had been avoiding people like the plague. But now that I was away from people and back on the plane, things really hit me.

Okay, so it probably looks like I am being melodramatic, but I cannot describe the empty and lost feeling that has been gradually accumulating inside my chest. It was just one thing after another and my body was too weak to soldier through it anymore.

I did not want to deal with Grandma leaving us.

I especially did not want to deal with everything I had left behind.

Carter. Mercedes. Aiden. Miranda.

My body jerked away from mum's touch. I grabbed fistfulls of my hair, pulling. I clamped my teeth down onto my lip to stop myself crying out. The physical pain would stop the mental pain. I just need to feel something else.

My fingers shook with the desire to have a razor.

"Honey," her voice said, snapping me out of it. Her gentle hands closed around mine, forcing me to let go of my hair. She squeezed me fingers tightly with hers. "I love you so much. Please don't hurt yourself. Talk to me."

"I am done talking," I whispered, refusing to open my eyes. "I am done with everything."

"Maybe we should organise visits with Dr. Marez again-" she started, her voice lining with panic at my possible relapse.

"Just stop talking. Please stop talking."

She fell silent beside me. I rested my head on her shoulder, trying to calm down my racing heart beat and my fast-paced breaths.

"I'm here for you. Always." were the last words I heard, before I shut out everything completely.

No matter who I had 'there for me', this was something I did not want to discuss with anyone. Me, myself and I had some serious issues to deal with. So when I locked myself inside my room for some mourning time, or so I told my parents, I took my alcohol stash and made a run for it.

Running away was my new speciality apparently.

I stumbled to the side, my fingers clinging to the gate beside me. I took another swig from the vodka bottle, the liquid burning my raw throat. I attempted to gain my footing and suddenly my legs were tangled. I tumbled to the floor, my bare knees scraping across the cement. A yelp escaped my mouth as I crashed down, the bottle shattering beside me. The liquid oozed out onto the cement ground, dampening my clothes in the process.

I rolled to my side, heaving. Slowly, I sat up and stared down at the sash of blood that was slithering down my shins. The pain felt good.

Mercedes.

Carter.

Miranda.

Aiden.

My grandmother.

My parents.

Images of Carter with his lips locked with one of my former friends burned into my skull. I reached over and turned the tap off, before resting my body back into the scalding water. I swallowed, my fingers running over the razor I held.

Honestly, it just started as a little thing. Every time Carter or my parents upset me, I would cut a small line on my upper thigh. It wasn't mean to hurt me much or scar me, it was just a coping mechanism I had come up with.

The sounds of shouting filtered through the closed, bathroom door. Mum and dad were fighting again. The 'divorce' word had been mentioned. I didn't want to even imagine them separated. Who would I live with? What would happen to us all?

I enclosed my slippery fingers around the bottle beside me and chugged down the remaining liquid. I grimaced as the foul taste erupted inside my throat. I gagged slightly, my head feeling light on my shoulders.

This time, I would not cut my thighs.

My wrists were the next best option. Without even thinking much of it, I began to slash my wrists. I bit my lip to not cry out at the welcomed pain. I kept going.

Blood began pouring down my skin, dropping like crimson ribbons into the water. Suddenly, the pain was unbelievable. Squinting through my blurry vision, I saw blood pumping out of my wrist at an uncontrollable rate. A scream left my lips as I realised I hit a vein.

I hadn't intended this. I just wanted something to distract me. I didn't want to kill myself.

Shouting and banging become a distant noise to me. The door was busted off its hinges, just as blackness began to embed my vision. What the hell was happening to me? Everything happened so fast.

This was it.

It was my time to die.

A scream tore from my throat as the memories bombarded my brain. I fumbled through my bag, seeing the razor that I had not thought about (much) for a long time. I licked my lips, my breathing suddenly had increased. Without a second more of hesitation, I slashed the blade across my skin.

I was so drunk I hardly even felt the sting. More and more slashes accumulated on my arm. A long sigh left my lips as I stared at the blood. My blood. I had missed the refreshing relief it brought as the physical pain distracted my over active mind. I squeezed my eyes shut, images and more images of that night tumbling through my mind. I made new scars over my old ones, not caring that they left jagged lines across my skin.

I honestly have no idea why I did this, but I did. I reached for my phone, the screen blurry. Somehow, I navigated my way to my contacts and rang him. He answered, surprisingly, on the second ring.

"Lacey?"

"I hate you for what you've done to me," I slurred, my words not even making sense to me. I felt the blood running down my arms and splattering on to the clothes I wore, but I didn't care. I was fixated on him again and what he has done to me.

"What? Lacey, are you okay?" his voice was urgent as he tried to understand.

"How could I love a monster?"

I didn't even realise I was crying again until I felt my wet tears land on my skin. I sniffled, wiping at my face, blood smearing across my chin.

"Where are you? Have you been drinking?"

"Don't call me anymore."

"What are you talking about?" he asked hysterically. "Let me come get you."

I let out a humourless laugh. "Oh yes, Carter Williams here to save the day. My hero."

"Lacey-"

I'm not sure what happened, but somehow the line was dead and my phone was back in my bag. I clutched at my head, the emotional tidal wave smashing back through my weak barriers. I began to clamber to my feet, only my body didn't seem to understand.

"What the-" I slurred, trying to make my body do what I wanted.

Black dots began to edge my vision and soon. I swallowed down a lump of something that had lodged itself in my throat. This was happening again. I never thought I would take this path again, but it happened. I felt the familiar sense of fear swell inside my chest.

"Carter," I tried to call out, but my mouth wasn't working.

That was the last thing I remembered before I completely blacked out.

Chapter 15

Carter's P.O.V:

I would have been less surprised if Hitler came back from the dead, than I was when Lacey's name appeared on my phone. Even though I was mad at her, without a moment of hesitation, I slid my thumb across the bottom of the screen.

"Lacey?"

Her words so slurred and inaudible, it took me a moment to understand her.

"I hate you for what you've done to me."

My stomach twisted painfully. My heart race increased as I felt guilt flood through my veins. She didn't deserve someone like me in her life. I only ever seemed to bring her pain. Saying that I didn't regret impregnating her best friend and that I would sleep with her again was harsh and definitely untrue. I only said that because she got back at me by hurting both mum and myself. I was angry and hurt, but it still gave me no right to say that to her.

She was like this because of me. I had to make things right.

I gripped my phone hard in my hand as I could hear her sniffling and crying. My heart ached at the thought of her sad and alone. She needed me. I needed her. I know I'm bad for her and it's selfish to want to be with her, but I do. I can't help the way I feel.

"What? Lacey, are you okay?" The words tumbled out of my mouth before I even knew what I was going to say. My heart was pumping rapidly inside my chest as I waited for her reply. I was afraid I actually wouldn't hear her, with my heart beat pounding so loudly in my ear drums.

"How could I love a monster?"

Even though she was hard to understand, those words were clear and cut me like glass. I physically felt her words as they burned through my flesh.

A monster.

I was one. I was a cyclone and tore everything down in my path. More specifically, Lacey.

I paused for a moment. My stomach dropped as I realised she was drunk. Her words weren't jumbled as one because she was crying and upset. It was because she was wasted out of her mind. I gulped, my throat suddenly feeling dry.

"Where are you? Have you been drinking?" I asked urgently, images of her abandoned on a street were flooding my mind.

I hardly even remember the conversation now. I was unsure of what I was saying, but I knew she wouldn't tell me where she was. I had to find her. Keeping my phone firmly pressed against my ear, I began to run towards my car in panic.

The engine rumbled to life and I burnt rubber getting out of the driveway. In my peripheral vision, I saw mum emerge from the door to see what the commotion was. I felt a pang of guilt in my stomach. We had been avoiding each other ever since the fact that I was going to be a father was out in the open. I knew that she was going to support me in every way possible and always be there for me, but I also could see the disappointment deep in her eyes.

I floored it as I realised the line was now dead. I cursed loudly, thumping my fist roughly onto the steering wheel. More curses flew out of my mouth as my eyes were darting everywhere.

Slowing the car down to a crawl, I swept my eyes through every inch of town, trying to find her. I had almost lost all forms of hope until I saw a motionless body sprawled on the ground about twenty minutes later. Slamming harshly on the breaks, I leapt out of the car. A guy was approaching her. Turning, I grabbed the baseball bat I kept in my back seat. Lacey used to always make digs at me for having that there. Who knew I would be using it to potentially save her life.

He squatted down and began rummaging through her bag. Low life scumbag.

"You low life piece of shit!" I seethed, practically spitting fire at the man

My fist connected with his nose and I heard a crack. He let out a stran-gled cry falling backwards. Before even having a chance to react, I lowered the baseball and pressed the end to his throat. He was someone I had never seen before which was odd. Having grown up in this town, I tend to know most people. At least this was better than someone I actually was friends with.

"I don't care if you have no roof over your head tonight. If I ever see you near this girl again, I will kill you. Now get out of my sight before I fucking kill you."

His eyes widened and he scrambled to his feet, nursing his broken nose. Blood was pouring down his face as he sprinted away from me, terrified. My entire body was trembling as I was so wired up. I dropped the bat and sunk to my knees.

"No, Lacey, no," I whispered furiously, my voice broken. "Oh God..."

Blood. There was so much blood. It flowed from her wrists and over her smooth, tanned skin. Her knees were scratched and bruised, but nothing like the blood that was coming from her wrist. I remember that day that her parents found her, almost dead in their bath tub.

It was the most terrifying day of my life.

Grabbing hold of her bag and the end of the bat, I picked her up, cradling her to my chest. Tears stung at my eyes as I realised if she died, her last memory of me would be saying that I would hurt her again and that I didn't regret doing so the first time.

It was moments like this that made you change your whole perspective on life.

"Don't you dare leave me," I hissed through my gritted teeth, as I jogged towards the car. "Don't you dare."

As quickly as possible, I lowered her on my back seat, her body flopping lifelessly. I sprinted as fast as humanly possible around to the driver's side, taking off towards the closest hospital. I had to get her there.

If she died...

It felt like hours, when only it was mere minutes, when I reached the hospital.

"HELP!" I screamed out dramatically, like people always do on the movies. I clutched her body, hugging her to me. Eyes of passing people were glued to us, all wanting to know what was going on. "Get out of my way! Move!"

I rushed through the sea of people and towards the emergency doors. The nurse's eyes bulged out of her head as she saw Lacey and the blood pouring from her. Her blood had matted onto my shirt, but I didn't care. All I wanted was her to be okay and safe again.

"Do something!" I screeched, my voice reaching an all-time high as she stood there, a little stunned.

As if that triggered her into action, she began dialling something and calling someone through a mobile-type device. Instantly, a group of paramedics and doctors flooded around me. She was pried from my arms and placed on a stretcher. Our lack of contact made me feel empty inside. I sprinted after them as they hurried her away from me, without saying anything.

"Sir-Sir!" the lady insisted, pulling me back. "You can't go past here."

"Like hell I can't," I growled, shaking her off aggressively.

"Do you want to be the reason she dies?" she barked at me, losing all patience.

That stopped me in my tracks. I flinched as her words hit a little too close to home. I swallowed the dry lump that had seemingly lodged itself in my throat, realising that I had been acting carelessly, like usual.

"I didn't think so. You can't go past here. Please go to the waiting room. We will keep you updated." her voice softened slightly as she realised what she said. She looked absolutely exhausted. She must get situations like this all the time.

Swallowing, I nodded and made my way back to the waiting room. What she said was harsh, but it made me listen. She took off into the room and the doors shut behind her, leaving me alone with my thoughts. I wasn't quite sure what to do next.

I stared down at my blood-drenched hands and clothes, suddenly feeling light headed. Collapsing down on the first chair I saw, ignoring the blood, I placed my head in my hands. The room started spinning. I clenched my jaw, trying to focus on my surroundings.

I'm not sure what happened, but soon I was on my hand and knees, dry heaving. My throat burned and my stomach ached as my body urged.

The thought of Lacey like this physically made me ill.

She had to be okay.

Lacey's P.O.V:

I didn't think I would be in this situation again.

Doctors constantly monitoring me as I'm on suicide watch. My parents staring down at me so confused and worried. My counsellor, discussing plans over with my parents at the sessions I would need to take again.

And Carter, again, being there for me even though we weren't on good terms. This overwhelming sense of deja vu was disturbing. The whole idea of being here again made me want to vomit up my entire life's consumption of food.

I stared at my hand, which was being clasped tightly in Aiden's. I stared at Carter who was glaring holes in the back of his head. Mum, had her hand over her face, her cheeks tear stained. After seeing her mother die, having me almost commit suicide probably wasn't helping her through this. Dad has his back to me and was in deep conversation with my former counsellor, Dr. Marez. Or maybe not-so-former.

"Lace," he whispered.

Carter was the first to realise I was awake.

It was like someone set off a bomb. Everyone jolted and rushed to my side instantly, asking me questions, invading my personal space. I squeezed my eyes shut, wanting nothing more then for them to all just leave me alone. I had a sudden urge to be sick again, but for different reasons this time.

"Hey guys, why don't we give her some space?" Dr. Marez said, instantly sensing my claustrophobia. I was surprised that no one else noticed the instant pressure they were putting on me. When I opened my eyes, they were all backed up, except Aiden, looking at me like I was about to blow up.

That was even worse.

No one knew what to say now. I pointed at the empty glass besides me. My throat was drier than sandpaper. Mum jostled forward and quickly filled up my cup. I reached for it and paused, staring at the thick bandages on my arm. I must have had a deep, antiseptic clean again to make sure no infections had started.

Swallowing, I reached for the drink again and sculled the water. It was refreshing and instantly soothed my throat.

"How do you feel honey?" Mum asked, sitting at the bottom of my bed. "Do your arms hurt?"

I glanced down at them again. Sure, they were stinging slightly, but it wasn't like I lost a limb or anything.

"They're okay." I managed to finally get out.

For the first few hours that I was awake, no one wanted to leave my side. It was as though if they went somewhere, they would come back to find me dead. Which I suppose is a fair call, this was the second time this has happened. But it still annoyed me. It was all my fault though, as usual.

I honestly didn't intend to do that much damage. Just the same as last time. The emotional pressure that built inside my head made me do irrational things. I needed the physical outlet, no matter who says what.

"I'm really tired." I said, void of emotion, cutting off the words mum was saying. "I want some quiet."

"O-okay sweetheart," she stuttered slightly, a little surprised at my bluntness. "Is there anything I can do for you?"

"No, it's fine. You guys go get some rest. I'm fine."

The doubt was obvious in her eyes as she pursed her lips. "We're not going anywhere."

"Suffocating me is not going to help. Please, just look after yourselves and stop worrying about me. I won't be alone anyway."

They knew I had brought up a valid point. It only took another twenty minutes of me begging them to leave, before they finally caved. With a kiss from both of them on my forehead, they parted, finally leaving me to some peace and quiet.

Except the two boys in my life had different ideas.

"Can I talk to her?" Carter said, his voice tense as he attempted to be polite to Aiden. "Alone?"

"I don't think that's a good idea-" Aiden began, but I waved him off, feeling exhausted all over again with everything.

"It's fine," I sighed. "Check in on us in five minutes to make sure I haven't killed him though."

Aiden offered me a smile, thinking I was joking. Reluctantly, he also walked from the room, leaving me alone with Carter. I swallowed nervously, avoiding eye contact. If my counsellor found out I was alone with him, she'd probably have a fit. She knows very well everything that has gone down between us. Better than anyone else actually.

"I can't believe you did this because of me," he began, sounding grave.

My head whipped to his in surprise, as my mouth fell open. "Are you serious?"

He lifted his head, confusion clear on his face.

"Yes, you were one of the leading reasons I had a meltdown, but it was not all about you. God, you're so selfish. It actually makes me sick how selfish you are." My voice automatically became louder with each word. I let out a groan of frustration. Of course he would make this entire situation revolve around him. A nagging voice reminded me that I was also selfish for doing this in the first place but I firmly ignored it.

His eyes widened, but he didn't say anything back, which I'm glad for. I took it as my cue to continue.

"I did not almost kill myself over a boy. I'm not that pathetic. Yes, your betrayal really hurt me, but the fact that I can't stand the person I've considered my best for the last two years, my grandmother, of all people you should know how close I am to her, dying, my inner conflict towards Aiden and the fact that I have been more alone than I've ever felt within the last few weeks. I just needed someone there for me. But the most important friends of mine betrayed me. With each other. Oh and my parents are probably hanging on by a thread as well, just to add to everything."

He opened his mouth to reply, but I held up my hand, signalling that I was not finished.

"So no," I continued, my cheeks flushed with anger. "I did not do this only because of you. I don't want to hear if you're sorry or whatever story you've rehearsed. Just leave me alone okay? I'm sick of you and everything. I'd really appreciate it if you could fuck off."

He jaw was clenching and unclenching the entire time I spoke. His teeth were gritted so tightly I'm surprised they didn't snap off. Silence hung heavily between us until he managed to get himself to speak.

"Okay." he responded, much to my surprise. "But we will talk soon."

"Yeah," I said, my voice softer this time as I slowly began to calm down. "Soon."

With a brief nod, he rose from his chair. He made it to the door, before turning back.

"I'm glad you're okay," were the last words he murmured, before disappearing out the door.

No matter how much he just frustrated me, seeing him leave left a little pang of sadness inside my abdomen.

I hated the fact that I immediately missed him as soon as he was gone.

"I don't think this is very healthy." Aiden murmured dubiously.

I glanced down at the number of chocolate wrappers that were scattered around me, the empty Nutella jar, a ripped open popcorn bag and my lemonade bottle. Okay, so when you look at it all together, it looks like a bit much. But when I was eating it all, it went really quickly...

"What episode are you on now?" he asked once I didn't reply.

"Season 3, episode 2."

His eyes almost bulged out of his head as he stared at me in shock.

"You've watched two seasons in two days?" he exclaimed.

"What?" I asked defensively, snuggling further under the covers. "American Horror Story is addictive okay?"

"You have a problem."

I have many.

"Well it was either this, or a run, but I don't have the energy to move."

Frowning, Aiden gently sat down, brushing away the various chocolate packets. He looked a little disgusted at how much I had eaten. To be honest, I was a bit disgusted myself. One human should not be able to wolf all that down within a few hours.

"How was school?" I asked, arching forward and pressing a gentle kiss to his lips. I pulled back quickly though, goodness knows what my breath smells like. I haven't moved from the lounge for a while now.

"It was okay. Mercedes tried to talk to me a couple of times but I managed to avoid her most of the day."

"What did she want?" I asked, trying not to sound moody at the mention of my former best friend. A scowl immediately found its way on my mouth though.

He jerked his shoulder up. "I probably don't want to know."

"Either."

"Spoken to Carter?"

"Not since the hospital." I sighed, leaning my head back and rubbing my hands over my eyes. "I don't really want to at the moment. I'm happy watching Tate instead."

"Isn't he only Tate in the first season?" Aiden questioned, confused.

"He will forever be Tate in my eyes." I replied passionately, clenching my fist.

"You need to get out of the house." Aiden laughed, looking at me like a freak. "Maybe we could go for a walk?"

"But I'd have to get up."

"You're a slob."

"Ugh, fine." I groaned dramatically, slowly going into standing position.

Dragging my feet, I gradually made my way to my room and began peeling my dirty clothes from my body. I glanced through my window, staring Carter's house. I had been home for a couple of days now, but I was having the week off school. Hopefully more if I can convince my parents.

We'd been spending a lot of time, just as a family, which was nice. Lots of board games and cooking. I think mum was just trying to distract herself as much as possible and was using me as her human prop.

I wasn't looking forward to my counselling sessions starting back up. My first one was tomorrow. It's weird, once I get there and start talking, it's really easy. And refreshing, actually. But it's just the idea of actually going there is what makes it hard.

Carter had tried to ring me once, but I didn't answer. He hasn't tried again. I just want to distance myself from him and be with my family. Aiden has been over twice now, making sure I still had a pulse. Things were going quite well with him. Okay, so we haven't really spent much time together, but anyway.

Slipping on a pair of dark jeans and a blue top, I began fumbling for a jacket. I threw my hair into a loose bun and made my way back out to the lounge. Aiden stood and grabbed both of my hands with his. He leaned forward and softly kissed the tip of my nose. I laughed, playfully pushing him away.

Hand in hand, we left the house. Fresh air had never been so sweet. The wind was cool and slapped my cheeks fiercely. I inhaled a lung full of air, drawing my jacket closer around me. Aiden removed his hand from mine and threw his arm around my shoulders, providing me with his body heat. I smiled gratefully at him, snuggling in as much as I could whilst walking.

"How are you?" he asked.

"Good, you?"

"No, how are you?" he said more seriously, squeezing me slightly as if to emphasise his point. I exhaled slowly. "Talk to me."

"I'm okay. I really am. I know it seems like I'm just doing nothing at home, which realistically I am, but I'm also recovering. Both mentally and physically. My arms are fine and I haven't wanted to hurt myself. I'm honestly just enjoying spending time with my family and doing nothing."

"Has Carter at least tried to contact you?" he kept his tone light but I could feel the tension build as soon as he mentioned him.

"He rang but I didn't answer. I will talk to him when I'm ready."

I felt his body relax beside me at my words. I rolled my eyes at his behaviour but decided not to comment. Carter was not my problem at the moment. I was enjoying the time away from him. Okay, I missed him like the pathetic person I am, but I generally am happy with myself at the moment. The first day out of hospital I spent the entire day sobbing whilst watching American Horror Story, but I soon ran out of tears, found more chocolate and began to move on.

Of course I was still sad about everything, but I had to deal with what was going on and move forward with my life. Which is exactly what I'm doing.

The park, which has been out former meeting spot, came into sight and I smiled slightly. This could be considered our place. Shrugging his arm off, I tugged at his hand so he came stumbling after me.

He grinned carelessly at me, clearly enjoying my affection. I jumped so that I was sitting on the ledge. He stepped between my knees and smiled down at me. Without hesitation, I kissed him, pulling him closer to me.

He responded instantly, his thumb making circular patterns on my chin as our lips moved together.

I didn't exactly feel electricity sparking my core like I experienced when kissing Carter, but it was nice. As nice as swapping saliva can be, anyway. I leaned back, his cheeks flushed from the contact. I kissed him gently once more and smiled.

"We should break up and get back together more often," he laughed, clearly impressed. I smirked slightly, half agreeing with him.

We spent half an hour there, just talking. It was a nice change, to actually just be with him, without all the drama.

"I love you." he whispered, pressing his lips to my cheek. "I love you, I love you, I love you."

"Okay, okay, I get it. You love me." I laugh, gently pushing him away.

He kissed my forehead, enclosing his warm fingers around mine. "You're beautiful."

"You too." I replied awkwardly.

He burst out laughing, stepping back. "Way to ruin the moment!"

"I didn't know what to say!" I laughed, getting to my feet. "But you are, I wasn't lying."

"I know," he said, battering his eyelashes at me.

"Don't ever do that again." I replied seriously.

He let out a chuckle, grabbing my hand. "Come on, let's get back before you get cold."

Something inside my chest swelled at this. At him and this moment. I quickened my pace so I could fall in stride with him, a smile plastered to my face. It felt like I hadn't grinned this much in a while.

We reached my house and I paused, my heart skipping inside my chest.

He looked amazing, as usual. It annoyed me that he could be sweaty but still look like a God. His white singlet clung to his body, showing off his defined muscles. His blond, floppy hair was stuck to his forehead. His chest was rising and falling, clearly still out of breath from his run. My mouth was hanging open slightly.

He always managed to steal my breath from me.

I shook my head, reluctantly dragging my eyes away from him.

Focus on Aiden, your boyfriend. Aiden, Aiden, Aiden. Think back to the park, he loves you, he thinks you're beautiful, you love him...

I felt Aiden tense slightly upon seeing Carter.

"Keep going," I urged, not wanting to look back at him.

Don't look, keep going, and pretend he's not there.

"He looks like he wants to kill me," Aiden laughed softly, although I knew it was fake. I'd be scared of Carter if I was in Aiden's position as well.

Knowing that I shouldn't, I glanced over my shoulder at Carter. His eyes were narrowed into slits as he glared at our entwined hands. I had never seen him look so angry. Without any warning, he spun on his heel and stomped towards the house. I stared at the muscles on his back, a little dazed. The slam of his front door made me jump in alarm and effectively brought me back to reality. I closed my eyes, annoyed at how distracted I got whenever I was in his vicinity.

I'm not sure why, but I instantly dropped Aiden's hand and began to hug myself. Although Aiden is technically my boyfriend and we just shared the most amazing time together, I felt wrong holding his hand. Swallowing, I shouldered around him, feeling terrible for no particular reason.

"Let's get inside and see what's for dinner," I said casually, not wanting him to pick on my mood change. I forcefully shoved all images of Carter outside of my mind and into a folder I do not want to open any time soon.

Why can't I ever get him out of my head?

Chapter 16

"**H**ow are you feeling today?"

"Annoyed to be back in this position to be honest," I stated bluntly, a sigh escaping my lips. I folded my arms defensively across my chest. At the end of our sessions, I had begun to feel quite comfortable with her. That had been lost since we stopped meeting regularly.

Today was my first session back with Dr. Marez, my counsellor. It was compulsory that I had weekly meetings with her as an agreement to being let out of hospital. I tried not to be annoyed but I couldn't help feel a little exasperated. The stupid stunt I pulled set me back months of therapy according to everyone. I was really beginning to regret my actions. I had been too self-absorbed, yet again, to consider what I would do to everyone around me. It made me question everything, really. I never thought I would be one to attempt to commit suicide (honestly wasn't my intention), but here I am, second time around.

She offered me a small smile which was filled with understanding. "I know it is hard for you to be back here, but it worked last time and it can work again. Help me help you."

I nodded, rolling my lips into my mouth. I felt uncomfortable. My spine felt stiff. My hands were placed awkwardly in my lap and my eyes were darting around the room. I wasn't sure whether to look her in eye or not.

"Lacey," she murmured softly, giving me a small smile. "Relax. You've been here before, it's not that scary, is it? I don't bite."

"It's been a while," I said, wiping my sweaty palms on my jeans. "I feel as though so much has changed within me as a person. I don't know where to begin or what to talk about really."

"How about we talk about school," she suggested, reclining back casually. "We will get to the bigger matters when you're ready."

I wonder who what will be about? I thought bitterly.

"School's okay, when I manage to make it through a whole day without getting angry and leaving."

"So your anger management strategies aren't working?"

"They do, kind of. The breathing, the counting and all that does work but I just hate going to school when I'm surrounded by fake friends and fake people, all dying for acceptance that will mean nothing once we leave." I felt my cheeks begin to grow hot. I swallowed, leaning back, tightening my arms in front of me. "So, I dislike going to school. I dislike the teachers, the classes and the people. There's really not all that much hope for me, is there?"

"There is always hope."

"Yeah," I muttered dryly, casting my gaze down. "For some."

"For all." she murmured softly. "It's hard for you to see that, but there is always hope. Have you tried sitting with a new group of friends? Or even considered changing schools?"

"Is there really any point though? The same drama will happen at a different school. Sitting with a different group will not change anything. My best friend, who I realised I actually haven't liked for a long time, is a back-stabbing liar and the love of my life is not much better."

"Carter?" she asked, knowing straight away who he was, from our last sessions. "Is he still giving you trouble?"

"I don't want to talk about it."

"It might be good to-" she began but I interrupted her.

"Can we change the subject?"

She stared at me for a few moments. I mean she really stared, as if calculating my every thought, trying to figure something out. After a stare-down, she did what I asked.

"Let's talk about your family." she began, jotting a few things down on her notepad, which I wanted to pry from her hands and look at. I sighed, rubbing my hands over my face.

Therapy sucks.

I trudged in through the front door, dragging my feet. I softly shut it and leaned back, feeling emotionally drained. I rubbed my hands over my face wearily, wanting nothing more than to curl up in bed and read a book. That was something I haven't done in a while. With that decision being made, I maneuvered myself towards the kitchen, to make myself some noodles before I entered my room for the evening.

Striding in, I made a beeline for the cupboard. I paused, seeing mum's back to me, her shoulders shaking. Her cries met my ears and my stomach clenched painfully. Slowly, I wandered towards her and rested a hand on her shoulder.

"Mum?"

She jumped in alarm, clearly not realising I was there. Her cheeks were tear-stained and her eyes puffy. She hastily wiped at her face. This moment caused a rush of panic in me. It reminded me of the time she told me I had to go live with Carter.

"I-I didn't see you there," she stammered, a little breathless.

"What's wrong?" I asked, my voice small and full of concern.

"I failed." she hiccupped, the tears flowing down her face. "I failed you as a parent and I am so sorry, Lacey."

"What are you talking about?" I exclaimed, grabbing both of her shoulders and squeezing. "You're the most amazing mother in the world. What would make you think that?"

"If I were a good parent, I would have seen you depressed. I would have realised there was something wrong. You wouldn't have tried to kill yourself."

Guilt flooded through me at her words. I felt physically ill. Pulling her to me roughly, I clutched her body tightly against mine.

"Don't you ever say that you're a bad parent for what I did. I was the selfish one who did this and didn't think of the others around me."

"When people are depressed they don't think of others, their own problems and worries consume them until they can't take it anymore. You told me you didn't want to go to Carter's but I sent you there anyway. If I lost you..." Her worlds trailed off and a heart-clenching sob tore from her throat. She engulfed me tighter, as if she couldn't squeeze me hard enough. "Y-you tried to tell me and I didn't-"

"Shh," I soothed, rubbing her back. "Stop. I'm here and I won't do it again. It wasn't you that caused this. It was a mixture of things. I didn't want to kill myself, I promise. I just wanted my emotional pain to stop. I didn't think about the consequences. I love you. I love dad. I'm sorry."

We gripped each other, as if our lives depended on it. Tears were streaming down my face, my mouth becoming hot and sticky. We stayed in each other's embrace for a long time. I didn't mind though, I just needed her to hold me.

"Tell me, okay? Tell me if you ever feel like doing that again." she murmured, her crying having seized.

"I won't ever do it again. Or want to."

"I hope not. I couldn't handle losing you, too."

More tears burned at my eyes and I buried my face against her.

This moment made me realise I really I needed to change.

The moment I saw her, I knew something was going to happen. I don't know how, or why, but I just did. Her vibrant red hair was the first to catch my attention as she made her way over to my table. She had bright green eyes and smooth pale skin. Out of the all the people who had vacant chairs beside them, I'm not sure why the teacher directed her to me, but I knew she would.

Anna was the new girl at our school. I noticed Mercedes watch with narrowed eyes as she maneuvered her way over to me. Yes, I was back at school. Yes, it sucked, but I was dealing with it the best I could. By 'best' I mean avoiding everyone and sticking to myself. Whispers followed me everywhere I went. I was the school gossip, yet again. A smile curved around her lips as she perched beside me.

"Hey."

"Hey," I replied, a little curious of her. "I'm Lacey."

"I know."

"Anna."

"I know."

She smirked back.

"How do you know who I am?" I asked her, quirking my eyebrow.

"Well, you're the talk of the school, of course." she said dramatically, her lip gloss coated lips still in a smirk. "Love triangles, attempted suicide..."

"I see your point." Not flinching at the word suicide, which she was expecting, I'm sure.

"I knew I had find this infamous Lacey Adams."

"You found her."

"Which one is Mercedes?" she asked me. Clearly, she didn't care about prying. I let out a laugh, surprisingly. She didn't muck around. Usually I would get miffed at someone wanting to know my business, but for some reason I wanted to tell her. I wanted her to be my friend. I suppose that's what happens when you're lonely.

"Mercedes?" I asked, rolling my tongue across my teeth. "That would be her, in the flesh."

I pointed across the room, not being subtle. Our eyes met and her mouth opened, as if she wanted to say something to me, but I turned back to Anna.

"We hate her, right?"

"She's pregnant with the child of my ex-boyfriend. So yeah, we hate her."

"Alright, duly noted."

I breathed a laugh, rolling my eyes. I liked her already. She was extremely easy to talk to, which meant whatever lesson I was in melted around me as we exchanged conversation. I jumped slightly as the bell rang. That class went quick. We parted ways outside the classroom as I made my way towards the door that would lead me outside. It was nice actually talking to someone. Yeah sure, I have small conversations here and there, but I didn't want to know many people from my year. I didn't like many of them.

"What are we doing this afternoon?" she asked casually, plopping down beside me as I lay sprawled in the shade of one of the large, chestnut, oak trees that boarded that yard of school. I squinted up at her, half shielding my face.

"I'm going for a run."

"You run too? Let's meet up and join circuits. Not that I have one yet, but I'll figure one out pretty quickly."

"Why do you want me to be friends with me?" I asked rudely. "Sorry, but of all people to choose from..."

"You're interesting." she shrugged. "I'm new, I need all the friends I can get and you don't look like you're all that popular right now either."

"Gee, thanks." I said sarcastically. "You're not going to gain many more being with me."

She rolled her eyes. "You know what I mean. You clearly are a bit anti-social though."

"I am, so if you don't mind," I said, shooing her away although I was actually enjoying interacting with another human apart from Aiden, my counsellor, parents or the teachers.

"Don't be like that. Where's Aiden?"

"You're relentless."

"Thank you," she replied with all seriousness.

I sighed, resting back. "He will join me soon I'm sure. You can meet him then."

"Yay!"

It wasn't long before I heard his footsteps ascend towards me and I knew it would be him. Lazily, I left my eyes closed. He crouched down beside me and patted my head awkwardly.

"Hey," he murmured.

"Aiden, Anna, Anna, Aiden." I waved my hand almost dismissively, still not opening my eyes.

They exchanged a few words, getting to know each other but I hardly paid any attention. I was too tired and enjoying my own thoughts at the moment.

"Want to hang out this afternoon?" Aiden asked, nudging me with his knee to get my attention.

"I have plans already with Anna," I said, peering through one open eyelid. "Sorry."

Anna turned her green orbs to me, one eyebrow quirked curiously. I stared back challengingly. She was going to interrogate me on that later, I just knew it, seeing as that I wasn't all that keen to give up my alone time this afternoon to spend with her anyway.

"Oh, alright."

I bit my lip, casting my eyes downward. Things were fine with him, but now that I was back with the counsellor and actually confronting the issues I have with Carter, the slight feelings of resentment that I had begun to previously feel for Aiden were coming back. I know I was so up and down, but I can't help it. I don't know what I want and I'm scared I never will.

After a few more attempts of conversation and me not really participating, Aiden retired back to his group of boys and I hated to admit I felt relieved. I cursed myself, wanting to physically face palm. I think I needed a break from all boys and have some much needed Lacey time.

"Why are with someone you don't even like?" she asked, going directly to the point.

"I do like him."

"Not sure who you're trying to convince here."

I exhaled deeply, rubbing my hands over my face. "It's complicated."

"Un-complicate it. Break up with him."

"I only just got back with him. I'm going to send him to the clinic if I keep this up."

"You're a girl, you don't know what you want. You're only human. If he really likes you, he will understand."

I peered up at her, a little surprised. Upon first meeting her, I knew she was a joker. Sarcastic, witty and sadistic. But serious? Now that surprised me. I grimaced up at her, knowing that she was right.

"I'm not going to do anything right now. I'll just see what happens."

"Whatever."

"What about you?" I asked, doing a little prying of my own. "What boy drama is going on in your life?"

"Ugh, don't get me started. A new boy is just what I need. I've had some drama with twins lately. It's really not as great as I envisioned it would be."

I scrunched up my nose at her. "You're terrible."

She shrugged. "That's life."

"Are we going running this afternoon?"

"Yep, I'll meet you at your place at four? Once I know directions of course."

"Sure. I'll show you the track I do. But I'm warning you now, it's long and I run the entire way. Sometimes I even sprint."

"You're going to kill me," she sighed dramatically. "But I suppose that's fine."

I stared at her for a moment. It was random how we just became friends. Just like that. But I was glad it happened. I needed some more females in my life.

The rest of the school day cruised by pretty uneventfully. Just as I was exiting school, I saw the back of Aiden's head and jogged up to him.

"Hey, sorry about earlier, I'm just tired. We can hang tomorrow, if you're free?"

"Yeah, movies or something?" he asked, coming to a stop. He reached out for my hand and I squeezed it, smiling up at him.

"Yeah sure."

"And it's okay. I know you don't want to be back here. I know what you're like."

I laughed, was it that obvious school was such a drag to me?

"What do you think of Anna?"

"I'm not sure yet. She seems a little scary."

"Scary?" I asked incredulously with a laugh. "How is she scary?"

"I don't know. She just seems a little full on. Like she knows something that she shouldn't."

"Yeah, I get what you mean. I'll suss her out when we go running this afternoon."

"You're taking her running with you? Have you warned her?"

"Yes," I laughed.

"Okay, I'll let you go. I'll see you tomorrow." He bent down and brushed his lips fleetingly against mine, before I pulled back. With one last smile, I began to briskly walk towards my car, only having fifteen minutes to get home, eat, change and meet with Anna.

This afternoon will be interesting.

"Okay, okay, stop." she panted.

For someone so glamorous, she sure didn't look so now. Her vibrant, red hair was tied back off her face and sweat glistened across her forehead. Her chest was rising and falling rapidly as she tried to catch her breath.

"We're not even halfway..." I pointed out, resting my hands on my hips. I watched in amusement as she doubled over, literally looking like she was ready to pass out.

"I'm fit but this is insane."

"I did warn you..." I trailed off, with a small smirk.

"Just - give - me - a - second," she breathed, wiping the excess sweat from her face.

I tilted my head back, trying to regain my own breath as I stared up at the pale, blue sky. The wind was starting to pick up now, meaning it was cooling down rapidly. The hairs on my arms bristled and I rubbed at them, just wanting to keep going.

"Ready?"

She groaned, her cheeks flushed. I just laughed and began my jog again. She begrudgingly followed suit, falling in step with me. Taking it slow, we managed to make it most of the way home without any more breaks. We were just coming onto my street when I saw him. No matter who he was with or what he was doing, he stood out to me. I felt my stomach clench.

"That's Carter," I grunted through my teeth, watching him run towards us as he was on his own jog.

"Woah," she breathed. "Can we just take a second to stare at him? I don't think I've seen someone so beautiful before."

"Oh please," I laughed, but definitely agreeing that his beauty was dazzling.

I did what she said and took a moment to stare at him. I realised then, he wasn't in his jogging clothes. He was sprinting towards me urgently, his eyes wide. My feet came to a stop before I even realised I had begun to slow down. I backed up slightly, suddenly feeling nervous. He didn't stop until he was inches from me, his hands gripping my forearms. Electricity spiked through my veins at his mere touch. I inhaled, his scent overpowering me, as usual. God, I had missed him. Just looking at him and being around him. I wanted to reach up and touch him, not caring at this moment everything that has happened. I missed my best friend more than anything in the world. He hadn't been at school today which means I haven't seen him for over a week. Doesn't sound like long, but it felt like eternity.

"Lacey," he began breathlessly, his voice automatically causing goose bumps to erupt over my skin. I swallowed, trying to not show how much he was affecting me right now. "It's not mine."

"What?"

"The baby," he said, his face red. "Mercedes' baby. It's not mine."

My mouth fell open. I stopped breathing. I felt light-headed at the sudden revelation. I don't whether I wanted to pass out with happiness or be sick.

Carter wasn't the father.

Chapter 17

His arms securely wrapped around me and I melted into him. I buried my face into his chest, just wanting him to hold me. My mind and body were still in shock. I couldn't comprehend what he was saying. I clung to him as though my life depended on it. I missed him. I missed his touch, his smell, everything.

"How..." I began, unsure of how to even form a sentence right now. I shook my head, my heart beating fast in my chest. "How do you know?"

"Mercedes confessed. I'm not the father. The timing isn't right for me to be the father anyway, once she explained it."

I stepped back. "You-I-what?"

"I know. We can be togeth-"

"Because you're not the father, doesn't change the fact that you slept with my best friend." I said sharply, stepping back from him.

He opened his mouth to reply, but no words came out. He was speechless, which was rare for him. It was as though this news was magically supposed to fix everything? I shook my head, stepping back from him. I kept backing up until there was at least a metre between us.

"Sorry, I just... I have to go. Sorry Anna." I stammered, turning my back on both of them. I strode back towards my house. It wasn't until I collapsed on my bedroom floor that I realised my hands were trembling. Swallowing, I ran my hands through my sweat-drenched hair.

What the hell do I do now?

"Get your lazy butt up and get ready."

"Go away."

"Don't make me do it."

"Do what?"

I shouldn't have asked. My toasty blanket was ripped from my body, the cool morning air nipping at my exposed skin. A dramatic groan tore from my throat. I sat up, shooting death glares at a perky, red head who was standing at the end of my bed.

"Morning." Anna beamed, revealing two rows of shiny teeth.

"Why are you here?"

"Well, I'm assuming the 'days of our lives moment' yesterday would have you pretty scattered. I can already tell how much you dislike school and assumed you would use this as an excuse not to attend."

She already knew me too well.

"You're correct, so if you don't mind..." I trailed off as I pointed rudely towards my door.

"I do. Get up before I make you."

"Why do I need to go to school?" I groaned.

"Because this is our final year! Make the most of it. Stop being a little cry baby. Read my lips. Boys don't control your life. Get a grip girl! Go to school, keep your chin up and don't let this drama get you down."

My mouth fell open slightly. She was right, not that I would openly admit that to her. I was letting boys control my life. That verbal slap in the face was enough to make me think about the way I had been acting.

"Now get up, get dressed and let's go."

Begrudgingly, I clambered to my feet and began my morning routine. I slipped into my uncomfortable uniform and ran a hand through my long, blonde hair. I stared at myself momentarily in the mirror. My face looked gaunt. My cheek bones were defined and my eyes tired. My collar bones stuck out unattractively. From a distance, I looked fine and healthy. But when you looked close, you could see how thin and frail I really was.

Rolling my lips, I added some more make up underneath my eyes, in attempt to cover the darkness that circulated underneath them. Slowly, I spread some gloss across my lips and stepped back, my appearance having improved.

"You ready or what?" Anna asked, materialising beside me. "We have five minutes."

"Yeah, coming." I said, taking one last look at myself before turning my back on the mirror. I exhaled loudly. "Let's get this over with."

"Love your enthusiasm." she snickered, nudging me with her elbow. "Come on, I'll drive."

I slipped into her car cautiously, staring around. It was like a bomb had exploded inside it. There were clothes, wrappers and bottles scattered all around. She noticed my staring and shrugged nonchalantly at me.

"I sleep in my car a lot."

"Apparently," I muttered, staring at the blankets piled on the back seat and her pillow smooshed against the floor. I reached over and placed it on the back, spreading it out. "You have a home, right?"

"Yeah. I have a home." her voice changed. It became surprisingly sharp. I quirked an eyebrow at her abrupt attitude change. She was allowed to know every detail about my life but one question about her and she closes up? I shrugged it off and pressed my forehead against the glass, not saying anything else.

"Sorry." She muttered.

I didn't reply.

"I do have a home. I just don't get along with mum, so I crash in my car a lot."

"Do you need-"

"No. I'm fine."

"Okay." I snapped back.

"Honestly," she said, her voice becoming soft. "Thanks though. I don't get abused or anything. I just don't like her."

"Fair enough."

"And we're here, yay!" she cried out, fist pumping. "I love school!"

"It's scary that you actually do."

"Shut up," she laughed, punching me lightly. "I like the social side of it."

"Of course."

"Negative Nancy." she muttered playfully.

We entered the school hallway and my shoulder connected with someone. I stumbled backward, glancing up. Mercedes. She stared coolly at Anna beside me. She seemed almost jealous? Like she had any right to be.

I had so much I wanted to say. I wanted to scream at her, hit her, something. But that wouldn't solve anything. The way I act doesn't define what she has done. It would only define who I am.

"You know," she said, her voice low, her eyes penetrating into mine. "Look Lacey, I'm sorry-"

I pushed past her in attempt to take the high road. I don't want to hear what she has to say. I don't want someone like her in my life.

"Good choice." Anna said quietly. "Although a little disappointed you didn't hit her. But with the pregnancy and all, I understand."

Rolling my eyes, I chose not to reply to that. After collecting our essentials from the lockers, we parted ways. I rounded the corner, my head connecting with Carter's hard chest. Can a girl get a break? I stepped back, avoiding eye contact, but I could feel the heat of his stare on me. Giving in, I looked up.

"Hey." he murmured.

"Hey yourself."

"How are you?"

"Okay, you?"

"Okay."

Silence followed after and I immediately felt awkward.

"Want to go for a walk tonight?"

"A walk?" I questioned, stepping back. His tan was dark due to the consistent sunlight we had been getting. His hair was sun bleached more than ever. "Where would we walk?"

"Anywhere you want."

I stood there for a moment, contemplating. I suppose it wouldn't hurt. A walk sounds nice, actually. It would be good to talk.

"Yeah. Okay."

His eyebrows rose. "Okay?"

"Okay."

"Eat your heart out Hazel Grace."

"Don't overdo it." I laughed, pushing back against him. I felt a flare as soon as our skin made contact but ignored it. "I'll see you later."

"Okay."

"Stop it." I laughed over my shoulder, rolling my eyes. I looked up and saw Anna entering the classroom, her eyebrows raised suggestively. I made a face at her and she laughed, walking into the room.

Is it bad that I'm actually excited for tonight?

It was cold. I shrugged a large jacket over my skin tight shirt, doing up a couple of the buttons. I dropped to my knees and snaked my hand underneath my bed, trying to find some nice boots to wear.

A voice cleared behind me, causing a grin to automatically spread across my face.

"I thought we were meet-" my voice came to an abrupt stop when I realised who it was. Aiden stared at me. That wasn't who I was expecting. "Hey."

"Forget something?" he asked, his voice sharp.

I thought for a moment but came up blank.

"We were going to the movies tonight."

Not so blank anymore.

"Oh crap. I'm so sorry, it slipped my mind."

"Our date 'slipped your mind'?" he questioned, arms folded across his chest. "What's going on?"

"Nothing is going on."

"You going somewhere?" he asked, staring at my clothes and ignoring my previous response.

"I was going for a walk."

He nodded slowly, his jaw clenched. "By yourself?"

I didn't reply.

"Why aren't you happy? Why am I not enough for you?" he whispered. "What can I do to make you happy?"

"You do make me happy," I whispered back.

"Not enough. Not as much as him."

My eyes drifted close.

"I can't keep doing this. I can't keep waiting around for you."

I bit the inside of my cheek, my eyes stinging. "I know. I'm sorry."

"Not as sorry as I am."

"Aiden-" I tried one last time but he stepped back.

"I just can't do this anymore. See you around, Lacey."

I stared at the ground, rolling my tongue across my teeth. It was the right thing to do and I'm glad he broke up with me. I sighed, sitting back on my bed. I sat there, just thinking for a long time. My body jumped in alarm as my phone vibrated against my leg. Carter was waiting outside. Getting to my feet, I wandered out the front, the cool air slapping me in the face.

"Hey. You okay?"

"Yeah."

"Okay."

I looked at him warningly and he held his hands up in a peace gesture. "That was unintentional that time."

"Sure it was."

"How's your counselling sessions been?" he asked when silence fell. I hugged my jumper closer to myself, feeling a little numb.

"Not too bad. Mainly revolve around you." I answered honestly.

"Understandable. I'm often a hot topic."

"Get over yourself," I scoffed, rolling my eyes. "How's life been for you?"

"Alright. I have been surfing a lot. That's mainly it really."

"I can tell. You're very bronze."

"I'm always bronze."

"Have you met Anna yet?" I asked, taking the initiative to keep the conversation going.

"Briefly. She seems cool."

"Yeah, she is." Our arms brushed and I held my breath slightly.

We continued to talk for quite some time. It was nice. It was just us, the way it used to be. We had circled the block twice and were back in front of my house. Admittedly, Aiden had slipped from my mind a while ago. It occurred to me that I had been waiting for him to do it. To finally end it. Deep down I think I knew he needed to be the one to do it for good, so that it was officially over. And honestly? I felt relieved. I'm glad he finally realised I was broken. That he could not fix me. He could do better.

"I should probably go." I found myself saying. The words tumbled from my mouth before I even knew they were going to.

"Yeah me too," he agreed, studying my face slightly.

He leaned forward and I held my breath involuntarily. Gently, he pressed his lips to my forehead.

"Goodnight, Lacey."

"Goodnight Carter." I whispered, not moving.

He stared at me for a moment, before dragging himself away. He turned, striding toward his house. I watched him go, a small smile on my face.

It were moments like this that made me appreciate having Carter in my life, despite everything that has happened.

The liquid burned my throat on the way down, but I didn't care. I stared down at the vodka with a sour expression planted on my face. I was glad I was drinking with another person right now. Last time by myself... didn't end so well. The taste reminded me of that dark time in my life. I didn't really want the flash back. It was too soon.

Anna, had convinced me to tag along to a party with her. It had been a little under a week since she started at school and already she was off with a bang. Sure, I was invited to parties but I never went. Too much drama when Carter was there. I didn't want to see him sucking faces with girls I have to face every day, not that I've seen him do that for a few months now.

I think I just needed some fun. And possibly the fact that I now actually have a friend to go to a party with made me actually want to go this time.

We looked pretty good, if I do say so myself. Anna's fiery red hair was straightened to perfection with a tight, black playsuit securely wrapped around her body. She had tall heels on and a clutch firmly planted in her palm, a vodka shot in her other.

I, on the other hand had settled with one of Anna's pretty red dresses that tied up at the back. Anna had taken it her duty to 'glamour' me up, so my hair was in ringlets shaping my face and my eyelashes longer than they'd ever been. I wore minimal make up on a daily basis, so seeing myself done up like this was actually pretty cool.

School hadn't been as awkward as I thought it would be. Aiden and I seemingly have mutually accepted the fact that we just don't work. We're not meant to be together. So he was back with his guys and I was with Anna.

I'd been talking to Carter more, which had been nice. Nightly walks had become an every night occurrence. He hadn't tried anything and I appreciated that. It was nice to just get to know each other again. Didn't stop me hoping that tonight would be different...

I slipped into some heels, again belonging to Anna, and grabbed my bag. Double checking that I had everything, I gave Anna the nod she had been waiting for. We decided to have pre-drinks an hour ago, which meant we were pretty much drunk already. That was good though, I didn't want to be in the 'awkward still getting on it' phase when arriving like most people do. I was focusing on walking straight and making sure I appeared sober, I carefully wound down my stairs.

"Ready to go mum?" I asked her.

She was perched on her back, legs folded over the arm rest. She gently placed her book down and slid her glasses back into her hair. It was nice to see her relaxed. She was usually bustling around the kitchen and organising forms for work. And yet, here I was disturbing her to drive me to a party.

"Yep. You girls look nice." She commented with a smile. "Whose party is it again?"

I didn't even know.

"Peter from school." Anna smiled. She spoke well but you could tell by her eyes she was drunk. Mum either chose to ignore this or was actually oblivious. "He's a bit shy so we're all going to try and make him actually have a good time."

"Aw, that's nice of you girls."

"Who?" I muttered when she came closer.

She shrugged at me. "First name I thought of."

I breathed a laugh, rolling my eyes. I followed them both out towards the car. I glanced over my shoulder, seeing Carter's bedroom light off. He was out. Out at the same party? I couldn't help but be curious. Did I want to see him? Yes, obviously, but what would I do if I saw him? Who knows what drunk Lacey is up too.

Trying to walk properly, I climbed into the car, my head spinning slightly. A smile made its way onto my face and I rested my head back. It was nice to feel this free again. It didn't take long before we were there. You could already hear the music. The bass vibrated against the floor. I quickly thanked mum and slipped out of the car, Anna not far behind. We waved as she left and stared at each other, smirking.

"Let's do this."

We linked arms childishly and made our way in. Our arrival instantly got attention, everyone already in love with Anna. Having her by my side made me feel more confident in every way. I was beginning to talk to people in my year again, that I hadn't in so long. It was nice. She gave me the push I have been needing. I was starting to actually make some friends again. I came to realise that being anti-social isn't as fun as I originally thought.

Straight away, we went to the beer pong game and began playing. I was pretty terrible, already too gone to focus as much as it is necessary in this game. I stumbled to the side, throwing my head back with laughter. I gripped the table and stared down at the jagged lines on my arm. They were still pretty fresh. I squeezed my eyes close, attempting to pretend they didn't exist.

"BRB girl," Anna called over her shoulder, sauntering towards a boy I've seen around school a few times. She didn't hesitate to wrap her arms around his neck and go in for the kill. I raised my eyebrows, a little impressed at her confidence. Well there you go. I couldn't help feel a little disappointed that she left, but I turned and continued a few more attempts at beer pong to kill time.

When I looked back up, both her and the boy were gone. I exhaled. Suppose I should go grab another drink. Watching the floor carefully, I waded through the small crowd of sweaty bodies toward my bag. I was almost there when a hand clutched mine. I was tugged roughly, hitting a couple of people on my way. I staggered outside, my head spinning.

"Hey," Carter said, his breath fanning my face. I could smell the alcohol on him. "I've been waiting for you."

"Have you?" I breathed, feeling a little exhilarated. "Why's that?"

Without warning, he cupped my face and kissed me. Tingles erupted through my body. With no moment of hesitation, I grabbed a fistful of his shirt, tugging him closer to me. Our lips moved together in synchronisation. I loved the taste of him and the feeling of his lips against mine. With ragged breathing, we parted. My chest was rising and falling, my cheeks flushed. He grinned at me, our noses still brushing.

"I have missed you so much."

"I have missed you too."

"You don't understand," he murmured, his lips brushing mine but not enough to be a kiss. "My body aches for you."

My eyes drifted close. I felt a sudden sense of content as he made a trail of kisses across my jaw. He moved toward the bottom of my ear, nipping slightly. A gasp left my mouth and I felt him smirk against my skin.

No other boy has ever made me feel this way. I don't think anyone else could. The heat underneath my skin was indescribable. I loved him. I always have, not that I could see that for some time, and I always will, no matter what he does to me.

"I love you," he whispered. I felt like I was on cloud nine. Grabbing his face with both hands, I forcefully pressed my lips against his again.

"I love you, too."

Our make out session was pretty hot. It was like we were making up for all the days we haven't been together. I couldn't get enough of him. I wanted more. I slid my hands underneath his shirt, our skin making contact again.

"Don't. Don't do that if you don't want to go further."

Reclining back, I let out a breath. I was drunk, I know that, but did I really want to go there again? Last time we did it ruined everything.

"I don't know what I want."

"Well then I'm not letting you go there." he breathed. "As much as I want to, I can't."

I squeezed my eyes shut. "Okay."

"You're so God damn beautiful Lacey." he murmured, surprising me.

My mouth felt dry. I needed some water. Swallowing, I averted my eyes. I had so many things I wanted to say, I just don't know how.

"We need to talk about this when we're both sober."

"Yeah, we need to."

I tilted my head back and our lips met one last time, before I pulled back. "I need to go get some water."

"Alright." He stepped back from me, our fingers entwining. "I know where Jacob stashed some water supplies."

"Who?"

"Jacob. The guy who is hosting the party?"

"Oh yeah, right." I agreed, pretending like I knew him. "Let me know if you see Anna, would you?"

"Yeah."

My lips felt swollen and my cheeks were hot. I ignored people's curious stares at Carter and my hands, which were still interlocked. I kept my head down as we made our way to a back room. He dropped my hand and began rummaging through the esky, pulling out a water.

"There you go."

"Thanks," I said gratefully, sitting back. I took a few sips, feeling a lot more hydrated. "Want any?"

"Yeah actually." He took a few sips himself before returning the bottle. "Party turned out to be good, huh?"

A small smile danced around my lips. "Yeah, not too bad."

"How are you getting home?"

"I'm just crashing in Anna's car, I think."

"That sounds comfortable. Do you want a ride home?"

"Oh it should be fine, but thank you for the offer."

We stayed out the back, just chatting again. We had been doing that a lot lately, which I liked. I hadn't realised so much time had gone by until I checked my phone, realising Anna had been trying to contact me. I had been with Carter for two and a half hours now. I squinted at the screen, trying to make out what she said.

'If you've ended up in a gutter, lying in your own vomit, I'm going to be very cross with you!'

'Omg, you're with Carter aren't you? Yay!'

'I'm bored and lonely, please be quick and find your way back to me my love.'

'Okay seriously. I'm bored. Come to me.'

'This party is getting lame now, can we go home?'

'Ugh, damn you and your perfect boy and your perfect life. Bye.'

'Sorry, I spoke out of anger. Can you come hang with me now?"

'Lacey pleaseeeee, I'm bored.'

'I'll be waiting at the lounge for you to return. I miss you. Please come.'

I rolled my eyes, laughing. "I think I need to go to Anna. She's having an anxiety attack."

"Alright, I can't keep you to myself all night, can I now?"

I was unsure of how to respond, so I chose to laugh instead. Just as we were at the door, he paused. He lent down, kissing me gently.

"Tonight was good. I hope we can continue our walks. It's the best part of my day. Call me if you want a ride home or somewhere to stay. Mike's brother is getting us all in his land cruiser. I'll talk to you tomorrow."

"Okay." I smiled up at him.

He shot me a smile as he disappeared through the door. Exhaling, I stood there for a few moments, making sure I was composed. I wandered towards the lounge, where Anna was perched, chatting to someone I didn't know. She leapt to her feet, completely ignoring them once she saw me.

"Thank God, get me away from this loser."

"That's not very nice," I laughed. I squinted at her, seeing some hickeys slashed across her neck. "Good night?"

"Yeah, yours?" she smirked, raising her eyebrows suggestively. "Lover girl."

"You can't talk."

"Touché. Let's go home, my head aches, my feet hurt and my hangover is already starting to kill me."

"I feel ya'," I laughed, grabbing her hand.

I was definitely glad I came out tonight.

Chapter 18

It felt as though a hammer had been inserted inside my brain and was having its own party there. My mouth was drier than sand paper and my stomach was churning uncomfortably. I slowly moved into sitting position, my head hitting the roof of Anna's car. Why I agreed to sleep here after the party was beyond me. Glancing over my shoulder, I saw Anna unattractively sprawled across the back seat, her make-up smeared across her face.

Scrunching my nose up, I tumbled out of the car, the fresh air feeling amazing. I gagged involuntarily and dropped to my knees. My mouth began watering and I squeezed my eyes shut, telling myself to never, ever drink again. I then proceeded to vomit my entire last night's alcohol across the newly mowed grass. Wiping my mouth with the back of my hand, I went back into sitting position and leaned heavily on the car.

Last night had been fun. I drank too much but had an awesome time, nonetheless. Clearly, since I was feeling the opposite right now. Carter's lips... A goofy smile danced across my lips as I remembered him. He had been so great. My grin widened as he was actually a gentleman and didn't give in to my 'wants' at the time.

I really should thank him.

Clambering to my feet, I realised I needed to get home. I began tapping furiously on the window, in attempt to wake up sleeping not-so-beauty from her coma. Like someone had poisoned her, she went into a fit.

"What day is it? What year? What country am I in?"

An unattractive snort escaped me as I stared at her. Her messy, red hair stuck across her face and she hastily wiped it away, genuinely looking lost. It was a little hard to believe someone as gorgeous as her woke up looking like this, although I can't say I looked a million dollars right now either. I opened the door and perched at the end of the seat, giving her a bright smile.

"Morning sunshine!"

"Woah," she said, holding up her hands. "Tone down the level of enthusiasm please. Too early to deal with that."

"It's actually almost afternoon," I pointed out, glancing down at my watch.

After my not-so-pleasant vomit, I was feeling refreshingly better, thankfully. Can't say the same for Anna, however. Sure, I still felt off and yuck, but at least I knew I wouldn't vomit again. That was the worst.

"I need a shower."

"Me too."

"Do you think I'm still over the limit?" she questioned, clutching her head in her hands, her skin turning visibly paler by the second.

"I don't think you would be. You stopped before me and it's almost 12 now, so you should be fine. You're not driving very far anyway."

"True. I'll drop you off and head home."

"Are you functioning well enough to drive yet?" I asked curiously as she staggered from the car, looking possessed.

"I'll be right."

I stared at her dubiously with a frown. She slid behind the wheel and I removed myself from the back seat and planted my butt in the passenger, where I had spent the uncomfortable night's sleep. The car rumbled to life and I immediately wound down the window. The rush of cool air around us was definitely welcomed. I rested my head back, the cool air fanning across my face feeling quite nice. I closed my eyes, deciding the sun was too bright.

We reached my house and I leapt from the car, dragging all my stuff with me. I gave Anna a salute and she stared back, looking like death.

"I shall communicate with you later, when I am functioning properly."

"Can't wait," I laughed. "Thanks for the lift!"

She cringed at the high tone of my voice and waved at me dismissively. I laughed and slammed the door shut. I wandered into my house and straight up to my room. I shed my clothes from last night and let the hot water of my shower swallow me up. The steam felt amazing to breathe in and the water running over my skin helped relax my knotted muscles. I sighed, leaning on the glass, feeling a lot more human already.

After spending longer than necessary in there, I emerged and slipped on a light, summer dress with daisies splashed across it. I let my hair naturally dry, letting it hang limply down my shoulders. I padded down the stairs and realised no one was home.

Making myself some toast and juice, I perched on the kitchen island and let myself eat. I began to feel better after that. After brushing my teeth, well, more like scrubbing them, I felt ten times better.

Now, to do what I had been planning to all morning. Visit Carter. Slipping on some sandals, with a deep exhale, I headed over next door. I knocked a couple times on the door, before slipping in. I met Miranda half way down the hall.

"Oh hi Lacey." she greeted. There was still a bit of tension between us from when I stayed here, but we'd known each other forever, so we were in the process of moving on. And by 'moving on' I mean pretending the whole 'running-away-dropping-bombshell-on-her' thing didn't happen.

Unfortunately the only thing left between us was awkwardness. "Carter's just up in his room studying."

A laugh automatically left my mouth. Carter, studying? What a joke. Never in his life has Carter studied for anything and yet, much to my frustration, aces any test he sits. It has been something that has bugged me ever since we were young. He was brilliant at most things and academically, was a star student without any effort in his behalf.

She frowned at me. "He really is studying. The last couple of weeks he hardly has done anything else."

My eyebrows shot up. "Really?"

"Really."

"Huh, there you go. I just have to see him briefly, I won't distract him for too long."

"Go on up." she smiled, turning from me although the smile seemed a little forced. "He could use the break."

What on earth was he studying for? Unless he was really making sure he was really prepared for the end of year exams, I have no idea what else there could be. As ninja-like as possible, I crept up his gigantic stair case and made my way toward his room. Much to my pleasure, his door was half-open. There was no ear-splitting music coming from his room, no angry grunts as he did weights. Just suspicious silence.

I inched closer and poked my head through the door. His back was to me as he sat cross legged on his floor. Books upon books were scattered in messy piles around him. My mouth fell open. He leaned forward and began scribbling on a notepad, which was thick of his writings.

Staring at him open-mouthed, my eyes bulging incredulously. Saying I was shocked, would be an understatement. I stood there for several minutes, just watching him. He was actually studying. I didn't recognise any of the textbooks he had, so I knew it wasn't school work. Well, none

of the classes we shared anyway. I doubt he would be studying this much
for football...

I leaned forward to try and see what the textbooks titled and the door
creaked loudly, successfully giving me away. His head snapped toward me
and I froze. Busted. He clambered to his feet almost in a panic. It was like
he was caught stealing or something.

"Hey."

"Hey?" I said back but it came out more of a question, my eyes still glued
to the books. "I just came over to thank you last night for looking after me
but you look busy so..."

"Never too busy to talk to you."

A genuine smile stretched across my face. I dragged my eyes to him and
felt a blissful sigh leave me as I took in his Godly appearance.

"How are you feeling?"

"Fine. You?"

"Better now." I walked cautiously toward him, looking down at the piles
of books around him. "What's all of this?"

"Promise you won't laugh?"

"Promise."

"I'm studying."

"Obviously. Studying for what, though?"

"To become a paramedic."

His answer was even more surprising than the fact that he was studying
in the first place. For a long time I always thought he would win some
sport scholarship and go on to be an athlete, despite having the ability
to probably become a neurologist. The fact that he was actually using his
brain instead of his muscles for something was... astonishing. It made sense
though, his father being a doctor and all. And he had been really obsessed

with Grey's Anatomy. He even called his car Meredith after Meredith Grey, the main star of the show.

"Wow, I didn't know you wanted to be a paramedic." I replied, not taking my eyes away from the books. "How long ago did you decide this?"

"I've thought about it for a few months and the last few weeks I thought I better study up on it. It's really something I want to do."

"Good on you." I grinned, genuinely happy for him. "I'm glad you figured out what you want."

He smiled at me. "Have you given any thoughts about what you want to do after school?"

Having a serious discussion with him felt so bizarre. Usually we would be bantering about each other's feelings for each other or just in the moment type things, but an actual talk about our future? We hadn't done this for a long time.

"I'm not really good at anything."

"That's a lie." he said almost angrily, much to my surprise.

He sat back on his bed and gestured for me to follow suit. I did. We stared at each other, both not really knowing what to say.

"I think you would be good something like a personal trainer or a nutritionist."

Both actually sounded up my alley. He always knew me better than I knew myself and I had often hated the fact.

"I have thought about being a personal trainer before."

"You'd be good at it. You're fit and you're mean." he said teasingly, giving me a light shove. "Plus, you're hot. I'd want to impress you."

I rolled my eyes at him. "Oh would you now?"

"Yep."

He smirked at me and I laughed. I decided to jump straight into the deep end and address what happened last night.

"Last night was fun."

"It was." he agreed. "What are you doing tonight?"

"I don't know."

"I'm going to take you to dinner." he announced. "Let's get take away Chinese and go eat it at the beach. We can star gaze, just like we used to."

An excited grin broke out on my face. "Okay, sounds good."

"Okay."

"I better let you get back to studying..." the words still sound foreign on my tongue. "I'll see you tonight?"

"I'll swing by your place at about six?"

"Sure."

"See you then." he said, leaning forward. It surprised me but didn't at the same time. Our lips met and I sighed in pure bliss, loving the feel of his against mine. He pulled back too soon and I got up. With an awkward wave over my shoulder, I left. I leaned against the wall once outside his room, my hands trembling slightly. My body went into freak-out mode whenever he touched me.

Anna was going to be ecstatic when she hears what my plans are for tonight.

It was 5:59pm exactly when he turned up.

I had been sitting in the lounge room, trying not to be excited for the last hour. I had on a dark maroon dress and my favourite black, leather jacket on, which I knew Carter loved. But I wasn't trying to impress him or anything...

My hair tumbled in natural waves, cascading down my back. I had on the jewellery he bought me for my sixteenth birthday and the perfume I knew he liked. He hardly had a chance to knock before I wrenched the door open, giving him a grin.

"Hey."

"Hey Lace." he smiled, his eyes dipping low. "You look amazing."

"Thanks, you too." I blurted automatically.

"Always do." he winked with a playful smirk. "You ready? I already ordered our food, it should be ready by the time we get there."

"Oh good, I'm starving." I replied gratefully, whisking the door shut behind me. He already knew exactly what I would eat anyway, so there was no point waiting for me. I was one of those annoying people that hogged the menu and looked at it for ages, but end up ordering the same thing they always do.

Immediately, his warm hand found mine and I let out a breath I hadn't realised I had been holding. Walking at night with him honestly had become my most favourite part of the day. I just loved being with him, despite everything we have been through.

We walked in silence for a while, but it was a comfortable one. I let my eyes sweep around and inhaled the cool, night air. I rolled my neck back so I could star up at the amazing stars. They contrasted perfectly against the dark sky. I loved star gazing.

"Carter, the paramedic." I breathed toward the sky. I'm glad Carter was leading me otherwise I probably would have ran head first into one of the electrical poles by now. "It has a nice ring to it."

"You think so?"

"I know so. You would be a great paramedic. You're intelligent, good with your hands, indifferent to blood, list of qualities needed for the job goes on really."

I glanced over at him to see him grinning. A small dimple appeared on his left cheek and I felt my own lips stretch into a smile at it. Reaching up with my vacant hand, I ran my fingertip across it. He came to a stop, facing me. He leaned down and softly kissed my own cheek, before he stepped back and tugged at my hand again.

"Let's pick up the pace or your rice will be cold."

That successfully got me moving. We made our way towards the restaurant. I rested against the park bench as Carter disappeared to go get the food. I smiled up at the sky. I looked into the window, waiting for Carter and a slight gasp left my lips. My eyes narrowed. Mercedes was there, at a table. I was so close that my forehead was literally pressing against the glass now and I think I was scaring the little boy to my right. But I didn't care in that moment, my eyes were fixated on her. The guy with her... I knew that neatly clipped hair cut from anywhere.

She was having dinner with Aiden.

Why were those two dining? I turned my back on them and focused on returning my breathing to normal. They always had that flirting tension between them, makes sense they would possibly pursue their 'thing' once Aiden and I finally ended.

"You okay?"

Maybe it's just a friendly dinner? A voice whispered in the back of my mind.

I shouldn't care though, Aiden was free now and could be with whoever he wants to be. It's just a shame he can't see her for who she truly is. He could do better. Well, he could have done better than me and look how long he stuck around.

"Er-Lacey?"

Maybe she would be a better person with him. Yeah, good, be optimistic Lacey.

"Lace?"

"Huh?" I asked, effectively coming out of my whirlwind of thoughts.

"Never mind," he laughed, resting a hand on the small of my back. "Let's head to the beach, shall we?"

"O-oh, yeah." I stammered slightly.

The smell of Chinese food washed over me and my mouth watered involuntarily. I picked up the pace, eager to demolish that fried rice.

"Slow down hot stuff," he laughed, jogging after me.

We successfully made it to the beach without any other shocking, or rather, disturbing revelations. If he was happy with her and she was happy with him, then I suppose I should be happy. I'm not really friends with either of them anymore, so it's none of my business. Even though I promised Aiden we would remain friends. I was contently happy with Carter right now and that's all that mattered. Those days of being meddled by them were behind me and I only wanted to move forward with my life.

I collapsed down onto the sand, Carter following suit. I savagely rummaged through the bags and grabbed my rice. He smirked at me in amusement as I shovelled a mouthful in without taking a breath.

"I'm hungry." I said, still with my mouth full, in defense.

"Clearly."

We ate in silence mostly and it wasn't until I was almost finished my food that I confessed what I saw.

"Did you see Mercedes when you got our food?"

He tensed automatically at the mention of her. "No?"

"She was with Aiden."

Slowly, he put down his fork and glanced over at me. "Are they a thing now?"

I shrugged in attempt to seem nonchalant. "Probably."

"What do you think about that?"

I almost smiled at his seriousness. He eerily reminded me of Dr. Marez.

"Honestly? I wish he was with someone else if he had to be with someone but it doesn't really bother me. If she makes him happy, then good for him. I'm glad. Don't know what is going to happen about the fact she is pregnant and all, but anyway."

"Yeah me either." Carter agreed. "Oh well, we'll see what happens."

"Exactly."

"How's your rice?" he asked and I was grateful for the subject change.

"Brilliant as usual, how's your... whatever you got?"

"Spicy and hot, just like my company."

I rolled my eyes at his lame joke.

We packed away the containers and put them to the side. I reclined back so that I was staring up at the sky. I patted my now slightly round belly, feeling satisfied.

"I love you." The words slipped from my mouth before I knew they were going to.

"I love you, too."

"I was talking to my stomach..." I trailed off teasingly.

"Oh, my mistake." He muttered with a laugh, rolling his eyes.

I turned to my side and he securely wrapped an arm around me. I snuggled into him and sighed, completely and utterly content right now. Even though what I saw was shocking and not something I liked to see, I wasn't going to let it bother me. I was here, with the love of my life right now and I was somewhat happy.

That was all that mattered.

Chapter 19

The crowd around us erupted into applause as Carter, yet again, slid across his stomach, making another try. I leapt to my feet, banging my hands together. A massive grin had been stretched across my face the entire game. He was playing brilliantly, as usual.

For a long time I didn't participate in watching the football games but now that I'm hanging out with Carter more, I decided I would come cheer him on. And by 'decided' I mean forcefully dragged by Anna. Even Aiden was playing, which was a first. He was only usually a reserve, as so many of the boys played. They had a lot of subs actually, so Aiden rarely got to.

"He is good." Anna nodded with approval.

"He's good at everything he does." I replied with an eye roll.

"Yeah, you'd know."

I slapped her playfully. It was a little over half time and we were up by two, which was good. Our football team wasn't fantastic, but this year it had been going pretty well. Anna was the one who convinced me to come (as usual with everything these days) as she was 'tuning' one of the boys on the team. I can't remember who she said it was but she was very excited to see him after the game. She pointed him out a few times but realistically, I couldn't keep my eyes off Carter.

After the game, I am accompanying Carter to a party at one of the boy's places. Anna would be there too but I think she was planning to go with whatever-his-name-is or possibly miss the entire party if she gets her way.

I'd like to hope she does manage to make it, partying with her is pretty fun. I had stopped all that for a long time, after Carter and I weren't friends. I have really missed going out. Anna has reminded me that I can do all those things, with or without a boyfriend. Boys don't have to always control my life, which unfortunately, have for so long.

"What's his name again? The guy you're talking to?"

"Josh," she replied with a satisfied smile. I glanced at her. She looked beautiful, as always. She had a high waisted, black skirt on with dark stockings underneath. She had a baby pink, long sleeved shirt and a matching headband with bow, wrapped across her head. The fiery redness of her hair contrasted well with the pink, which was surprising. She looked the definition of "pretty in pink". Her dimples only added to the look. My best friend, ladies and gentlemen, was an absolute stunner. And here I was, a skinny rat beside her. "Number nine out there."

I focused on him but with the distance and what he was wearing, it was hard to distinguish what he actually looked like. I made a mental note to have a closer look later. I dug my hand further into the chip packet and realised there wasn't any left. (Yes, I have started eating properly again and by properly, I mean regular food normal people eat). That was one of the worst feelings ever, reaching in and having none left. I got to my feet and headed towards the bin. Conveniently, it was the same time Aiden had come over to grab a drink from his bag.

"Hey," I said with a small smile. He was subbing briefly. Sweat glistened across his forehead and his breathing was still irregular from the exertion. His expression was soft as he stared, as though he was unsure of how to act around me.

He wouldn't even meet my eyes as he mumbled a quick, "hey," before scuttling back toward the bench. I frowned after him. I know things were a bit tense between us but that was a bit immature. I sighed, shrugging it off. If he didn't want to try and be friends, there wasn't anything I could do about it. If he was going to be childish about it, he's not someone I want to be around. I did feel a pang of sadness though as I thought about us not being able to return back to the good friends we once were. I suppose that's what relationships do. They can ruin everything.

Just as I was mounting the stairs back up to the grandstand, one of the boys scored, causing everyone to stand. I momentarily lost where I was sitting but used Anna's radiant hair to guide me back. I slithered in beside her. I laughed as her cheeks were flushed pink and her eyes bright with excitement.

"You really love these types of things, don't you?" I asked with a genuine smile. I was glad she was having a good time. It made me happy. Seeing her smile made me forget about Aiden's behaviour. I suddenly had an overwhelming sense of gratitude towards her.

"Yep." she replied, popping the 'p'.

I leaned forward and embraced her quickly, before pulling back. She glanced at me in surprise, quirking an eyebrow.

"What was that for?"

"Just a thanks for coming into my life when I really needed you to."

"Don't get all serious on me now," she said lightly, pretending to wipe a tear from her eye. "But you're welcome gorgeous! And don't think I'll be going anywhere, anytime soon."

I grinned, actually feeling a little teary. "Thanks Anna."

She grinned back, giving my shoulder a light squeeze. I re-focused on the game, unable to wipe the grin from my face. The game continued with a lot more cheering and a few more scoring on behalf of Carter and another boy whose name I don't know.

The buzzer blared loudly and screams tore through our side of the grandstand as we won. I kind of wish we had cheerleaders and a mascot like they do on American movies, but this was still fun. Anything to do with Carter, I would find fun, if I'm honest. Speaking of, I was supposed to meet him at his car. I turned to Anna and she gave me an excited grin, clapping her hands with excitement.

"You're meeting Carter, yeah?"

"Yep, will I be seeing you at Damien's tonight?" I asked, hoping that she would make an appearance.

"Most likely, depends how quick Josh is."

"Oh the double meaning."

"Get your mind out of the gutter," she smirked but we both knew full well what she had been implying.

"I'll catch you later," I laughed, making my way down the steps once more.

I paused as I saw Mercedes and Aiden walking off together. Good for them. If they're happy with each other, then I'm happy for them. I just wish that Aiden and I could go back to being friends, even if he is with Mercedes. Possibly even go back to speaking terms with Mercedes...

Key word: Possibly.

I turned and headed towards Carter's car. I leaned against the window and gazed up at the sky, watching my breath gather in front of me. The night air was cool, which had me hugging my thin cardigan to myself. I watched as the team milled toward their cars, all hyped up from the game. They all piled in, one after the after, loud and obnoxious as usual. I frowned when I didn't see Carter. The cars began splitting quickly, everyone eager to go get drunk in celebration of tonight's win. Eventually, there wasn't anyone left.

I waited a few more minutes, before I pushed off the car and went back out to the field. Carter's bag was still on the bench. No one else's was there. My mouth involuntarily turned dry. Scanning the area, I hurried over to it. I fumbled through his back and let out a sigh of relief when I found his keys. That relief only lasted briefly when I found his phone as well. I now had no way of contacting him.

He wouldn't have left without saying something to me, surely? I swung the bag onto my shoulder and continued to swivel my eyes around the field, looking for any signs of him. Deciding on waiting at the car until further notice, I began the short trek back. I was just passing the stands when I heard grunts. I paused, my stomach clenching uncomfortably. Swallowing the dry lump that had lodged itself in my throat, I peered through the cracks of the seats. A slight gasp left my lips at what I saw.

One guy was holding up Carter, while two others took turns repeatedly beating him. I felt sick as I watched them. Three against one was cruel and cowardly. His head was hanging forward and the guy behind him was literally the reason he was still standing. Blood was gushing from his nose and mouth. I took a few steps back, panic spiking through my veins.

I dropped to my knees and fumbled for Carter's phone. I dialled 000 and waited impatiently for them answer. After requesting the police to be sent, I hung up. I watched in horror, fist in my mouth as they continued to beat him. My entire body was trembling. I knew it was cold, but it wasn't the abrupt cool weather that had me shaking.

"You're not so big now, are you Carter?" The bigger guy of the two grunted, his fist connecting with Carter's jaw.

"Where's all your 'friends' Carter? If you're so popular, why isn't anyone here to save you? Why has no one noticed?"

My heart was thudding against my rib cage so loudly, I'm surprised they couldn't hear it. I couldn't just sit here and wait around for the police to show. Carter could be unconscious by that point. The boys, who are members of the opposing team, didn't seem like they were going to stop any time soon, which was a terrifying thought. How far were they willing to go? This seemed a little full on just for some opposition team rivalry.

My chances of making them stop were very slim. I could hardly fight them off, since I was under average weight and the one and only time I tried to bench press, I almost crushed my entire chest. I'm not going to admit what weights I had on the bench press either...

"How does it feel having no power, Carter? It's not fun is it?" the smaller guy spat, but not actually hitting him. Carter's blood was smeared across both of their knuckles. That sight alone was enough to have me gagging. "This is how I felt when you hooked up with my girlfriend. Right in front of me."

Of course. Of course Carter did. The anger and resentment in the boy's voice caused me to shiver.

"Not only did you end our winning streak and stopped us going to the championship, you took my girl too. You know what? It's my turn to take yours."

"Don't you touch her." It was the first time Carter had spoken since I had been there. His words were hardly audible as his breathing had become ragged.

"Lacey, is it?" the bigger guy asked, flexing and unflexing his fingers. "She seems like she could be a bit of fun. You think so Brian?"

"Yeah," Brian, the guy holding Carter, agreed with a dirty smirk.

I felt bile rise up in the back of my throat. I began rummaging through Carter's bag. There had to be something in here I could use. But then again, if I did distract them, that would only turn their attention to me. The issue of three against one would still occur, since Carter is in no position to fight back. Carter, even in this state, would probably be more successful in this fight than me.

My skin touched something cool and I pulled out a baseball bat. Why on earth was he carrying a baseball bat around in his football bag? My head shook slightly, him and this baseball bat really are inseperable. I shrugged it off and chose not to question his decision, but be grateful instead. Clutching the bat with sweaty palms, I shakily stood, peering around the bench one more time. Carter had dropped to his knees.

"Isn't she waiting for you?" one of the boys sneered, getting in his face. "All alone? By your car? Would be a shame if anything happened to her."

A shiver rolled down my spine at his words. This felt like a scene out of a movie. Things like this just don't happen. It was incredulous. This is why I never come to these games, although for Carter's sake, it's good I actually did.

"Don't. Touch. Her." I hardly even recognised Carter's voice. It was animal-like. He attempted to get to his feet and began swinging, but the smaller guy kicked out, striking him in the ribs. Carter collapsed in a sprawl, dry heaving from the impact. It was painful to watch. My body urged to go and help him.

"Brian, why don't you go check on her?" The bigger guy suggested. "I think we've got it from here."

He grunted in reply. A man of many words apparently. I ducked under the bench and held my breath. He let go of Carter roughly and began marching toward the car park. I shivered at the thought of me being there, waiting. What would have happened if I hadn't come looking for him?

This was good though, this meant one was gone, just two left. I waited until he was out of sight before I began my mission. As both of the boys' backs were to me, if I was quick and silent, I could sneak up on them. I decided on taking the bigger one out first, liking my chances with the smaller one better, if it came down to it.

Exhaling slowly, trying to build up the courage to go, I tip-toed out. I waited until I was close before I swung the bat out and struck the big guy in the back of the head. He staggered forward, tripped over Carter's body, before collapsing on the ground with a groan. I swung around wildly with my eyes shut, hoping to hit the other guy. As I kept just swinging and making no contact, I peeped through a narrowed eye to see the guy staring at me with a mixture of shock and amusement.

"Put the bat down before you hurt yourself, young lady." he scorned me like I was a child misbehaving. If this moment wasn't so serious, I would have laughed at him.

Sounding possessed, I let out a ragged scream, running toward him. I swung the bat and it connected with his shoulder.

"That's for hitting Carter!" I yelled. He hunched over in attempt to protect himself while a feminine scream escaped him. "That's for sending the other guy after me!"

Smack.

"And this is for-"

The bat was wrenched from my hands as the larger and noticeably angrier guy was unfortunately back on his feet.

"Might have to let Brian know you're here, shall we?" he asked, narrowing his eyes at me. One hand was gripping the bat, the other holding his head. I was pretty proud I took at least one of them out. Clearly I wasn't very good at this fight situation, otherwise I would have seen him get to his feet. I glanced down worriedly at Carter and my blood ran cold. He wasn't moving. The blood on his face was beginning to dry. He laid there limply, immobile.

"Thank God," The smaller guy said, standing up right, rubbing his shoulder. He winced as he gingerly touched his arm.

"Pussy," the other one muttered, looking at him with disgust. I wanted to point out that I actually took him out so he couldn't talk, but I suppose he did recover from it quickly. He swung the bat so that it was resting on his shoulder. I began to step back, not liking the look of this situation. He grinned at me maliciously. "That hurt, Lacey. Now I'm going to have to make you hurt."

My body was trembling as I began to back away faster. Suddenly, the wail of sirens could be heard and I wanted to cry in relief. I have never been so glad to hear the sound of police. He narrowed his eyes at me, looking even more terrifying, if possible.

"This isn't over."

I wanted to reply with some witty comment, but the words got stuck in my throat. Never before have I been in a situation like this. I never want to again. Dropping the bat, he inclined his head and the smaller guy fell in step with him. They began a mad dash away, but it was too late. The police had spotted them. I would laugh if I wasn't so scared. Now that I was somewhat safe, I ran towards Carter, dropping to my knees. He was still breathing, but had gone unconscious.

"Carter," I begged, pulling at him. "Carter please wake up."

One of the police ran toward me, slightly out of breath.

"We need an ambulance," I cried out, tears falling openly down my face. "We need one right now!"

Now thinking about it, I should have rang the ambulance before the police. I guess it's hard to think clearly when you're having a meltdown. He nodded, grabbing out his phone. Pressing my palms to his chest, I gripped his shirt tightly, the tears rushing down my cheeks faster than a waterfall.

"Carter, please be okay," I pleaded with him, hiccupping. I buried my head into his chest, sobs wracking my entire body. I know there was medical assistance on the way, but if anything happened to him and he didn't make it... I honestly couldn't bear it. I began crying hysterically, unable to control my emotions. The officer crouched beside me and awkwardly patted my shoulder.

"Honey, can you take a step back?" he asked me in a soft voice. "I need to take a look at what we're dealing with here."

With a nod, I clambered to my feet and watched the officer go about the series of tests, in attempt to get Carter to respond.

Well... this night had taken a turn for the worst.

The last time I was in hospital I had my wrists bandaged and was forced to take counselling sessions again. This time, I was the one perched on the uncomfortable seats, with a bad tasting coffee beside me.

Carter was awake, although badly injured. He has rib bruising, a concussion, a broken finger and a mass spread of bruises colouring his skin. Somehow his nose had managed to not break, which was good. The blood had all been cleaned away so you could clearly see all the bruises and swelling now.

Slowly, he rolled his head to me. His fingers twitched and I walked over, sitting on the edge. I slipped my fingers through his.

"I'm so lucky you were there."

I gave him a smile. Squeezing my hand, he lifted my hand to his mouth (wincing the entire time) and pressed his lips to my knuckles.

"Thank you."

"I'm just glad you're alive," I breathed. "You should have seen what you looked like. I have never been so terrified in my life."

"I wish you didn't have to see that."

It fell silent for a few moments, but I had to ask the question that had been whirling in my mind all morning.

"Do you know why they attacked you?" I asked quietly.

"It was a while ago, Lacey. Months ago when I was with his girl. I swear it wasn't recent."

I nodded slowly. "Were they still together when you hooked up with her?"

He didn't reply but his face said it all. I nodded slowly.

"That's disgusting, Carter."

The word hypocrite slammed into my mind, but I determinedly ignored it. This was different. Carter and I had a major, major history together. He barely even knew this girl. She would have meant nothing to him.

"I know but he's a jerk. You think I'm bad? Wait until you get to know him. Every party he cheated on that girl. I just wanted to show him what it could do. Plus, he had played really dirty that game. I was angry and drunk, which is no excuse, but I just saw her there... I took the opportunity."

"And look where it got you."

"Yeah, lesson learnt." he grimaced, moving in attempt to get more comfortable.

Miranda reappeared back in the doorway, Matthew beside her. Matthew was Carter's father. I hadn't seen him in a while. He was rarely there when I had stayed there and when he was, I was either out or he was in his office working.

Carter and his father looked very alike. Matthew was tall, tan and had clear, blue eyes that stood out from a mile away. He had blond, sun-streaked hair and the body of an athlete, even though he wasn't one. They were an amazingly gorgeous family. The height different between the two of them reminded me of what Carter and I would look like at their age. Miranda was smaller than him, by a noticeable amount. She had long, blonde hair that was styled to perfection, as always. They looked beautiful together and younger than you would think.

Matthew gave me a nod in greeting. Miranda had already been here for an hour or two, and only left to get Matthew. I stood slowly, pulling my hand from Carter's. I think I should give them some family time.

"I'll be back later," I murmured softly to him.

"You don't have to leave, Lacey." Matthew said to me, going over and fiddling with some things in Carter's bedside table. "You're a part of the family."

"Oh it's okay, you guys just spend some time together. I should probably go fill mum in with what's happened anyway. She's not replying to my texts."

"Alright," he nodded. "Thanks Lacey, for what you did. If it wasn't for you, his injuries may have been a lot worse. We're very grateful."

I nodded. Grabbing my bag, I shrugged it onto my shoulder and slipped out of the room. I was just wandering through the hall when I heard a dramatic groan. I glanced through the window and narrowed my eyes, seeing the bigger guy whom had beaten Carter, getting tended to by one of the nurses. A smug smile danced on my lips as I was the one who hit him.

One of the officer's that had chased him was still here, sitting in the corner of the room. Good. I had had to give a statement and thankfully, didn't get charged for hitting them, as it was clearly self-defense. Carter's reasoning for having a baseball in his back was that his friend Izack (who turned out to be the guy scoring almost as many points as Carter, go figure) and himself had played some softball before the game. Thank God for that, who knows what would have happened otherwise.

Not wanting to stick around, I kept moving. I rounded the corner and froze. Mercedes' mother was there. With Aiden.

"You're sure?" Aiden asked slowly. "Absolutely positive?"

"Yes." she said, her tone indicating she was annoyed. Her voice was clipped and professional, like always. "The non-invasive Prenatal Paternity test is the most accurate process to test who the father is. I've researched it, it is 99.9% accurate."

"God," he choked out, rubbing a hand through his hair. "What a mess."

Her eyes bulged as she stared at him incredulously. "A mess!? Are you the one carrying a child in your stomach? Is it your daughter who fell pregnant at the age of seventeen? You're just an immature boy. You're not fit to be a father."

With that verbal slap in the face, she spun on her heel and marched away from him. My heart felt like it had dropped into my stomach. This could not be happening.

Mercedes emerged from the room, wandering over to Aiden. She had one hand on her stomach, as the other reached to grab his hand.

"I told you," she murmured quietly, squeezing his hand with her own. "You're the father."

Chapter 20

Well if that verbal revelation isn't enough to send me back a year in counselling, I don't know what will.

My mouth had become dry as I saw Mercedes clutching Aiden's hand, her other gently resting over her unborn baby.

The baby who apparently belongs to my ex-boyfriend.

I felt utterly and completely disorientated, unable to decipher one thought from another. Backing up, I quickly exited the hall. I leant against the wall, my stomach churning uncomfortably. I gripped at my sides feeling starkly empty.

Shoving my fist into my mouth, I pushed from the wall and strode the other way. Tears burned at my eyes and I felt bile rise in the back of my throat. For him to be the father... the timing... he would have been with me.

We would have been together.

The tears flowed openly down my face before I could stop them. I ignored the curious stares of people around me and the disturbing smell of antiseptic. I wanted nothing more than to just curl up in a ball and forget everything.

Karma was kicking me straight in the face. I cheated on Aiden with Carter, only fair he cheats on me with my best friend. Both the boys in my life, with her... I dropped to my knees, unable to stop the vomit from coming up my throat. A nurse ran towards me, asking me a series of questions. I clambered to my feet, hastily wiping my chin with the back of my hand.

"I'm fine, I'm fine," I kept repeated, trying to force myself to believe my own words. Pushing away from her, I staggered towards the exit, feeling indescribably sick.

The next few hours were a complete blur. Even to this point in time, I can't remember how I managed to successfully get home. Currently, I was lying in a pool of icy cold water, the shower raining down over my skin. I sat, feeling miserable, the fierce coldness of the water successfully making me feel numb.

I had made the decision to remain calm until Aiden talks to me. I think, even after everything, he will have the decency to speak to me about this. He would have to before I "found out" through rumours and whatnot, right? My head hung forward and I pressed my face against my drawn up, bare thighs.

Slowly, I got to my feet and twisted the knob as I stepped out, absently towelling myself off. I dressed in a daze, going down the stairs. Mum was perched on the lounge, watching T.V. She had a mug beside her and an opened packet of fruit-nut chocolate.

"Mum," I croaked out. Instantly, her eyes snapped to mine. "You told me to tell you if I felt like cutting again."

Her mouth fell open. She clambered to her feet, her face reflecting a look of complete shock and terror. I raised my hands in a peace-like gesture.

"I don't want to kill myself, that has never been my intention. I just feel crap."

"What's happened?" she asked me urgently, her hands fluttering over my body like unwanted flies. I groaned, lightly pushing her away.

"Don't. Please just listen. I'm not going to do anything drastic, I promise. I just need someone to talk to."

"Okay," she said slowly, backing away from me as if I were mere seconds away from exploding. She sat back down rigidly. "What do you need to talk about?"

So I told her. I told her everything that has happened from my sixteenth birthday until now. She didn't interrupt which I was thankful for. The words tumbled out of my mouth and it felt so refreshing. Sure, I had told this story to my counsellor on countless occasions, but it was different telling someone so real and constant in my life. Dr Marez is real, obviously, but she isn't my mother. She will never play the role my mother does.

Finally, I was at the end. A sigh escaped me as a surprising surge of relief filtered through my body. She reached forward, hesitantly at first and engulfed me in a bear hug.

"I must be the most oblivious parent in the world."

"No, you're just a realistic one." I pointed out. "You're busy, I've been busy. I haven't spoken to you like I should have."

"I want you to tell me things. I want to be involved in your life. I'm not too busy for you, Lacey. I had no idea..." she trailed off, her eyes slightly watery.

I shrugged pragmatically. "It's in the past."

"Mercedes and Aiden?" she asked quietly, still shocked. "Who would have picked it..."

"I know." I muttered distastefully. "This is one giant mess."

"Don't get yourself down about it, as hard as that is going to be. Clearly Mercedes is someone you don't want in your life. With Aiden, I think you deserve to give him the chance to explain. Despite this predicament, I still think he is a good guy who really loves you. Let him explain before we jump aboard the 'I hate Aiden' train, okay? As for Carter, I think he is trying very hard to make things right with you. But all in all, you need to do what is best for you."

"But deciding what is best for me is the hardest part."

"It will work out." she said, giving me a small smile. "You'll see."

"When?" I asked with a groan.

"God will give you a sign."

"I hope it's a clear one."

I swivelled my eyes to the T.V and reclined back, wanting to spend some quality time with mum. A loud knock echoed through the hallway and mum got to her feet. I reached over to the chocolate and broke of a couple of squares. I had just popped it into my mouth when I heard footsteps stop at the entry in to the lounge room.

"Lacey," was all mum said.

Turning, I stared back curiously and my stomach clenched.

Aiden.

I leaned back into my pillows, my body slowly sinking into them. He was perched at the end of my bed awkwardly, not knowing where to look. I folded my arms across my chest.

"You know." he stated.

"I was at the hospital last night. I saw you together. I heard the news when you did."

He exhaled deeply, pinching the skin in between his eyes. "I don't know what to say."

"So when you were comforting me about Carter, you had been with her? Or you were with her?" I asked, sounding a little too cavalier. I tried my hardest to keep my voice firm, so I didn't break down.

"Look, Mercedes and I have been close for a while. But I was with you and I thought she was with a guy named Tom. But apparently that was just a lie so she could get closer to me. It was the day you told me you had been with Carter... I was with her. I was upset and she was there... one thing lead to another. It happened once and hasn't happened since, but yes, it did happen. Do I regret it? Yes, I'm too young to be a father and now I really will never be able to be with you. But I can't change what has happened. I'm going to support her and be the best father I can be. I can only hope that one day, you and I can return to the good friends we once were."

A humourless laugh left my lips as I shook my head incredulously. "Wow. You're no better than Carter. I was wrong about you."

"Either are you."

"Huh?"

"You're not better than either of us. All of us have cheated. You had Carter on an unreachable pedestal and that's why it hurt you so much when he came tumbling down from it. But what's worse is that you and I are just as bad. Probably worse, actually." he shrugged nonchalantly, giving me a hard stare. "So you're not the only victim. All of us are. You focus on how much Carter has hurt you but you've hurt him just as much back."

My mouth fell open at his words. His truthful words. We were all as bad and corrupt as each other. I swallowed uneasily, wishing I could increase the distance between us.

"That doesn't justify what you did."

"I know."

"Things aren't going to go back the way they were."

"I know."

I sighed, rubbing my face, feeling weary. "Just go."

His lips parted, as though he was going to say something but changed his mind. He got up and half-turned back, before disappearing through my door. I fell back, letting my blankets swallow me. I didn't feel like crying. I didn't feel like doing anything. Numbly, I stared up at the ceiling, unsure how to feel.

"Are you alright?" Mum asked, her voice soft. From my peripheral vision I knew she was hovering near my door.

"Yeah, just fine and dandy."

"Want to talk about it?"

"I will later, I just want to lay here and pretend I don't exist for a while."

"Why don't we go out? Let's go watch a movie or go out for dinner. Just get out of the house for a while?"

I fell silent for a moment, pondering her suggestion. After a few seconds, I rolled my head to the side.

"Alright. That sounds nice."

Spending time with mum is just what I need.

Last night was pretty cool.

It was so refreshing spending time with mum. Dad came home earlier than we expected so he joined us. We ended up having a family outing and I realised how much I missed us doing things together. When I was first let out of hospital, we played board games and such, but that was because they were scared to leave me alone, not out of spending actual time together.

"I'm glad you had a nice time." Carter said, wincing as he moved himself into a more comfortable position on his lounge.

He has been released, obviously. Both Miranda and Matt were out at work so I volunteered to babysit him. He was still very bruised and sore from his encounter with his football rivalries. I cringed at the thought of them. When I close my eyes at night, it's their faces I have been seeing in my mind. It's disturbing, to say the least.

"You okay?" I asked him, worried he was in pain.

"Yeah fine," he waved me off lethargically, his eyes drifting closed.

I settled back into the lounge, hugging my thin cardigan around my body. Carter always liked to have the air-conditioning set to icy cold temperatures for some bizarre reason. I, on the other hand, am the type of person to wear jumpers mid-Summer and sleep with five blankets and a dooner when it's hot.

"You're cold aren't you?" he sighed in annoyance. He had sweat literally forming on his forehead while I'm next to him with goose bumps erupting over my skin.

"It's not unbearable but it is a tad cool."

"Want me to turn it down?"

"It's fine."

I was trying not to get frustrated with the fact that he was. He was really annoyed but I understood why. He is a very active guy. If he's not surfing or out with his mates, he is running, or doing something with his car. Carter's not the type of person to just sit around and watch movies, like I do. So that fact that he's basically immobile right now letting his body recover is infuriating him. Me? I think it's awesome. It gives me an excuse (not that one is necessary) to re-watch Prison Break.

"Is it time for your painkillers yet?" I asked, glancing at my watch.

"Yeah I think so."

I reached forward and unclasped the bottle, tapping it. After washing the pills down with a glass of water, he rested back on the lounge and fell silent. His breathing was deep and even, indicating he was asleep. My phone began vibrating. As silently as possible, I slipped out of the room and slid my thumb across the bottom of my screen.

"Hey Anna, what's up?"

"Random question: What are you doing with your life next year?"

"I'm well thanks, how are you?" I replied back sarcastically with an eye roll.

"Serious man."

"Honestly? I'm not sure. I was thinking of just working while I figured out what my next move is."

"I was hoping you would say that. Would you be interested in travelling? I am looking at flights now and I think I want to move overseas for twelve months. What do you think?"

I furrowed my eyebrows as I plopped down onto the chair behind me. "You want to move away?"

"I want us to move away. Just for a year. Imagine how fun it would be! We get to explore a different culture, get life experience, get away from this place for a while. Come on, say yes!"

A laugh escaped me. "Well this is very sudden!"

"Not for me, I've known for a while I wanted to move and besides it's next year. I just want someone to move with! Would you though? Be interested, that is?"

I leaned back and contemplated her offer. Surprisingly, the whole idea sounded appealing. To get away from here and travel sounds awesome. The thought of being away from Carter literally tore at my heart, but at the same time, time away from him is exactly what I need. I need to know what life is like without him.

"Surprisingly yes?" I said but it came out more of a question.

"Yay!" she exclaimed. I let out a laugh as a foreign feeling of elation rushed through me. The idea of getting away from here was actually amazing. I would love to travel. "I'm going to keep researching and get back to you. We shall discuss this at the school camp this week. Get ready for the best year of your life!"

With that, the line went dead. I placed my phone down and stared at Carter's backyard for a few moments, deep in thought. The rich, blue sky was illuminant, stretching across my vision. This place was beautiful and I shouldn't want to leave it, but I think I have to. Travelling for a year is just what I need. Time for me, myself and I.

With that decision made, I felt like a weight has been lifted off my shoulders.

Chapter 21

A scream of frustration tore from my throat as I threw the Wii controller up into the air. Carter laughed beside me, shaking his head. I folded my arms across my chest and began glaring at the wall opposite me.

"How is it possible you still smash me? You're injured!" I cried out.

Carter and I had always been highly competitive against one another, video games included. A cocky smirk stretched across his face as usual. He rested back, wincing slightly. He clearly finds this a lot more amusing than I do.

"You do realise it's not real tennis?"

"Only strengthens my argument." I scowled. "I'm over this, let's do something else."

"You're such a sore loser."

"Bite me."

As Carter was still cooped inside, again, I volunteered to be his babysitter. I forgot how frustratingly good he is at everything he does. It irks me to no end that he is naturally greater at everything than I am. He was moving a lot better now, but still had quite sore muscles and bruises from the incident.

I clambered to my feet and stretched, feeling the muscles in my back crack. A yawn left my lips as I was ready for another nap. Time sure does go fast when you wake up at lunch. The weather outside was cold, dark and miserable, making it perfect movie and snuggling weather. For me, anyway. The rain never stopped Carter. If anything, he was only keener to surf, claiming the water was 'warmer' or something.

He cleared his throat. "So about this dance."

"Ugh," I said with a groan. I collapsed roughly back onto his bed.

"Well that's not the attitude to have." Carter frowned, quirking an eyebrow at me.

It was coming up to our annual dance at school for the seniors. Every year our school threw an elaborate dance. The themes were always awesome, the music got louder every year and the punch was always spiked ten minutes in. It was a typical high school dance. Of course, I used to not be able to wait until I could go. Mercedes and I used to gab about it all the time. I envisioned myself wearing an elegant, expensive dress with Carter beside me, wrapped in an equally expensive and sleek suit.

We would look perfect together.

Carter and I then had our falling out, ruining my dream. Even now that Carter and I were back in good terms again, the dance wasn't the same. I was dreading it now. Especially since I was on the outs with Mercedes.

"I don't really want to go."

"Why not? You're going to have a hot date?"

"Up yourself much?" I scoffed, shoving him lightly.

"Who said I was talking about me?"

I frowned at him and he laughed. Slowly, he rolled to his side and gingerly propped himself onto his elbow.

"I don't like anyone. I don't have any friends to go shopping with. It's all just crap."

"Alright negative Nelly, that's not correct at all. I was being truthful - you do have a hot date because you're taking me. You have Anna to shop with and trust me, she will help you find something. You have other friends, you just choose not to be social. One good friend is better than having a bunch of fake ones anyway."

I just groaned in response.

"You don't have a choice anyway. I'm taking you whether you like it or not. So you better get yourself organised."

"I hate you."

"No you don't." He laughed, leaning forward. I noticed his automatic cringe as pain flared up his sides. He flicked my nose and leant back, acting as though that didn't hurt.

"You're still in pain."

"It's nothing. Doc said I'll be fine in a few days. I'll be ready and roaring for the camp. You just wait."

"Do you really think it's a good idea to go?"

"Yes Lacey," he sighed in exasperation. "We're seniors now. We need to be involved in everything before school is over forever. Stop being so sulky about everything."

"I'm not being sulky!" I retorted indignantly, jutting out my chin.

"You are."

"Fine. I'll go to the stupid camp and the stupid dance."

"Atta' girl," he grinned, ruffling my hair. "Now let's keep playing. We can even do Wii Bowling again if you want."

That was by far my strongest sport. A small smile danced on my lips as he said this. I rolled my eyes and clutched the Wii.

He was going down.

The vine swung back, slapping me directly across the face. I hissed, wincing at the sting of it. Anna glanced back apologetically.

"Oops."

I muttered some disgruntled profanities under my breath as this was the fifth time she had 'accidentally' smacked me in the face. Since her shoulders were shaking every time she turned back around, it was obvious she found my discomfort and annoyance quite entertaining.

We were currently at our annual senior school camp and I was not finding it nearly as fun as I thought it would be. Just kidding, I knew this was going to be torture. I enjoyed the hiking but not the constant battles of peeling leeches from my skin, swatting away mosquitos and getting bitten a million times by ants.

I wiped my brow with the back of my hand, feeling the mixture of sweat and sunscreen smeared across my forehead. We had been walking for about two hours now and I was famished. My stomach was aching with hunger, my eyes stinging from the sweat leaking into them and my muscles were strained.

Anna, who is the most glamorous human being I've ever been around, was obviously enjoying herself more than I am. I think anyone was, really. Her vibrant, red hair was piled messily into a bun on the top of her hair. She had a tight, red singlet on, thick tights and matching red shoes, making her look like she was about to step into a fitness commercial.

Me, on the other hand, was sweating like I had just run a marathon and felt like collapsing on the ground. I was fit and ran a lot, but I wasn't used to the endurance in this humidity. I needed to stop skipping breakfast.

Of course, Carter was leading the group, despite still being sore from his confrontation with his football rivalries. He was injured and was still probably the fittest and strongest of us all. I frowned as I saw him leap elegantly over a large boulder, as everyone else just shouldered around it.

Show off.

I couldn't help be a little annoyed. I wish he would hang back and walk with me. Of course I wanted him to go have fun and be with his friends. However, the whole walking a thousand kilometres (okay, I'm exaggerating a little) might have been a little more bearable if I had him by my side.

After what felt like an eon, we managed to make it to the waterfall. The sound of water rushing and the smell of the spring water had never been so pleasant. The kids we were accompanying whooped with joy, propelling themselves forward in a rush. I laughed as they hastily clambered over the rocks. As we were the seniors, it was our duty to be the 'leaders' of the year sevens (the youngest year in high school). I didn't mind most of them as they were timid and shy about everything, but some were real pains, spreading my already thin patience.

By the time I reached the waterfall, most people were already in the water. My mouth dropped open as Carter was leading a group of adventurous year sevener's up a slippery rock climb, to reach a cliff. It wasn't the dangerous part that had my jaw dropped. It was his tanned, muscly back with water glistening over his skin like marbles. Even the yellowing of his bruises weren't enough to ruin his perfection.

"Stop gawking at your lover and get in the water." Anna scorned me with a playful shove, peeling her clothes off.

I rolled my eyes but obliged, jogging after her. The water was surprisingly cold but refreshing nonetheless. My body sank low, the cool water lapping over my face and through my long, blonde hair. I emerged from the water, slightly breathless. Sounds of crying and cheering could be heard and I glanced up, seeing Carter performing an almighty flip. I cringed, only hoping he wasn't taking it too rough with his injuries. His bruises had begun fading and his body was back to its usual state, somewhat, anyway. His internal injuries must not have been too serious, as he recovered pretty fast. He was clearly taking his new found energy to full advantage.

After paddling in the water for a while, both Anna and I retired to the bank, where we spread out, soaking up what little sun shone through the canopy. I closed my eyes with a sigh. Thankfully, Mercedes had given the trip a miss, obviously thinking hiking while pregnant may not be a fun experience. Not so thankfully, Aiden was here. What's worse? We were all jammed into the same group.

The talk of our 'love triangle' was still buzzing through everyone at school and the tension was more than obvious when we found out Carter, Aiden, Anna and myself were all partnered in the same group. Luckily there were also some others with us so Aiden could be separated from Carter. No one missed the heated glares between them though. Especially not me.

Eventually, I peeped through my lids and gazed at everyone splashing and playing in the water. Aiden was resting back against a set of rocks, an easy-going smile on his face. My stomach clenched slightly as it always does when I see him. There was so much regret between us.

I dragged my eyes from him and watched Carter fooling around with a few of his friends, loving every second of being back outdoors and adventuring. It baffled me how someone could have so much energy. It was draining just watching him.

Soon enough, we were all toweling off and marching back towards our camp, all eager to grab some food and sit around the fire. The trip back was a lot faster as majority of the trek was downhill. Again, Carter lead the way, with me struggling for breath at the back. My limbs felt heavy, my eyes were sore and I had a head ache accumulating behind my eyes. I was ready for some marshmallows and a nice nap. I lost Anna in the sea of bodies, so I kept to myself mostly and didn't speak much.

Relief flooded through me as we got to the glade where all our tents were set up. I'm not sure how but many of the people ran towards the campsite, still full of energy. I was dragging my feet. Carter dropped back so that he fell in step with me. He reached into his backpack and withdrew a powerade.

"Here, have this." He told me, shoving it into my palm. "It will give you sustenance."

"Thanks," I replied weakly, giving him a wan smile.

"Is my poor baby tired?" He cooed, ruffling my hair.

"Stop it."

He chuckled, wrapping a supportive arm around my shoulders. His warmth felt nice against my cool, clammy skin. I snuggled into him as we slowly made our way back to camp.

"That walk was invigorating, don't you think?" He breathed, tilting his head back slightly at the darkening sky above us.

"Yeah. Thrilling." I deadpanned, brushing loose tendrils of my hair off my face as they had begun to stick to my forehead. "I'm going to shower."

"I'll get some marshmellows ready for you," he grinned, smirking at my lack of enthusiasm about nature. I rolled my eyes and ducked into my tent. I began rummaging through my bag, grabbing all the essentials I needed. It was evident that Anna had already beat me to it and was already heading off to shower.

The showers were extremely disgusting here. The floor was full of grime, the curtains were stained and the walls had mould accumulating across them. It smelled like wet, old clothes that had been locked in a room for too long. Wrinkling my nose, I entered. I could see Anna's toiletry bag on one of the stools outside, along with her signature red towel that she takes everywhere. There was another shower running somewhere around the corner, but I preferred not to go around there, as it was even worse than these ones and the lightbulb had blown. I went to enter the cubicle next to her when she giggled. I paused. Why was she laughing so flirtatiously?

"Stop, you're going to get us caught," she breathed with another teasing laugh. My eyes bulged out of my head as I looked down and saw that another pair of legs was in the shower with her. I quickly turned and exited the shower block, unsure how to feel. I was marching back to my tent when I realised I had dropped my shorts. With an exasperated sigh, I headed back. Just as I was walking in, I ran head first into someone's chest. I stumbled back in surprise.

The person quickly steadied me. I looked up and locked eyes with Aiden. His hair was wet and his chest was glistening with water. His cheeks were flushed red. My stomach fell. No. He couldn't have been the one in there with Anna.

This trip suddenly just got a whole lot worse.

Chapter 22

The rest of the trip had gone painfully slow but I was finally home. As soon as I stepped foot into my house, I sprinted to the bathroom and scrubbed myself clean of the grime and dirt that was spread over my skin. After spending an excessive amount of time shampooing and exfoliating, I emerged from the bathroom feeling one hundred percent more human.

I was wringing my hair when my phone rang. I sighed, knowing it was Anna without having to look. I had avoided her like the plague the rest of the trip, which had been hard since we were in a tent together and placed in the same group. I couldn't believe she would betray me like that. Out of all the boys she could be with, she had to choose him. I spent as much time with Carter as I could, even sitting with him on the bus ride home. She knew something was up and decided constantly calling me was going to make me talk to her. I know I should answer and talk this through with her, but I was too afraid of the answer. Honestly? I was afraid to lose her. Anna is the first friend I have genuinely gotten along with and trusted for the first time in a while. I didn't want to risk knowing she had been with Aiden. It would ruin everything between us.

I turned my phone off, eventually unable to stand the constant vibrating. I tried to distract myself in more ways than one. I went for a run, had another shower, read for an hour, watched a movie, but my thoughts still went back to Anna and Aiden together. I felt sick and betrayed. I knew there was only one person that could distract me from my turmoil of thoughts. Conveniently, he lives next door.

Slipping on a loose pair of shorts and a shirt, I headed over. I squinted as the too-bright afternoon sun met my eyes harshly. Walking in without knocking, I wound my way up the stairs to his room, his house having a rather cool chill in contrast to the humid air outside.

"Hey." I said, barging rudely through his door. He was sprawled across his bed, a textbook in his hand. I did a double take. The thought of him studying still seemed incredulous to me. I shook myself mentally and crawled onto his bed, falling back. I stared up at his ceiling.

Carter, the paramedic. Has a nice ring to it.

"Hi?" He replied, the word coming out more of a question. "What's up?"

Oh nothing, I just think my best friend and my ex-boyfriend are hooking up and I feel sick about it.

"Just wanted to come see you."

"You've been by my side the last couple days," he pointed out, placing the book beside him. He leaned over and easily dragged my body towards him. I settled back, half resting on his lap. I closed my eyes and he began massaging my scalp. "Obviously I'm not complaining, but is something up?"

"I just like spending time with you."

He was quiet for a few moments before a cocky smirk danced across his lips. "That's understandable."

"Am I distracting you from your study?" I mumbled, his fingers feeling like Heaven. A blissful sigh escaped me. In moments like this, it was easy to picture Carter and I the way we used to be. As if that night never happened. That we were still dating and completely, obliviously in love. It was easy to forget that he broke my heart and we hated each other for over a year. Now, here we were, together but not really together, just like we were growing up. We were back to the start.

"You're always distracting me," he laughed. Carter leaned forward and pressed his lips against my forehead. "I bet you're glad to be back home."

"No kidding."

"Are you avoiding Anna?"

"What gives you that idea?" I asked with fake shock, staring determinedly at his bed comforter. His fingers ran tantalisingly slow through my hair and I let my eyes drift closed. I felt the need to seek his advice about this situation, but at the same time, I didn't want to talk to him about it.

"I'm not blind."

"Okay, I'm avoiding her." I gave in, withdrawing myself from his embrace and reclining back onto his bed. I stared up at the ceiling once more, not wanting to look into his clear, crystal eyes.

"Why?"

"I think she's hooking up with Aiden."

He grew silent beside me. I swallowed uneasily and peered up at him. His lips were spread into a thin line, a crease forming over his brow. Every time a frown formed on his features, I wanted to lean forward and smooth his face into the handsome, entrancing smile I used to be so accustomed to. He hardly smiles like that anymore. His trademark smirk was indented permanently on his lips.

"That has you pretty upset?"

"Yes."

"Because you still have feelings for him?"

Yes.

"Carter," I sighed and he shook his head, getting to his feet.

"You need to figure out what you want, Lacey." He frowned. I felt panic rise in my chest. Clambering to my feet, I reached out to him but he stepped back, shaking his head. My stomach clenched. He looked pained for a moment as if struggling with what to say to me. "You can't have us both. You need to either let him go, or me."

"I don't have feelings for Aiden," I lied.

I am still physically attracted to Aiden, yes. I can't help it.

"Stop being immature and talk to Anna about it. You're not helping anyone by being childish and avoiding her."

I flinched at the verbal slap in the face. He shook his head, his cheeks growing redder by the second. Agitatedly, he ran his hand through his hair. I didn't have anything to say back. I bit my lip, casting my eyes down to the floor.

"I really need to study." He said quietly. He wandered over to the door and opened it. I swallowed uneasily. He was kicking me out. "I'll talk to you later."

Without another word, I strode from his room. I thought spending time with Carter would help distract me from thinking about Aiden, but it only made things worse. My stomach clenched uncomfortably in my stomach, making me feel sick. I stepped out onto his veranda, the hot hair washing over my body.

I was walking through the gate when I glanced up, seeing a familiar flame-haired friend of mine, standing on my porch. She had her arms folded across her chest, a frown etched onto her face. A deep sigh left my lips as the knots in my stomach only grew tighter.

Confrontation time.

I kept walking and brushed past her. I left the door open behind me and wandered up to my room. I collapsed onto my bed and waited for her to follow. She quietly closed my door. I felt the end of the bed dip as she sat. It was silent for a few moments as the tension accumulated between us. We were both waiting for the other to speak first. Anna finally gave in.

"What have I done?"

"I think you know."

"Obviously not." She frowned. I rolled over and stared at her accusingly.

"I saw you in the shower block."

Her cheeks began to turn red. "Oh my God, you saw me naked? That tattoo was done by a friend of mine and I was drunk at the time..."

"Er- no. I heard you with him."

She cast her eyes down and began playing with a loose thread on her denim shorts. "I was going to tell you. It's only just started."

"How could you?" I asked, feeling my eyes burn with the urge to cry. My cheeks grew warm as I glowered at her. "How could you do that to me?"

"How has this got anything to do with you?" She asked in bewilderment. "Do you like him?"

I stared at her for a moment, as if she had three heads. "Are you serious?"

"I am so confused." She groaned. "I didn't know you liked Ryan?"

"Out of all people- wait what?"

"What?"

We both stared at each in utter confusion.

"Who are you talking about?"

"Ryan Steppard, who are you talking about?"

I was such an idiot. I felt my cheeks turn hot. Aiden must have been in the shower cubicle around the corner. I jumped to the wrong conclusions, letting my emotions get the best of me, yet again.

"I thought-" I began, unsure of what to say. How do you tell your best friend that you thought so low of her, so quickly? "Oops."

She quirked an eyebrow at me. "Did you think I was with Carter?"

"Aiden, actually."

"Wait, rewind." She said, holding up her hands. "You still have feelings for Aiden?"

"No."

She gave me a pointed look.

"Maybe."

She cocked her head to the side.

"A little."

"Lacey!" She cried out in exasperation. "Honestly, you are the most frustrating person I've ever met in my life."

"Gee, thanks." I retorted sarcastically.

"You want Carter when you're with Aiden but want Aiden when you're with Carter?"

"I'm not with Carter, we've just been hanging out."

"Have you...?" She asked, her round eyes penetrating mine. I leaned back a little, her intensity hitting me like a wave. If I had, I knew she would be giving me a solid lecture about needing to figure out what I want, before letting myself get into a situation like that, blah blah.

"With Carter? Not since my sixteenth birthday."

"Okay." She nodded, folding her legs neatly underneath her. "I think you should stop hanging out with Carter if you're still confused about Aiden. Clearly you're way over your head with both boys."

"But I'm really enjoying spending time with Carter. He asked me to the dance." I whined, sounding like a spoilt brat.

"Bloody hell." She sighed, pressing her fingers to her temple. "Don't go with him. Go stag, with me."

"That's a bit slack of me, don't you think?"

"Hmm. He would look amazing in a suit." She pointed out, tilting her head, as if visualising what he was going to look like.

"And it has been my dream to go with him ever since I was five."

"Okay then." She said, actually looking a little hurt that I rejected her idea of going together. I rolled my eyes, reaching out to her.

"We'll still be there together. Besides, aren't you going to go with Ryan?" I asked.

"If he asks me."

I exhaled, knowing that I needed to apologise. I was damaged, making me being a terrible friend. Anna deserved a lot better and yet, for some reason, she still stuck by me. And for that, I owed her.

"Anna, I'm sorry about avoiding you and thinking the worst of you. I let my emotions get the better of me."

"I knew becoming friends with you would be drama, Lacey." She admitted with an eye roll. "I know what I'm in for."

"Ouch."

"Truth hurts."

I sat and stared at my best friend for a few moments. I was suddenly thankful for having her in my life. I was so stupid to distance myself from her. She was important to me and I needed her.

"You just went very serious."

I rolled my eyes, letting a playful smile dance around my lips. "Do you want some tacos?"

"Always."

With a grin, I got to my feet and pulled Anna's hand. I wound down the stairs, feeling like a weight has been lifted from my shoulders.

"Hell to the no." Anna said in disgust, shrivelling up her nose. "No, no, a hundred times no. Take it off, it's hurting my eyes."

I snorted, staring down at the emerald, shiny, green dress that was wrapped a little too tightly around my body. I picked it up as a joke. She played along at first but had to be honest in the end. It really was a hideous dress. With my skin colour and hair, it did not work.

Anna was probably the easiest person I've ever shopped with, believe it or not. The second dress she tried on looking positively amazing on her.

First shop too, might I add. She chose a lacey, black dress that clung to her petite figure wonderfully. Her vibrant, red hair contrasted perfectly against the dark material. Her deep, dark eyes were enhanced. She was going to look beautiful. With her fiery red hair and lips, she was going to be jaw-droppingly gorgeous.

And then there was me.

Three hours in and I hadn't found anything that remotely looks nice on me. Okay, there had been a really nice navy dress that I adored until I looked at the price tag. It wasn't so nice then.

"I honestly think you would look great in red." She said for the umpteenth time, withdrawing a long, off-the-shoulder red gown from the rack. "Try it?"

"I like the idea of wearing red but when I put one on, it looks gross."

"No it doesn't." She frowned, shoving the dress into my hand. "Try it."

Grumbling under my breath, I stomped into the change room. Wearing jeans and a singlet was a poor decision on my behalf. I have had to wriggle myself back into my jeans about sixty times today and I was starting to get chafe from the rough texture of the denim. I was tired and over it. I was beginning to think there was no dress that would work for me.

I slipped the silky fabric across my skin. I cocked my head to the side as I stared in the mirror. This was by far the nicest red dress I've tried on, but still, something wasn't quite right. Begrudgingly, I wrenched the cubicle door open.

"Oh, I like that." Anna said, much to my surprise. She had disliked every dress (besides the beautiful navy one) almost more than I had, bar a few red ones. "But I don't like the top."

I pivoted and stared at my reflection. The bottom was beautiful, flaring out. The middle part highlighted my petite waist, which was very flattering. It was just the top, that didn't work. As the straps fell off-the-shoulder, my hideous collar bones were poking out aggressively. I honestly could use them as a defence weapon, they were that sharp.

We met eyes in the mirror and Anna was nodding, knowing my exact thoughts. "We need to cover those collar bones. They're freakishly prominent."

"So it's a no?"

"It's definitely the best one so far. I say we get it if we can't find anything else but we should keep looking in the meantime."

"Yes sir."

She smirked at me. I disappeared into the change room. I was just putting my foot through one of the left parts of my jeans when another dress was flung over the door.

"Try this."

I screwed my nose up as I stared at it. It was a light-pink, loose-fitting dress. Not my style at all. With a heavy sigh, I reached for it.

Scowling at my reflection, I began feeling utterly defeated. There was nothing that suited me. Maybe I should go back to the navy and beg my dad to buy it for me, pleading that the dance was a monumental high school moment for me and it was worth the three digit price tag.

"Well? How does it look?" Anna demanded.

"Terrible."

"Show me!"

With a deep frown, I walked out. Her face fell. "Aw man. Okay, pink definitely isn't the colour for you."

"You think?" I muttered, ready to stab her as this isn't the first pink gown she's forced on me.

"Okay then, what colour do you want?" She sighed, throwing her hands up. "Since all my suggestions are useless."

"Blue."

"Okay, fine. I'll go look."

I glanced up and met eyes with the shop assistant. She sighed as I handed her the red dress. She couldn't catch a break. Just as she'd put one away, she'd turn to have another two on the 'go back' hanger.

"Not the one?" She said sarcastically, looking more over it than I was.

"No." I snapped, not appreciating her attitude. She was meant to be encouraging me to try on more dresses, not make me feel even worse.

I tried to do a dramatic stride into the cubicle but the stupid pink dress didn't allow me to move at a normal, human pace as it wasn't so 'loose-fitted' as I had originally thought. I hardly had time to get the dress off before another was flung over the door. I closed my eyes and focused on my breathing. I counted to ten in my head and exhaled, feeling a little calmer.

After carefully stepping out of the pink dress and handing it out to Anna, I stared at the blue dress. The colour was amazing. It was a medium, striking blue. My favourite colour. With my fingers crossed, I slipped the smooth material over my body. I clipped it up at the back.

I held my breath as I stared at myself. It was a high neck style, covering my collarbones. It had beaded diamonds across the top. It was a very simple dress but definitely me. I did up the belt clip. It gathered in the middle, showing off my figure, but in a way that I was still comfortable. It was shorter at the front, showing off my tanned legs but fell elegantly longer at the back, making it look very formal.

"What do you think?" Anna asked in a bored tone.

"It's the one."

"Oh thank God," I heard her mutter.

I stepped out, a grin on my face. Her eyes popped open and her lips parted.

"Woah, that definitely is your dress."

"Hallelujah." The shop assistant cried out and we both just frowned at her. That was great customer service. In her defense, we had been here for hours, taking up the change rooms and complaining 80% of the time. Maybe make that 90%.

The price was a little higher than what I had been looking for, but it was worth it. I finally found a dress that not only did I feel comfortable in, but looked equally as great, if I do say so myself. Blue is definitely Carter's colour, so I know it would work well. The electric blue would contrast well with our golden-tanned skin.

I placed the dress gently down onto the counter, feeling like it was a precious, fragile item that could be easily broken.

"Is that all today?" She asked with a fake smile and over-enthusiastic voice. She must just be trying to play nice and get us to leave the shop.

"Yes, thank you." I clipped, withdrawing my Eftpos card, forcing myself to beam at her.

After purchasing my now favourite item of clothing, I looped arms with Anna. "Thank you for putting up with me."

"What are best friends for?" She asked with a playful smile. "Besides, it was worth the time finding the perfect dress. We're going to look killer."

"Hell yeah we are." I grinned.

It was funny how one dress had abruptly changed my mood. I now felt relieved, satisfied and excited. The dance was going to be awesome, I was going to make sure of it. I was going to drink enough to be buzzed and enjoy my night. With Anna by my side, I was going to most certainly have fun. Nerves bubbled under the surface of my happiness, as Carter and I didn't leave things on good terms. We had been texting and agreed to give each other space until the dance. Afterwards, we would have a 'talk'.

I'm not looking forward to that.

"Shall we have pre-champagne toasts at your place before the dance?" Anna asked, a shine to her eyes that I hadn't seen before.

"Definitely."

Thursday couldn't come quicker.

Chapter 23

Twice in my life, I have seen my father cry. The first time was when I was admitted to the hospital after cutting. The second time was today.

He stared at me with such admiration that even I was choking up. He beamed at me, his eyes watering.

"I am so proud of you, Lacey." He said to me, his voice breaking slightly. Tugging me forward, he roughly pressed his lips to my forehead.

"Thanks dad," I laughed, lightly pushing him. "Don't go getting too soft on me now. I'm not even in my dress yet!"

"I know," he laughed, wiping at his eyes. "It's just a proud moment in my life. To see you grow up into an amazing young woman. Just as amazing as your mother."

Rolling my lips into my mouth, I blinked away the desire to cry. Mum had just spent an hour perfecting my make-up, I wasn't going to go ahead and ruin it now.

As Anna was getting her make up professionally done, she wasn't here yet. I have been demanded to not get in my dress under any circumstances. We were meant to be doing that together, apparently. We still had two hours until we had to be there, so we were running well with time.

The nerves had begun to bubble in my stomach. I was ready to pour myself a drink soon to calm myself.

I hastily walked to the bathroom and leaned against the sink. The nerves that were ferociously bubbling in my stomach made me feel nauseous. I gently pressed my hand to my stomach, as though that would ease my worry. Dragging my eyes up, I gazed at my reflection.

My skin was glowing. It was smooth and clear, contrasting with my golden locks perfectly. My hair was draped around my shoulder, twisting down my collarbone in a stylish but messy braid. I had a simple, diamond clasp at the bottom that matched the beads at the top of my dress. My make-up was simple but elegant. The dark eyeliner around my eyes enhanced the green, making them appear to have a sparkle to them. I must say, I was impressed with my own appearance. I couldn't usually say that. The desire to run and put my dress on was increasing with every moment. I wanted to feel perfect.

There was a loud knock down stairs and my stomach clenched slightly. Anna was here. It was time. Rushing down the stairs, I almost knocked dad over.

"Slow down, hot stuff!" He cried out, finding his feet.

"Sorry," I laughed, wrenching the door open. My jaw fell to the ground. She. Looked. Amazing.

Her fiery, red hair was piled into a bun, loose tendrils spilling around her face. They were curled to perfection, contrasting with her porcelain white skin. She had smoky, grey eye shadow and her lips were as bright as her hair. She looked stunning.

"I know, I look hot." She smirked and I snapped myself out of my trance. I rolled my eyes at her, taking a step back. "You don't look too shabby yourself!"

"Cheers."

"Well? What are you waiting for?" She asked me, stepping inside. She brushed non-existent dirt off her shoulder and beamed at me. "Let's open the champagne!"

Two glasses later, my head was beginning to spin. I had just slipped the silky, smooth fabric of my dress over my skin. Anna's cool fingers brushed the back of my neck as she did up the clasp.

"Well don't you look gorgeous." She said to me quietly.

I grinned in response. I stared at myself and couldn't wipe the smile from my face. This colour was killer on me, not meaning to sound conceited. As expected, Anna looked like a Goddess. Her dress clung dangerously well to her petite figure. I couldn't take my eyes off her. In that moment, I wished we weren't arriving together.

"Let's go get photos before you get too drunk," she teased, clutching at my arm, pulling me from my thoughts.

She was right. I was already beginning to feel the alcohol take its course in my body. I had to slow down or I wouldn't be allowed in the dance. When I'm drunk, I'm not too good at hiding it.

The camera lights put me in a daze. I was grinning so wide that my cheeks were hurting. Dots dancing across my vision so I just smiled, unable to see exactly where the camera was.

After getting a thousand photos with Anna and some with my parents, it was time to go.

"You girls really look beautiful." Mum beamed at me, rubbing my arm soothingly. "Now Lacey, don't get too drunk tonight. That dress is way too nice to ruin."

I rolled my eyes. "No promises."

"Do enjoy yourself though," she said with a smile. She glanced sheepishly at dad. "I know I did at my senior dance."

"Ew."

Anna snorted and covered it up with a cough when I glared at her. Mum glanced down at her watch.

"The boys should be arriving within the next few minutes. Have you got everything you need?"

I did a quick scan through my bag. It was a tradition at our school for the parents, friends and relatives of the students to watch them arrive at the dance. Everyone was very cliché with the whole arriving in a limo or fancy car. Therefore, we decided to go in a done-up kombi. It was awesome. It was painted like it was the beach and was so realistic as well. As it was shaped in a ute, Carter was driving with Ryan in the passenger seat whilst Anna and I would sit in the tray. As mum and dad were coming to watch, dad was going to drive it after we exited, so that the next car could come up. We were definitely going to stand out, not being so traditional.

The sound of the ute made my bubbling nerves erupt like a volcano in my stomach. I looked at Anna and let out an embarrassing squeak. As expected, she was at total ease. She grinned at me. With our arms looped together, we emerged from the house. The cool hair hit me and an automatic shiver ran down my spine.

My mouth went dry as I gazed at Carter. He was leaning nonchalantly against the kombi ute, an easy-going smile on his face. He pushed off the ute and strolled towards me.

"You look amazing." He said, entwining our fingers and planting a kiss on my cheek. A blush crept up my neck as I awkwardly stared down at my shoes. His finger gently prodded my chin, lifting my face so that I was staring at him. He leaned down and kissed me softly. I thought I was going to melt. He inched back, his lips still brushing mine. "You may look stunning, but we still have to talk."

The happy rush of feelings inside me froze. He stepped back, his smile unfaltering as he stared at me. I swallowed uneasily.

"You look gorgeous, Anna." He said charmingly, as Ryan and her had stopped gazing at each other adoringly.

"You don't look too bad yourself Carter," she smirked back, basking in the attention.

"Shall we?" he asked formally, gesturing to the ute.

I pushed my troubled feelings aside and forced a smile onto my face. With a lethargic wave in my parent's direction, I let Carter help me scramble into the back of the ute. It was quite difficult in heels.

The trip was only short to school, but the wind was enough to give me goose bumps. I rubbed my arms, nervously nibbling at my bottom lip. I hope my hair doesn't get too messed up before we get there. The bump of the tray made my already queasy stomach feel worse. I was beginning to think I was going to vomit over the side soon.

"Hey, you okay?" Anna asked me, squeezing my shoulder.

"Fine." I smiled.

Looking unconvinced, Anna gave my hand a reassuring squeeze. Soon enough, we were amongst the rest of our peers in the long line waiting to enter to dance. It was getting beyond cool now and I was shivering uncontrollably. I desperately wanted Carter's jacket but there wasn't much point, seeing as I would have to take it off in a few minutes.

My nerves were burning holes in my stomach by the time we were a few meters from the door. This was probably a terrible idea. What if I get tangled getting out of the ute? Why did I want to stand out? If Carter drops me I'm going to cry and never show my face around here again.

The questions whirling around inside my mind seized as the ute jerked to a stop. Carter smoothly exited and glided around to the back. He undid tray and gave me a heart-stopping smile. It was the smile I needed to see. Even if we weren't in a good place right now, he was with me. I slowly got to my feet, scanning the crowd. I met a bunch of eyes, all watching me. I tried to breathe normally. My head was spinning.

Mum and dad were there, a phone in one's hand, a camera in the other. The flashes were making my light-headedness worse. I leaned down and Carter gripped my waist, easing me down from the ute. I felt a dizzying sense of relief when my feet met the secure ground. I heard the light thud of Anna landing beside me. We all posed for the professional photographer, before making our way in. Carter looked completely at ease, of course, while I was having a mini meltdown with everyone's eyes on us.

As we entered the hall, the music was vibrating the floor underneath us. I needed another glass of wine to settle myself. Clearly the previous two glasses weren't enough.

"You look like you're going to pass out." Carter murmured. I strained to hear him over the loud music.

"What?"

"I said you look like you're going to pass out." He repeated, gripping my shoulders. "Are you okay?"

"I need alcohol."

"Let's see what we can do about that." He laughed, rubbing my arm and guiding me towards the punch bowl. "I'm sure it's spiked."

He was right. I winced as whatever the mixed alcohol was slid down my throat. I downed the drink like it was water and refilled it. Carter laughed, doing the same.

"Let's go get a couples photo before we dance." Carter urged, tugging at my arm. I let him drag me over to the booth where another photographer was set up. There weren't many people on the dance floor yet anyway, as most were still arriving.

I awkwardly sat on the uncomfortable chair, Carter taking position behind me. He rested a hand on my shoulder. Trying to keep my eyes focused on the camera, I grinned.

"You guys make a gorgeous couple." She said, beaming at us.

My stomach clenched. Carter shot her a charming smile, before helping me to my feet. My shoes were already digging into my skin. I needed more alcohol to numb the pain. I began to head towards the punch bowl, but Carter snaked his hand around my waist, drawing me to him.

"Let's dance."

How could a girl resist that? I let him pull me towards the dance floor. I was a shocking dancer. My feet were always in the wrong spot, my eyes always cast down and my rigid posture made everything look awkward. Carter, of course, was smooth and elegant, as though he took regular lessons. He probably did just to show off at events like this.

Luckily for me, we just settled on a slight shuffle-type-thing. I wrapped my arms around his neck, feeling his warm skin radiate against mine.

"You truly do look beautiful."

"So do you."

He rolled his eyes. "Thanks babe."

He leaned down, gently pressing his lips to my nose, before drawing back. I glanced over, seeing Ryan dip Anna back, her laughter able to be heard over the music. A small smile danced on my lips as I stared at her. She looked so happy right now. It was good to see.

Suddenly, Carter stepped back. I pivoted on the spot as he gripped my leg, pulling it up. I gasped as I dipped, the back of my head almost touching the floor. My cheeks burned crimson as I hoped no one could see up my dress. I was flung back into standing position, my body pressed against Carter's. He ferociously kissed my lips. Electricity sparked down my veins as our lips moved together. Too soon, he drew back, making me almost beg for me. He smirked at my shocked expression.

"Couldn't have Ryan show me up."

I was exhausted. My feet were aching, my eyes stinging and my stomach churning from all the spiked punch. It had honestly been such a great night, but I was almost ready to go home. We hadn't even gotten to the after party yet. There was no way in the world Anna was going to let me miss the 'biggest event of our high school career', direct quote.

I let my eyes wander over the hall. Dribbles of different blue streamers hung from the roof. Blue and silver balloons were scattered across the walls, some having come loose, littering the floor beneath us. The decorations were amazing. The student council committee really had out-done them-selves this time.

"I hope I get a good one." Anna's voice brought me back to the present.

It was a tradition at our school, for the couples to separate at 10, grab a mask and then find each other. The lights would dim and the music would get louder. It was just meant to be a bit of fun. You were meant to make it hard for the other person. Almost like a hide and seek type game.

Anna and I had been in line for about ten minutes now, waiting for our masks. Thank goodness we were almost at the front. My feet were killing me.

Anna tied her mask up and looked over her shoulder at me, smirking. Her mask was black and feathery, contrasting well with her dress. I stepped forward.

"Sorry, hun. We're all out of blue." One of the teachers was handing out the masks, but she wasn't someone who has taught me before. Typical. I sighed, shifting my weight from one foot to the other. "But we do have silver, to match your shoes."

She planted a smooth, silver mask in my hand. It had no embroidery or anything fancy. It was plain and simple, but I liked it. I shot her a grateful smile and slid the mask up my nose. I turned and froze. Mercedes was behind me, talking to another girl. Her dark hair was twisting down her shoulders in aggressive curls. She wore a dark, purple, floor-length gown wrapped around her once, petite body. Her baby bump was prominent but she still looked quite nice.

She glanced up and locked eyes with me. Even with the mask, it was quite obvious it was me. The blue dress stood out. I swallowed uneasily. I began walking past her, but she grabbed my arm. I flinched as her cold fingers wrapped around my bicep.

"You look really nice, Lacey."

My eyes were bulging through the cut out of my mask. I cleared my throat.

"Thanks, you do as well."

I pulled my arm from hers and continued walking. I needed more alcohol. Well, technically I didn't since I was kind of drunk already, but I didn't care. I was on my fifth cup of the punch. My head was well and truly spinning at this point. It made the pain in my feet more bearable though, so I wasn't complaining.

The boys were the hardest to distinguish. As they all had similar black suits, except for the odd few, and matching plain masks, it was hard to tell who was who. Therefore, I wanted to hide, to make it harder for Carter. The last couple who find each other, get free tickets to the theme park across town. It's one of the funnest places I've ever been to. This game lasts a while, unfortunately. The teachers chaperone to make sure people aren't cheating.

"Hey, what was all that about?" Anna asked quietly. Her eyebrows were furrowed over her mask as she peered down at me. "With Mercedes?"

"She said I looked nice."

"How thoughtful of her." She remarked dryly. "Oh, there's Ryan, gotta go."

She spun on her heel and briskly walked from me, covering her masked face. I glanced at Ryan who watched her in amusement. He turned, pretending to not have seen her. Cheat.

I took a sip of the punch and grimaced at the foul taste. As the drink got lower, the more spiked it became. People were putting anything they could in there, so now it tasted even more terrible. A yawn escaped me as I placed my cup on the table. I stumbled slightly to my left. A warm hand steadied me and I gasped, not realising someone was behind me. I was spun on my heel. His lips met mine in a rush. They moved together in complete synchronisation. He stepped back. I breathlessly looked up. The blood inside my veins froze.

The eyes behind the mask were dark brown.

Chapter 24

What. The. Hell.

One minute, I was by the table, having a drink. The next, Aiden suddenly appears and thinks it's alright to kiss me? Um, excuse me? I'm practically back with Carter and the mother of his unborn baby is in the very same room as us. What the hell was he thinking?

After the passionate kiss, he took off from me. Okay, so I didn't see his face - it's dark and he was wearing a mask. But I knew those eyes. I knew those lips. It was Aiden.

I was still shaking. Should I tell Carter? I don't particularly want to have that conversation with him. Do I even need to? It's not like we're definitely together. I should. I need to. My stomach clenched at the thought of it.

The game was over now - I hadn't bothered hiding from Carter. I was still in shock. He had gone to round up the other's and we were about to head to the after party.

Unfortunately, we didn't win the tickets. Not that I really cared about that now anyway. Did I still like Aiden? I'm so confused. I couldn't be with him.

1- Because we have tried and tried before, it just doesn't work. Carter is too apart of my life. It's too hard.

2- He now has a child to think about. To my ex-best friend. Awkward? Extremely.

"Ready to go?"

And it's not like I am in love with him or anything. Yeah, I think he's attractive. Yeah, I think he's a nice, genuine guy (except cheating on me with my best friend, but hey, we're all as bad as each other, so I shouldn't pin that on him when I cheated on him too).

"Lacey?"

"What?" I asked, not having realised Carter and the two others had re-joined me.

"Are you ready to go?" Carter asked, placing a hand on my lower back.

"O-oh yes. Yeah, sure." I stammered. I stared at him. We were already on shaky ground. This would definitely push us over the edge.

My drunken mind decided then and there. I'm not going to tell him.

Anna gave me a curious stare. She knew something was up.

"Later," I mouthed to her.

We started to make our way out of the venue. I focused on keeping my feet steady as I was practically drunk. I glanced towards Mercedes. Aiden was with her, holding her hand. I grimaced, turning my head the other way. Are they together? I know they're having a child together, but it doesn't mean they're dating. And it's not like I kissed him. Although, well, maybe I did kiss him a little bit back...

Carter's mum was waiting outside and we all piled into the car. The warm air was a nice change to the fierce cold of the wind outside. I gripped Carter's suit jacket tighter around my body, still shaking despite the recent climate change.

We were making a quick pit stop at my house, so we could get changed into something a bit more comfortable for the party. Ryan and Carter were going back to his to get ready as well. I'll have a chance to fill Anna in and seek her advice. She is good with these types of situations. She's more reasonable than I am.

I slipped the cream coloured dress over my body, doing a little wiggle until the dress was sitting correctly. I glanced at the mirror, impressed that my makeup and hair still looked pretty good. Anna was wearing a tight, grey dress that showed literally every curve in her body.

It kind of annoyed me, if I'm honest. Not the dress, but her. She was so pretty. It made me feel inadequate beside her. Half the time I just felt self-conscious and gross. Not only did I feel like a skinny rat, her bubbly, out-going personality made me seem even more stand offish than I already was. In ways though, her constant chatter and smooth flowing words did encourage me to speak. She both did and did not boost my confidence. If that makes sense.

"Wow, who are you trying to impress?" I asked her with a laugh, as I shrugged into my black, leather jacket, firmly pushing back all my negative thoughts about my best friend. I've already lost one this year, I didn't want to lose another.

"We're ending our senior year. I'm impressing everyone." She smirked, sliding into her own, knitted jacket. It was going to be cool out tonight, but we still wanted to wear dresses. You just had to at the formal after party. You could say it was almost tradition.

My eyes had become slightly unfocused. I took another sip of my drink, although I really do need to slow down.

Mum had bought me these really nice boots back from when she was away. They were suede and knee high in length. They made me look taller than I was and made me feel way cooler. With my leather jacket, I was going to look pretty fresh.

"Woah, they are hot!" Anna gushed, leaning down and running her hands on the fabric. "Bitch I'm borrowing them soon."

I laughed as I began to re-do my lipstick. "I guess you can maybe borrow them. If you're lucky."

"You're not getting a choice in the matter."

My phone vibrated. I stumbled to my desk, trying to find it.

"It's in your hand, idiot," Anna laughed. "How drunk are you?"

"Carter says hurry up," I stated, ignoring her.

"Typical boys," she muttered.

We were practically done anyway. Just as we were exiting my room, Anna reefed me back. I cried out in shock, not having expected it. I grabbed the wall, as my legs suddenly becoming tangled together.

"What?" I whined, rubbing my arm.

"What was up with you before? You were acting like you'd just seen a ghost."

"Oh my God, you won't believe it!" I said, actually having forgot for a moment the whole thing had happened. "When we were playing the mask game, Aiden kissed me! Mercedes was right across from us!"

"What?" She squealed, her already ginormous eyes somehow getting larger. "For real?"

"Yeah! Isn't he like dating Mercedes now?"

"You guys are all so bloody confusing," she said in exasperation. "I give up."

"What should I do?" I asked as we began going down the stairs, ignoring her comment. "I can't tell Carter, he'll go ballistic."

"You need to confront Aiden."

"What should I say?" I asked, pausing at the front door.

"Um, bitch, what you kissin' me for?" Anna suggested.

I snorted. Okay, maybe drunk Anna doesn't quite give me some life-changing advice.

The car horn beeped.

"For Heaven's sake Carter, don't get your knickers in a knot." Anna snapped, slamming the door shut behind us.

The cold air slapped my cheeks and I hugged my jacket to me as I half jogged towards the car. The heated air inside felt really nice.

"You all ready to go?" Miranda asked.

"You bet," Anna smirked, giving me a wink.

Tonight's going to be interesting.

I was drunk. Like, really, really drunk.

I had planned to spend the night making out with Carter and dancing with Anna, but somehow I ended up being off with some girl named Olivia. I don't even know her. She's not in our year but somehow managed to make it to the party, claiming she was partnered with some guy in my year.

We had been game hopping, bouncing from beer pong, to never have I ever, to king's cup and so on. The drinking games had left me, well, drunk.

The flash of Olivia's iPhone camera almost blinded me. I staggered back, a million dots dancing across my vision.

"Sorry, that was blurry, go again," she muttered, shoving the phone back in front of our faces. I scrunched up my face and squeezed my eyes shut in attempt to shield myself from the fierce light.

"Aw!" she cooed, grinning from ear to ear. Her cheeks were crimson and her lips just as red, from the alcohol she was consuming. I squinted through the dots in my vision, vaguely able to see the image. It somehow turned out to be kind of cute. Except I did kind of look like a monkey. She was pulling a silly face, her tongue sticking out. "I'll send it to you later!"

"Yeah, okay," I said, not really caring too much.

"You're so cool," she said, pocketing her phone. "We should hang out some time."

"Yeah, sure," I said distractedly, searching for Carter. I had hardly seen him all night. I guess he was avoiding me a bit. We still had to talk. It seemed like he was just having a guy night. Which was okay, I guess. I'm lucky I found someone like Olivia to hang out with, seeing as Anna has been MIA with Ryan, doing God knows what.

Mercedes had, thankfully, not attended tonight. Not that I am aware of, anyway. Eventually, I was probably going to have to face her and sort through our issues. But honestly? I couldn't really be bothered.

"Hello, Lacey?" Olivia asked, her big, brown eyes mere inches from my own. "You, like, totally just spaced out."

"Huh? Oh, yeah, sorry."

"I was asking your advice on-" she stopped and looked at her phone. She quickly began looking around for someone. I quirked an eyebrow at her.

The bass of the music was beginning to give me a headache. I was heavily contemplating finding a room to pass out in.

"I have to go - it was nice meeting you Lacey!" Oliva said, kissing me on the cheek. It was sloppy and made me stumble. I didn't even have a chance to say bye before she was scampering off towards some guy I vaguely recognised.

I began wading through the clumps of sweaty bodies, trying to find Anna. I suddenly was feeling quite alone without having Olivia beside me. She was pretty cool and kept me company most of the night. Was a bit random, really.

A sigh left my lips as I was losing hope of finding Anna. I turned to go back to where I was, when I saw him. Aiden. As I was heavily intoxicated and not thinking clearly, I obviously thought confronting him in front of a public audience was appropriate.

I stormed towards him. Jabbing my finger into his chest, pushing my face close to his.

"Why the hell did you kiss me?"

He grabbed my wrists, stopping me from jabbing him further.

"Don't touch me!"

He tugged on my arms and dragged me towards one of the quieter rooms. He kept repeating "shh" as my protests became louder. Was he bringing me in here to kill me or something?

"Shut up for a second!" He whispered. I did as I was told. He dragged me further into the room. I snatched my hand from his grip and folded my arms defensively across my chest. I was swaying dangerously and his figure was blurry.

"Look, I'm sorry - I didn't plan for that the happen. I just... I miss you."

"Aren't you dating Mercedes?" I asked.

"Not officially."

"You still shouldn't have done it."

"I don't regret it."

"And you - what?"

"I love you," he murmured.

"Stop it, Aiden."

"Why?"

"Because it just doesn't work between us. We've tried. And tried again. It just doesn't, okay?"

He edged closer to me. I stepped back and somehow tripped, landing in a painful sprawl on my backside. He grabbed my hand, pulling me with ease, back to standing position. Before I had any time to react, he fiercely pressed his lips to mine. Okay, I'm going to say I kissed him back because I was drunk, not because I wanted to. Yeah, that's definitely the reason.

His tongue brushed mine and his hands tightened around my body. I gripped his arms, feeling his muscle underneath my fingertips. His hand ran down my back, landing on my butt. He squeezed it hard, making me gasp into his mouth. All the time we were together, he never did anything like this. It was always soft, gentle kissing. This kiss was hot and urgent, like he thought this was the last time he'd get the chance. He pressed his body to mine, gripping my head with both hands.

Suddenly, I snapped back to reality. I stepped back breathlessly, feeling guilty but yet, slightly exhilarated. I kind of liked doing something reckless. Something I wasn't meant to do.

That kiss just made Aiden hotter. I wish he had took some control like that in our relationship. Might have worked out a bit better if he didn't treat me like I was made of glass. Maybe that's why I find Carter so alluring? Because even though he treats me like a princess (sometimes), he knows how to take control.

He stared at me, his lips slightly parted, also breathless. Our stare was heated and I didn't know what to say. I quickly turned, planning on making a hasty exit, when I met eyes with Carter. He looked so hurt. I guess it has always been Carter with someone else. Although I had dated Aiden, it was when I was on the outs with Carter. But now that we were practically together, me being with Aiden was something different.

"Wow, Lacey." he said, his eyes watering. My stomach was clenched so tightly I felt like I was going to vomit. "You really know how to hurt a guy."

What the hell do I do now?

"Carter!" I cried out.

He strode from me, his back rigid. I attempted to run after him, but Aiden's warm hand swallowed mine.

"Don't go."

"Aiden, leave me alone. You've caused me enough trouble as it is."

"You kissed me back."

"Well, yeah, Aiden, I'm drunk!" I yelled out, slapping his hand away. "You know I've always been attracted to you, of course I was going to."

"You shouldn't have if you don't like me."

"I don't know what I want, okay? Just, let me go after him-"

"Why? I treat you better than he does! Trust me, it will be different this time-"

"You have a child to think about now. I want to travel, explore, live. I can't be tied down like that! Not when I have no idea who I am!"

"Lacey, come on." he pleaded, reaching out for me.

"No." I snapped, shoving him. My wrists ached in protest but the pain hardly registered in my mind. "You should have thought twice before fucking my best friend."

My words were like venom. The sting on his face was heart breaking. I couldn't help it though, I needed to get through to him. I needed to severe the ties between us, once and for all.

"Look," I said, feeling too guilty to leave things like this. I let my face soften as I stared intently into his eyes. "I'm a total bitch. You deserve better."

This time, he let me go. But now I had no idea where Carter would be. Probably long gone by now. I hastily dialled his number. Straight to voicemail.

"Carter," I whined, sounding like a seven year old. "Please talk to me. I'm so sorry. Call me."

I rang Anna but there was no answer as well. My heart was hammering inside my chest. I hope Carter wasn't about to do something stupid.

"Hey, Lace, you alright?" I turned, seeing a guy to my right. It took me a second to realise I went bowling with him once, when Anna and him were talking. Right now, I could not remember his name for the life of me.

"Oh hi, yeah, um, have you seen Carter anywhere?"

"Yeah I passed him like a minute ago. He was heading upstairs."

"Alright, thanks," I said, giving him an awkward pat on the shoulder. I jogged upstairs. I instantly regretting doing so, suddenly feeling nauseous. I bit my tongue, refusing to vomit. I had to find Carter and sort this out.

I reached the top and met his back. He was leaning into a girl's ear. I had seen her earlier. It was hard to miss her. She was a foreign exchange student from France. I couldn't even tell you her name. She was attending our school for six months as someone in our year had stayed with her in France six months prior. She had worn a bright, fuchsia dress with diamonties scattered across the top. It was a bit blinding, if I'm honest.

She grabbed his hand and tugged him towards a vacant room. My stomach was in knots by the point. My eyes were burning with the desire to cry.

He turned back. His eyes meeting mine. They were void of emotion. The old Carter that I finally had gotten back, was gone. He gave me his trademark smirk. The one I had grown accustomed to and hated.

A tear slid down my face. I began to walk towards him.

"Don't," I whispered, my voice breaking. "Don't do this."

He reached toward the door, never breaking eye contact.

In one fluid movement, he slammed the door in my face.

Chapter 25

My legs collapsed underneath me. That's it. I'm so done with him.

"Miss, are you alright?" a voice asked me.

My vision was blurry and my head was spinning. I tipped my head back so I could stare up at the person addressing me. He was crouched down so we were level, but I couldn't see his face. He had a faded, blue skater hat shielding his face. He had broad shoulders and even from this angle, I could tell he was pretty solid. He looked kind of familiar.

"Um, no, not really," I answered, my wrist aching from where I had fallen on it.

"Why don't you come with me?"

"Why would I do that?" I asked, a little taken back.

"Because you don't have a choice."

He met eyes with me and I froze. My entire body went rigid. It was one of the football guys that bashed Carter. The one I hit on the head. He grabbed me roughly, pulling me up. His touch somewhat triggered my muscles and I was able to move again.

His arm snaked around my waist and I screamed. His knuckles jabbed my jaw and my cries died down. He gripped me hard, dragging me off towards a room. This situation just went from 0 to 100 real quick. And I didn't like it.

"CARTER!" I screamed, despite everything that had happened between us in the past twenty minutes.

The door was shut and locked behind him, quicker than I could blink. As everyone was equally, if not more, intoxicated than I was, no one ventured to my rescue. I never thought I would be that girl. The one you read about in online articles or hear on the news. The girl that everyone feels sorry for. And now, this very situation could be happening to me.

"What the hell do you want?" I hissed, stepping away from him. The back of my knees hit the bed and I fell back. My eyes began darting restlessly around the room, trying to find anything I could use to protect myself.

"I don't think I have to spell it out for you."

"You lay a hand on me, I swear to God," I threatened, starting to slowly sober up, but not fast enough. My brain was still foggy from the alcohol. My body still unable to function at normal human speed.

"What?" He questioned, cocking his head to the side. "Your little bitch boy will come save you? He looked pretty occupied a few minutes ago."

"Yeah and he'll kick your ass." I spat, ignoring the hurtful, yet truthful, comment about Carter's actions. I began crawling back as he was inching towards me.

"He didn't do a very good job last time." He smirked.

Reaching forward, he grabbed my leg, easily dragging me forward. I kicked out, jolting him in the cheek. He hardly even blinked. He leapt onto me, his full body weight crushing mine. My heart was slamming into my rib cage. I could hardly hear anything over the sound of my heart beat drumming in my ears.

"Lace? You in there?" Anna called out. I wanted to cry with relief.

"ANNA HELP!" I screamed as loud as I could, before he literally head butted me.

Pain skittered across my forehead and I cried out. I could feel blood trickling down my nose. My vision was blurry before, but now I could hardly see a thing. I was so close to passing out. It was extremely difficult not to close my eyes.

The banging on the door was distant to me. I could hardly comprehend what was happening.

Sudden light flooded into the room. The guy, whose name I don't even know, was pulled off of me.

Ryan had him pinned against the wall. Anna tugged at my hand. I stumbled after her, bleary eyed and still drunk. We practically fell out of the room, into the gaze of a bunch of people, all confused about what was happening.

Amongst the crowd, Carter was trying to push through, to get to me. The collar of his shirt was unbuttoned and his hair messy.

"Lacey!" he called out, grabbing me.

I flinched at his touch.

"Not now," Anna snapped, pushing him from me.

I gazed up at him as she was dragging me away.

We were never going to be the same.

Carter's P.O.V:

My thoughts were in a whirlwind. All I could see in my head, was Aiden's hand on Lacey, their lips glued together like magnets. I wanted to be sick.

After us being so close again, how could she betray me like that? Had she been hooking up with him this whole time?

Her tanned arms were slender as they wrapped around me. I blinked, trying to focus on the girl in front of me. She began murmuring something in her regular language. Obviously, I didn't understand French.

Her warm, soft lips met mine. I kissed her back at first, before shoving her from me. This wasn't right. After being with Lacey again, I couldn't be with anyone else. It felt too wrong.

"What's wrong?" she asked, her voice laced heavily with her accent.

She was hot, I must admit. But I couldn't go through with it.

"Nothing," I muttered, tearing at the top button my shirt. I was feeling short of breath, for some reason.

She rushed forward, her lips meeting mine. She ran her hands roughly through my hair, as if thinking this passionate act would get me to give in. I pushed her back again, shaking my head.

"I can't, I'm sorry," I groaned, my stomach feeling tight.

"CARTER!"

The blood inside my veins went cold. Was that...?

"Where are you going?"

I hadn't even realised I was running for the door.

"I have to go."

"Do you not find me attractive?" she asked, stepping between me and the door.

"Look," I tried to think of her name, I really did, but I came up blank. "You're smokin' hot. You're probably a really nice girl, but I'm in love. I'm in love with someone else and I can't be with you. I'm sorry. Please, I need to go."

Her face fell. I couldn't stay to comfort her, not when Lacey needed me. I attempted to get through the bodies. Anna was there, beating at the door. I shoved Ryan out of the way and booted the door in. Anna reefed me back by the shirt, making me almost fall over backwards. Ryan rushed in, doing exactly what I had planned to.

"What the hell?" I yelled.

I faced Anna and she slapped me. She literally slapped me. And it hurt like a bitch.

"You're an asshole. Get away from her," she hissed, shoving me roughly back.

I staggered. For a small, petite girl, she sure was strong. She rushed in, grabbing Lacey.

I tried talking to her, but when I met her eyes, they were cold.

She was never going to look at me the same.

Lacey's P.O.V:

Last night had been a complete fucking disaster. And I have no idea what to do about it.

I was in the wrong. I shouldn't have kissed Aiden back. That's only going to send him even more mixed signals then I already had. And frankly, it wasn't worth the drama now between Carter and I.

I thought he'd grown up. Matured, from last time. But the first thing he does again, was lash out and hurt me back. I hadn't intentionally hurt him to begin with. It all happened so fast.

This place was toxic. I needed to get out.

I'm not sure if it's from my hang over (high chance) or the sudden feeling of suffocation and claustrophobia from this place, but something had me running to the bathroom to vomit.

Carter had tried ringing me several times. Obviously, I chose the mature response of ignoring him. So, he sent me a text. The text held a detailed description of that fact that he did not sleep with the French girl. I'm glad, of course, but it doesn't change that he wanted to hurt me again. Like he has so many times.

I'm over it.

I'm over dealing with Carter and his bullshit and I'm over Aiden.

Honestly, I need to get the fuck out of this place.

Anna was coming over later this afternoon. Her aunty works at the flight center in town and has emailed her a bunch of flights, quotes and information about travelling. I can't wait. The urge to leave this place behind me was growing with every second. I wanted out and I wanted out now.

Briefly this morning, I had flicked through some study plans and universities in other countries. But I'm tired. My mind, body and soul is honestly exhausted. I'd like to just travel, and work. Save some money and see the beautiful world around me. I want to get to know me for once.

The last couple weeks, Anna and I have been sending each other website links or articles about a certain place. So far, we were thinking of Hawaii. To just chill out for a year, learn to surf, spend our days on the beach and just relax. I'd fit in well natural golden tan, although most natives had darker hair. Anna would stand out like a flamingo in a pod of pelicans, but she'd probably like that.

Sighing, I rest my chin in the palm of my hand and continued to scroll through tourist travel ideas of Hawaii.

I suddenly couldn't wait to pack my bags and leave.

The sudden urgency I was feeling about leaving was obviously mutual. Anna and I, without too much mucking around, began planning our trip to Hawaii. This was serious and it was actually happening. Our parents have okayed it, knowing that there wasn't a chance in hell to stop us anyway. Anna's mum seems to want Anna to leave and honestly, my parents probably want me to leave too. I think it would help everyone if I just left.

My parents, could breathe again. They wouldn't have to worry about me so much. They can just focus on their work and their marriage.

Aiden, can further develop his relationship with Mercedes. They can grow to be the happy family I'm sure they will eventually be.

Carter, can focus on his studies in becoming a paramedic. He can settle down, get his head in the game and become the extraordinary person he's destined to be.

And me? I can get drunk whenever the hell I want, on a beach I probably won't be able to pronounce, getting tanner than I have ever dreamed of being.

This is the most excited I've been about something in a long time. It was a good feeling.

"You're sure you want to do this?" Anna asked me for the upteenth time. "I really can't have you backing out last minute, okay? If we're doing this, we need to be ready to go all the way."

"I'm ready." I replied with determination.

At first, I freaked out about expenses. But since nan passed, she had left me quite a solid amount of money in her will. Plus, my parents are willing to lend me a hand. Anything to just help me get out of the horrible, dark place I'm in now. I'm not sure about Anna's finances, but she seems fine with everything. I'm not going to ask how she's doing it. As long as we're in it together, everything will be great.

I decided, I'm not going to tell Carter I'm leaving. I'm going to write him a detailed letter, pouring out my heart to him. I will slide it under his door and then be gone. I will do the same for Aiden. The letter's, are going to be entirely different. I don't really know where to start with either of them.

"That's a good idea," Anna said, bringing me back to reality. "I think a letter is definitely the way to go. That way you won't get dragged into any, like, passionate kisses or, like, hot break up sex..."

I rolled my eyes. "I'm done with that."

"Sure you are."

"Seriously." I said firmly, shutting my laptop lid. "I'm so done with both of them. I don't want that negativity controlling my life anymore."

"That's the smartest thing I've ever heard you say."

I smiled up at her.

I'm finally ready to move on with my life.

Chapter 26

I could not begin to express the relief I felt when I heard that final tick on the clock, indicating the three painful hours I just endured, was over. I was free. All I wanted to do was leap from the table, kick it over and spit on the hand written essay that will barely pass. I hadn't studied, so sitting here for three hours and knowing I was going to fail, made me feel worthless and pathetic. But thankfully, my exams were over and I was officially finished high.

Thank goodness.

I cannot wait to step outside this school and never return. It will be one of the best days of my life. The sooner I leave this hell hole, this sooner I can leave the horrible, toxic drama that has plagued my life for so long.

Aka, leave Carter and Aiden.

After having to wait, what I feel to be quite an unnecessary amount of time, we were relieved from the gym. The sunshine, although the air was cool, hit my face and I inhaled a lungful of the fresh air. My neck was stiff, my back rigid and my hands had cramped within the first ten minutes. My legs felt wobbly from sitting uncomfortably for three hours straight.

"How'd you go?" Anna asked, her flaming red hair vivid in the afternoon sun.

I responded with a deadpan stare.

"That good?" she laughed, slipping her bag over her shoulder, glancing down at her watch. "Why don't we go for a drink?"

"It's like, two o'clock," I cocked an eyebrow.

"So? We just finished high school, Lace. Let's go celebrate!"

She had a point. I shrugged, a small smile making its way onto my face. "Why not?"

"Yay!" She squealed, clapping her hands together. "How about we swing around to yours and we can walk down town from there?"

"Sure," I said with a nod, falling in step beside her as we made our way out of the school. I had to come back to officially sign out of my classes, but other than that, I was definitely finished with this place. "You don't need clothes from your house? Would look weird walking around with alcohol in our school clothes."

"I have everything I need in my car."

Right. I forgot Anna practically lived in her car. It definitely looked like it. I rummaged through all her stuff, attempting to find the front seat. She began throwing clothes towards the back seat, seeming unfazed about the clutter spread around us. I guess she would be used to it. To me, it made my OCD go into overload, but I stared determinedly out the window.

As we were underage, I'm not sure how we planned to get this alcohol, but knowing Anna, she already had a plan, so I didn't bother to question it. We pulled up at mine, at the same time Carter's car pulled smoothly into his driveway.

He waved at us. He looked like he was about to come over, but Anna firmly turned her back to him and grabbed my hand, pulling me inside. She obviously has not forgiven him about what happened at the last party we went to. I hadn't really either. I don't know what I would have said, or done, if he had come over. Knowing Carter, he would just start casually, asking me about exams and then I would get wrapped up in him and totally forget all the stuff that has happened recently.

That's how much of a pull he has over me.

My house was quiet as we entered the front door. Both my parents were at work. I face planted onto my bed, feeling like that was appropriate. I felt mentally drained and was ready to lay like this for the rest of the night.

"I'm going to text Jerry and see if he's working at Celebrations today," Anna said, more to herself than me, I think. I slowly moved my head, so that I could peer up at her. Celebrations was our local liquor shop. I quirked an eyebrow, waiting for her to elaborate. She rolled her eyes. "I hooked up with him a few times, he usually gives me free alcohol. If he's on, I'm going to order us some champagne."

"You never seize to amaze me." I muttered, once again, burying my face.

It didn't take Jerry long to reply and apparently he was doing a home delivery. I took that as an opportunity to take a long walk. One, I knew Anna was really excited right now and wanted to start celebrating immediately - whether it be with Jerry or any one of her guys, probably. I didn't care if she started her party without me, I just wanted to clear my head a little. And that way she can repay Jerry for the favour. Gross.

I felt my muscles relax and unwind as I began walking. Not sprinting and pushing myself this time was actually nice.

I took the time to look around me. I lived in a beautiful place. It's hard to believe that I felt so complete living here once. The last twelve months, however, have been dark and toxic for me. I honestly believe the only way I can ever connect with this place again, would be to leave. Not forever, but definitely leave for a while.

A shiver ran down my spine as the cool wind slapped my exposed skin. I forced myself to walk a little further, before turning around and heading home. I thought I hadn't gone long, but the walk had been about forty minutes. It was nice to just hear my own thoughts for a while and not be so distracted with reality.

It began to sink in that this was it. This is the time where my life is going to take off. I have finished school - I no longer have any commitments to this place, bar my family. I think the idea of leaving was a distant concept to me but now is a pure possibility. And I cannot wait.

I lingered in my driveway momentarily, staring at the almost-mansion beside my own house. So many memories. So much love had been in that house. I could never have imagined how everything would turn out. With a sigh, I walked back to my house, finding Anna, thankfully, alone. She looked bored and had her bottom lip puckered.

"I missed you."

And, she was almost drunk already. I shook my head at her.

"Sorry, just needed to get some air."

"You were gone forever!" She whined, sounding childish.

"So, what happened with Jerry, hmm?" I asked suggestively.

A grin spread across her face. "It was very good, thanks."

She reached behind her and grabbed a glass, which was almost overflowing with champagne. I rolled my eyes. You were meant to have less then half of what she had put in there. Typical Anna.

"A toast," she declared, holding the wine glass up in triumph. "To us and the future."

"Yes," I agreed with a laugh, clinking my glass to hers.

Finally, there was something I could look forward to.

Three Months Later

Considering I feel like I don't have that many, the amount of clothes stuffed into my giant-size suitcase was actually ridiculous. I found some tops I bought like five years ago, that still had the tags on them. Luckily, I have never grown and still remain the same size since I was like twelve. Pretty sad, when you think about it.

After a long, kind-of-exciting, kind-of-dragged-out process, we had managed to knuckle down and sort out our travel plans. And I was planning to leave tomorrow. The amount of organisation that had gone into this was mentally draining. We were so lucky to have Anna's connections because it was short notice to organise flights - but somehow everything has worked out.

The last three months, I have been doing relief work at the new display home in town - dad set me up with it. I've been working about three days a week, which was been awesome experience. And, it forced me to leave the house and actually do something. A lot of my organising had actually been done there, in between walking people through the model home and whatnot. I definitely took advantage of the free wifi.

In between then, I have been spending time with Anna and my family. I've seen Carter around, but he's studying or partying with his friends usually. A few times we've passed by each other and he has tried to contact me, but I don't have the energy to be around him anymore. I've decided that I'm going to write three letters.

One to Carter.

One to Aiden.

One to Mercedes.

I was going to do a drive by to their houses on the way to the airport, drop them off in their letter boxes and then be on my way. I've already discussed my plan with mum and she thinks that it's a good idea. I hope it is.

Nerves had been bubbling in my stomach for the past week. Tomorrow was the day I was going to leave this place behind. I was going to begin my new life and I was beyond excited for it. Also, nervous as hell.

Anna acted like she did this all the time and wasn't fazed at all. I was almost having a panic attack. There is so much that could go wrong. What if I don't like it? What if we get mugged? What if Anna and I get in a huge fight over there and she leaves me?

So many thoughts and scenarios were whirling my mind, making me feel nauseous. But it was going to be okay. Because anywhere would be better than being here right now. I was ready to take on this new adventure, with my eyes open and my head held high. Everything was going to be great.

A sigh was heard behind me and I glanced over my shoulder, seeing mum leaning against my door frame. She actually looked a little teary.

"You're really going, huh?" she said, a faint smile on her face.

I nodded, sitting down beside my too-stuffed suitcase. "I need to go."

"I know," she murmured, coming to sit beside me. "God, I hope Hawaii is going to be better for you than this place has."

"It will be." I whispered, casting my eyes down. "It has to be."

"I'm going to miss you like crazy."

"I'm going to miss you too." I leaned my head on her shoulder, fighting back my own tears. My mouth felt hot and sticky.

"You're going to have to go through this 'skype' thing with me again."

I laughed, wrapping an arm lazily around her shoulders. "You bet, mum."

If only I could pack my family up with me, too.

"You started?" I looked up at mum, to see her staring at the three pieces of paper, neatly spread across my desk.

"I've tried."

"I'm sure the words will come to you. You just need to write what you feel." With that, she slowly stood. I think she wanted to leave before we both burst into tears.

I watched her walk from my room. Slowly, I maneuvered myself to my desk. With a sigh, I picked up the cold pen.

Dear Carter...

Chapter 27

D ear Carter,

What happened to us? Why were we destined for such heart break?

I don't even know who to blame anymore. Maybe everything is beyond us. Maybe the universe didn't want us together. I don't know. All I do know, is that I need to go. And you can't come with me. I don't why we are like this. I don't know why we just end up hurting each other over and over. But it has to stop. I'm tired of this.

By the time you read this, I will be on my way to Hawaii. I'm travelling with Anna. We plan to work, drink, tan and just relax. I hope this is what happens anyway. I need a break from reality and I'm hoping Hawaii can do this for me. I'm going to miss you like crazy, despite everything. I hope you take me leaving as a positive to change. I want you to study hard. I want you to grow. I think me leaving is going to benefit us both in multiple ways.

I'm not moving there forever - even though I have thought about it. I'm going for a year. Maybe two. I don't know yet. It's hard to tell if I'm going to like this place or not. I really hope so. A year is a long time.

In this year, I want to discover myself. Maybe for the first time. I want to do this just for me. No drama, no commitments, just me, myself and I. I think you should take some time to do that for yourself, but that's up to you.

It's strange, you know. For three months I have tried to write this letter and I couldn't. I just stared at a blank page, for sometimes up to an hour and just gave up. And now I'm leaving tomorrow and I feel like I don't have enough time to say what I want to say. It's funny how things work out like that.

I do love you. I always have and I think I always will. But we can't be together right now. I need to grow up and honestly, so do you. This is going to be the longest time we've ever been a part, but if we really do love each other, it is only going to make us stronger.

With me, I'm going to take the best of the best memories of us to Hawaii. All the horrible stuff we have done to each other, I'm going to leave that here. When I come back, I hope we can have matured and not relive any of those things. I don't, ever, want to repeat any of this year. If we do, then we have our answer. We don't belong together.

I wish things had been different. I wish a lot of things. I just hope you can move forward with your life, like I plan to.

This year will tell us one thing. Whether time a part will make us realise that there is more out there and we're just not meant to be. Or, it will allow us to grow and finally be ready to be together. I guess we will just have to wait.

So, this letter is not a goodbye, Carter. It's a see you soon. I wish you the best for whatever you choose to do. I hope you know that I will miss you every day, but I need to do this.

I love you.

See you soon,

Lacey.

Chapter 28

Dear Aiden,

Imagine if someone told us a year ago where we would be now. Who could have predicted all of this?

You deserved so much better than me. I wish you had met someone else and been happy with them. I do not regret us, though. I'm glad I met you and got the chance to be called your girlfriend. You're such a kind person. I have no idea why or how you put up with me for as long as you did.

But that one time. That one mistake from you has changed your whole life. You sealed your fate the moment you chose Mercedes over me.

I don't even know what's going on inside your head. One minute you want me, the next you don't. I'm the exact same, I know. Honestly, we're all as bad as each other. Well, me more so than you. Anyway, that is why I have decided to do what I'm doing.

A year gap. A year to have a break from reality. Hawaii, will be my temporary home. Who knows, I could end up never coming back. Kidding. Kind of.

I hope you treat Mercedes well, even though I choose not to associate with her anymore.

I wanted to write you this letter, to tell you that I don't regret us. I don't regret it at all. I regret how I treated you and how it ended, but not us. And I wanted to apologise for everything that I have done.

I hope that one day, we can move on and be friends. I'd like that. I hope this year, you can find yourself and find peace. And be happy. You will be a great father. Don't ever forget that.

Sorry this letter isn't going to be very long. I'm not all that good with words. I know what I want to say, but it's hard to actually say it.

Please move on with your life. Do not hold a place for me in your heart. I don't deserve it. We don't work, after all the times we tried. I think it's better off to just end it for good. I will cherish that last kiss we shared and never forget it. Because it will be the very last one for us.

A lot is going to happen for you this year and I wish you all the best luck for it.

For now, I'm not in your life. I don't want you to treat me like I'm in your life. I want you to focus on your family, not me. One day, I hope we can grow to be in each other's lives again.

Good luck with everything,

Lacey.

Chapter 29

Dear Mercedes,

It feels weird to write that since we have not spoken for a long time. I was a terrible best friend. So were you. But I started it.

I want to apologise for everything that I have done. I couldn't leave without telling you that.

I really am sorry. I didn't treat you well at all. I made all of this happen. I'm honestly, really sorry. I hope that we can forgive each other one day.

I'm planning to do a year in Hawaii. I need a fresh start and to leave this place. I hope that you and Aiden can grow and be happy, with whatever happens.

We did a lot of bad things to each other. I don't know why we grew into such hatred, but we did. It's time for me to stop blaming everyone else and blame me. I am the sole reason for everything to have become so screwed up.

That's why it's time to go.

I'm sorry, but this isn't going to end with friendship, although I don't know if that's what you want or not anyway.

I don't think we can be in each other's lives the way we used to. A year can change a lot, so who knows. But for now, I'd rather just cut ties once and for all. I don't want to be forever thinking that we should have apologised to each other. I don't care (that much) if you don't apologise for what you've done. But I'll feel better knowing that I have, at least.

I hope that your future is bright. I hope everything goes well during birth and that your child will be healthy. I wish you all the best for everything.

In a year's time, we will see how things are. I don't think we will ever be best friends again, I'm sorry. Too much has happened. We both can't ignore it. In saying that, there could be hope. It's hard to say now, however.

I have a flight to catch. Thanks for reading this letter.

Lacey.

Chapter 30

In the midst of all my excitement, I almost forgot how sad leaving was going to be. Let's just say, it had been one emotional morning for my family. My father's hug almost broke my ribs and mum hadn't stopped crying for the last two hours. Both of us had been a sobbing mess, so dad had to drive.

Anna was sprawled out on the back seat, completely nonchalant. It looked as if she was just on the way to school, not on her way to leave the country for a year. Although I actually don't know much of the details, I know that her and her mum don't have the best relationship. Regardless, I thought there would at least be some reaction out of her. I frowned at her, hoping she was alright. Wouldn't want her to be having second thoughts now, of all times.

For some reason, I had wanted to leave Carter's letter to last. I guess it was because it was the most important. Which meant we had to do a loop, but I don't think my parents really cared.

I glanced at Anna, hoping for a supportive smile but she just gazed emotionlessly out the window. I looked at mum who gave me an encouraging smile. That was all I needed. With wobbly legs, I slid out of the car. My hands were trembling as I placed the sealed envelope into Carter's mail box.

Panicking for a second that he might look out his window and see me, I made a dash back to the car. My heart was racing. This was it. I wasn't going to see him for at least a year. That was a long time. Dad pulled smoothly out from the driveway and I stared back at his mansion, biting my lip.

I suddenly wondered if writing a letter was a good idea after all.

Most of the trip was silent to the airport. I think we were all a bit nervous. I was playing with a loose thread in my shorts, to the point I ripped some of the material. With a sigh, I pressed my forehead against the cool glass.

I'd only been outside Australia once. I went to New Zealand with Carter's family. We went snow skiing. It had been pretty awesome, but that was years ago now. I felt very new to this. Anna would be there, but it still felt weird not to be travelling with someone more adult-like. I suddenly felt very amateur, like I wasn't ready for this kind of adventure. All the confidence and excitement I had felt for the past three months, suddenly warped into a sick feeling of nausea.

The car came to a stop and I snapped my head up, having been so deep in my thoughts, I hadn't realised we'd actually reached the airport. This only made me feeling one hundred times worse.

Dad hauled our suitcases out of the car and they landed with a heavy thud on the pavement.

"Alright, see ya," dad said with a wave, hopping back in the car. My eyes boggled from my head. He began laughing, re-emerging from the car. "Joking, Lace."

I slapped him lightly on the shoulder. That did not help my sudden tidal wave of anxiety.

"You'll give the poor girl a heart attack," mum murmured.

I peered over my shoulder nervously at the sliding doors, that had people walking through, dragging their luggage behind them.

"You're going to be okay, Kid." Dad said to me, patting my shoulder a little too roughly.

I gave him a wan smile in return.

As a group, we began our short journey into the terminal. Mum completely transformed into business mode and basically got as organised with everything. Thank God, because my whole body was trembling and my mind was running a million kilometres per second. I could hardly walk straight, let alone think straight, too.

The next hour was a complete blur. I think I somehow entered a trance. I followed mum's orders as she acted like she actually worked for the air port. We then got to the part where my parents couldn't come with us.

My stomach did a flip. "What if I-"

"Shh," mum hushed me, wrapping her arms securely around me. "You will be fine. You're so strong, Lacey. You're going to have a great time."

She kissed my cheek. I glanced at dad who gave me a lope-sided smile. "Go get em', Kid."

I was so not ready for this. What had I been thinking!?

With one final hug, tears began pouring down my face. They turned to hug Anna, and finally, I saw a crack through her nonchalant facade. It was good to see her come back. Her eyes were teary as she hugged my mum. I wonder if she was wishing that was her mum instead.

It was time to go.

With one last wave, I followed Anna's flaming red hair towards the final waiting room.

This was it, no going back now.

Carter's P.O.V:

Once again, I woke to complete silence. This was common for me, considering my parents were hardly home and I never had any friends over much anymore. Or girls, for that matter.

With a groan, I rolled out of bed. I wasn't particularly motivated to go straight to study today. So, I decided to make myself a coffee. I scrolled through facebook, taking tentative sips. I had been trying to go out more and actually do something other than study, these last couple of months, but I still felt like I wasn't achieving much.

I turned the water to scolding hot and stepped under it, the steam filling the room. I inhaled a lungful, running the water through my hair.

I missed Lacey. I wish things hadn't gotten so screwed up with us. It was lonely in the big house with just my own company. But hers is the only one I want. At the slowest rate possible, I toweled off and stepped into some jeans.

Mum had left me a post-it note, asking me to do some jobs. I sighed. At least it would give me a reason to procrastinate my study some more.

I loved learning, don't get me wrong, but I could not stand being stuck inside all day. I'd rather go do something fun, but I guess this is just life.

After doing some basic chores, I pulled the bin bag out, scrunching up my nose. Didn't we have a house cleaner for this? With a disgruntled mutter under my breath, I stomped out to the bins outside. I glanced at Lacey's house. It looked like there wasn't anyone home. She'd been pretty busy, from what I've creepily observed. I glanced at the mail box, seeing the little red flag in the air. With another unnecessary sigh, I wandered towards it.

The envelope felt cold in my hands. I quirked an eyebrow. It was hand written and addressed to me. That was odd. I was half expecting excessive junk mail about who to vote for in the next election, not something personally written to me. I hardly ever got mail, unless it was my phone bill.

I stretched as I began the short trek back to my house. I poured myself a glass of coke. I sat down and stared at the writing. It had a familiar slant to it. Curiously, I opened it.

Dear Carter...

It happened so fast. My body was reacting faster than my mind was. I tugged on a shirt, the first I saw and ran to the door. I tripped, attempting to get my shoes on. No time for socks. I ran to the car and punched it, having forgotten my keys. This couldn't be happening. She can't leave. I rushed back inside, basically turning everything upside down until I found them.

My heart was slamming inside my chest from the rush of adrenaline. I broke countless speed regulations as I floored it to the airport.

A letter? After everything we've been through, she wrote me a God damn letter? I guess I deserved as much, but it still hurt. She knew I would have asked her to stay. I was that selfish.

Maybe she will have second thoughts and back out of everything?

One can only hope.

I felt like I was in a movie. I'd never imagined I would be chasing Lacey. Begging her to stay with me. If all else fails, I'll at least see her one last time to say goodbye.

I needed to see her. I needed to feel her lips against mine.

I left my car unlocked and I think my door might have still even been open. I sprinted, as fast as I humanly was able to. I pushed past people and ignored their curious stares. Some people followed me, probably waiting for the dramatic, movie-like-moment to happen.

After running around in circles, I finally decided to ask someone for help.

"Umm, hi, err, I need, oh God," I said breathlessly. A wave of frustration rolled through me. I didn't even know what flight she was on. I realised I hardly knew anything. Didn't know the time, the terminal, nothing.

"Calm down," the woman said sternly. "What do you need?"

"My girl- I need to, ugh, I don't even know the flight number or anything!"

"Please slow down," the woman insisted, looking irritated. "I can't help you if you don't tell me what's wrong."

"Has the flight the Hawaii left?" My chest was heaving. I stared at her, waiting. She couldn't be gone. Not when I was this close.

Considering our airport wasn't as large as a city one, there would only be one flight to Hawaii.

She slid back on her swivel chair and pushed her glasses further up her nose. Was she deliberately slow walking me? I wanted to slam my fist onto the desk, but that wouldn't help the situation. I fidgeted nervously, practically ticking.

She turned to me, her gaze hard and unsympathetic.

"It's gone."

I staggered back, feeling defeated. I felt my body shut down. I was too late. I clutched at my chest. What the hell was I going to do? I felt like I was physically in pain. I bent over, clutching at my sides.

I couldn't believe it.

I was too late.

Epilogue

L acey's P.O.V:

It was weird to be back.

So much time has passed and yet nothing seemed that different. Well, I felt different, but that was about it. I stared at my house. Not one thing has changed and in a way, I'm glad it hasn't. It's nice to come home to something stable.

I was absolutely exhausted. I had so, so much fun while I was away. I pushed myself to the absolute limits - going out of my comfort zones in ways I could never have imagined. I even went swimming with sharks. Voluntarily. I know, Hawaii changed me.

"Where's mum again?" I asked as dad attempted to haul my humongous suit case towards our door. I must have developed some new muscles, carrying that around with me. It probably weighed more than me.

I was a little taken back that mum hadn't come to pick me up. I thought that was odd. She had been in constant contact with me, throughout my whole trip and kept repeating that she couldn't wait to see me, blah blah, but didn't show to pick me up from the airport? That just seemed weird. It's been over twelve months - yes, Anna and I prolonged our trip another three months. We just didn't want to come home. We'd been having too much fun.

"I think she's home," dad said, sounding a little distracted.

"If she's home why didn't she come pick me up?" I asked, feeling whiny. And a little annoyed. I would have gone to pick her up if our roles had been reversed.

Dad didn't answer as he fumbled to get the door open. A grin broke out on my face as a banner was splashed across the wall.

"WELCOME HOME!"

"Aw, dad," I laughed, my grin somehow getting wider. "That's awesome."

There were sets of balloons at the bottom of the stairs. It was pretty cute. I guess this was the part where people would usually have a full house party. You know, if they actually had friends, unlike myself.

"Where's mum?"

"Hello, Lacey."

I turned and my jaw fell to the floor, along with my carry bag. Mum stood there, but that wasn't the shocking part.

"What?" I asked stupidly, staring at her. "How? What?"

"Please don't ask how," dad shuddered and mum just laughed. Yeah, I guess that was a pretty gross question to ask. I didn't want to know the details.

I shook my head, still in complete disbelief. "How did you hide this from me?"

She smirked, proud of herself. "It was easier than I thought it was going to be. I guess you don't notice changes as much when you're not seeing me in person every day."

I wandered over to her slowly.

"I already have a name picked out."

I guess skype was only of our faces...

Still in shock, I gaped at my mother's protruding belly.

"You know the gender?" I whispered, scared to even touch her.

"Yes," she smiled, rubbing her pregnant belly. "It's a girl. Time to meet Allie, Lacey."

I dropped to my knees, my eyes burning. I gently traced my finger across my mother's belly.

"Hi, Allie."

Mum laughed, shifting her weight from one foot to the other. I wonder if she thought it was weird that I was speaking to her, but not really to her. I felt a little strange myself. I've never spoken to someone who wasn't really in front of me before (excluding phone calls). I've never had much to do with pregnancies.

"How far along are you?" I asked, staring her up and down as I rose to my feet. Her belly was scarily big. "You sure you're not having twins or something?"

Dad choked on his water. He looked absolutely horrified at the the thought of having twins. That made me laugh.

"Eight months."

"You guys are so reckless!" I exclaimed, shaking my head. "This was obviously not planned, right?"

Mum shrugged. "It wasn't, but I don't regret it. It's time for a new stage in my life. Or, a repeated one, you could say."

I could not believe this. What a bomb shell to arrive back to. I thought I was going to have one from Carter, not from mum. I shook my head at her, a small smile on my face.

"Well, who's going to help me decorate Allie's room?"

"Oh Lacey," mum gushed, her cheeks turning pink. "I'm so glad you're accepting this."

I rolled my eyes. "Like I had a choice."

Tears welled in her eyes and her cheeks became flushed.

"Kidding..." I trailed off, glancing to dad.

"It's not you," dad sighed, going over to my now weeping mother. This was weird. She never cried - unless it was something like me leaving. Or grandma dying. To see her openly cry over, well, nothing, was really bizarre. "She does this all the time."

"Oh, right, the hormones."

Mum wandered into the kitchen to sit down. Dad and I followed suit. Dad was so cute. He was acting so protective, even when she was just walking. This whole situation was so weird!

"Now come on, fill me in with what's been happening! Any other crazy news you want to slap me in the face with?"

Dad laughed, ruffling my hair like he used to when I was younger.

"Ah, Kid. I've missed ya."

I think it was safe to say, I missed them, too.

I decided to take a walk. It's what I used to love doing and I'd actually missed the place, believe it or not. I glanced down at my dark skin. It was the darkest it had ever been and my hair was bleached from the sun. I felt really surfy. I looked the same, but to people who hadn't seen me in a while, probably wouldn't realise it's me from first glance.

I didn't even realise where I was, until I heard the water splashing against the water. It had been a long time since I had walked here. Squinting, I stared over the water to the other side of town, where Carter and my cubby sat.

Carter and I used to sprint here from my house, before having to swim across to the cubby. We could never just do it casually, it was always a competition. I missed it.

The wind was slightly cool, as it tussled my hair. Mercedes had written me a letter back. In the letter, it explains as she did not know where to post it, and since I don't have any social media, she dropped it off at my house. It probably laid on my bed for over a year.

There wasn't anything too exciting in the letter. She apologised, which I'm glad for, and basically said what I did: too much has happened. We just aren't going to go back to being friends. But she suggested that we go for coffee one day. I don't think that's too bad of an idea, actually.

I was half curious in knowing what was happening with her and Aiden. I wonder if they were still together. In saying that, however, I kind of liked not knowing. It was peaceful.

It was strange. In some aspects, a year is a long time. I felt like all the drama that plagued my life was a life time ago. But in saying that, it had only been a year, which wasn't very long at all.

With a sigh, I sat heavily, placing the letter inside my jumper that I plonked next to me. I stared at the calm water. I had slept like a baby last night. I had been so exhausted from everything. But now, I was feeling regenerated and needed some fresh air.

"Long time no see, stranger."

His voice was smoother than silk. A shiver ran down my spine just at the sound of it. God, how I missed it.

I peered up, seeing Carter basking in the afternoon glow. He looked amazing as ever. His hair was slightly longer and his tan slightly darker, but he relatively looked the same. I noticed, having studied him a little further, that he had some stubble on his chin. I liked it. He looked more mature.

"Carter," I said, my voice sounding a little hoarse. I cleared my throat. "How's it going?"

He collapsed beside me. "Your mum told me you took a walk. Surprised to find you here, though."

"Me too," I admitted, unable to look away from him. I have missed his mesmerising face. He was so beautiful. I longed to run my hands over his golden skin, like I had so many times before. "Guess I missed this place more than I thought I would."

"Funny that," he replied, giving me a lope-sided smile. "How goes your mum, hey?"

"I still can't believe it," I said, shaking my head. "She didn't tell me anything!"

"Oh wow."

"Yeah, I know!"

"Must have got bored, not having you around to cause trouble," he laughed, nudging me playfully.

I scrunched up my nose. "Yuck, Carter."

"So, how was Hawaii? Meet any cute boys?" he teased and I knew he tried to keep the question as casual as possible. It worked. Kind of.

"It was amazing. So much fun," I grinned, feeling my cheeks heat up as he mentioned other boys. Of course not, I was still in love with him. "And, err, no guys."

"Really?" he asked, looking pleased at my answer.

I bet he had been dying to ask that since the second he saw me.

"Really. You?"

"Nope, no guys for me." he smirked, stretching. My lips parted as I stared at him. He was honest-to-God the most handsome boy. Well, I am bias of course, but he is very attractive.

I rolled my eyes. "Be serious."

He held my gaze. "There's no one else compared to you."

My stomach suddenly turned into the spaghetti circus. I squirmed under his intense gaze. Looks like we have our answer.

I swallowed uneasily. "O-oh."

He gave me a boyish grin, reaching out and tucking a loose tendril of my hair behind my ear. I sighed as his skin made contact with mine. I'd missed feeling the body warmth of another human, so close to me.

It was strange. I felt nervous around him, like I used to when we were younger. It was a nice feeling, as weird as that sounds.

I decided to interrupt the tension-increasing-by-the-second moment. "Have you seen much of Mercedes and Aiden?"

He didn't seem fazed that I asked. Was probably expecting it, really.

"Eh, a little. The birth went all good, as far as I'm aware. I don't think they're dating, but they're, like, together. If that makes sense. They're living together now and stuff, but it's not official dating or anything. I think it's just for the kid. It's a boy - Toby, I think his name is."

"I'm glad everything has worked out." I said, meaning every word.

Carter caught my eye. My breath hitched in my throat. He leant towards me. I had been waiting for this moment, ever since I left. I closed my eyes, waiting to feel the rush of exhilaration. I had missed his lips.

Instead, his lips went to my ear.

"Last one to the cubby has to make the other dinner tonight."

Suddenly, I was met with a whirl of wind. I gasped, falling back slightly. Carter was up and whipping his clothes off before I could blink.

"That's so unfair!" I whined, jumping to my feet, not even having time to check him out.

I was already too late. He was sprinting towards the water, in only his jocks. He plunged into the water and I panicked, having trouble getting the zipper of my jeans undone. After falling over in the process and ending up in a tangle, I ran after him as fast as I could.

The water felt icy on my skin, but I couldn't let the cold slow me down.

He was not going to beat me.

Although I had adventured a lot, I realised how truly unfit I was. My body felt heavier than lead by the time I reached the other side. I dragged myself out of the water, seeing Carter sprawled out the front of the cubby, looking hotter than ever.

"And the champion makes a comeback," he cheered with triumph.

I rolled my eyes. It was all I could do, considering I was panting and gasping for breath. He just laughed, coming towards me.

"God, I've missed you." In two strides he met me. His hands cupped my cheeks. He pressed his warm lips against mine and I moulded into him.

I guess things were back how they used to be.

Finally able to form a coherent sentence, I rested my forehead against his, utterly breathless.

"Guess we're not just childhood sweethearts anymore."

He stepped back, staring at me with complete certainty.

"We were never just that."

9 781944 260170